MEET
THE COSMIC CORRESPONDENTS
OF SATELLITE NEWS . . .

RIKKA COLLINS—ace reporter. She's got brains, beauty . . . and a built-in microphone.

HARRY SNYDER—anchorperson. As an intergalactic newsman, he's tops . . . when he's not tipsy.

JHONNY—cameraman. He's a robot, he's illegally employed . . . but no one's perfect.

MICHELANGELO—technician. He may look like a grizzly bear, but this alien troubleshooter knows his nuts and bolts and microchips.

"ACE" DEITRICH—the brains, literally. His body died almost three decades ago, but his scientific mind is still ticking.

"BOX" AMBOCKSKY—program director. He gets the team into the heat of the action, brings them back to the studio . . . and sometimes bails them out of jail.

They're the Satellite News Team—beaming your broadcast light years ahead of the competition.

Catch all the news! Don't m̶i̶s̶s̶ ̶ ̶ ̶ ̶ ̶ ̶ ̶ ̶e̶ *Night News*—the first b̶o̶o̶k̶ ̶ ̶ ̶ ̶ ̶ ̶ ̶ ̶ ̶ ̶ ̶e̶ thing stands in the ̶ ̶ ̶ ̶ ̶ ̶ ̶ ̶ ̶ ̶ ̶ ̶ ̶ ̶ ̶ ̶ ̶ and a nova-hot stor̶ ̶ ̶

D1022882

Ace Books by Jack Hopkins

SATELLITE NIGHT NEWS
SATELLITE NIGHT SPECIAL

SATELLITE NIGHT SPECIAL

JACK HOPKINS

ACE BOOKS, NEW YORK

To Peter Delellis,
the man who introduced
me to science fiction.
Thanks, *bon ami.*

This book is an Ace original edition,
and has never been previously published.

SATELLITE NIGHT SPECIAL

An Ace Book / published by arrangement with
the author

PRINTING HISTORY
Ace edition/October 1993

ISBN: 0-441-75047-8

ACE®
Ace Books are published by The Berkley Publishing Group,
200 Madison Avenue, New York, NY 10016.
ACE and the "A" design
are trademarks belonging to Charter Communications, Inc.

PRINTED IN THE UNITED STATES OF AMERICA

10 9 8 7 6 5 4 3 2 1

CHAPTER ONE

"GOING ONCE!" CRIED the human auctioneer, his gavel raised high above the striking pad on the hovering podium.

Frantically the museum auditorium of millionaires consulted with their reeling accountants to see if the staggering bid of 16 billion dollars could be topped by even a single penny. Heads shook no. Heads shook yes. Some just shook. Banks and loan sharks were hastily consulted via cellular phone rings and golden Rolex wrist radios. Jewelry was ripped off tan wrists and plump necks and thrust into the hands of harried butlers who immediately dashed toward a convenient line of video booths in search of the nearest twenty-four-hour pawnshop onboard the orbiting L5 colony.

"Going twice!"

Ebony canes cracked into splinters from nervously twisting hands. The tiny monitor panels on pocket-docs flashed a wild strobe effect in the crowd as the miniature robotic physicians struggled to control blood pressure, throbbing migraines, heart attacks, and nausea. Hip flasks were drained. Wallets consulted. Pockets searched for spare change. Eyes rolled. Teeth gnashed. And a horde of calculators overworked past any conceivable warranty simply exploded into a pyrotechnic display of electrical sparks and tortured transistors.

Sitting stately and serene amid the boisterous turmoil, the Honorable Gertrude Trump-Rockefeller smirked triumphantly. The billionaire Congresswoman from Mercury knew that nobody sane would even dare to top her bid!

However, since sane was the operative word, that meant

1

she should definitely expect trouble from the infamous lunatic royalty of Mars and practically anybody from California.

Minutely adjusting the cuff of his impeccable black tuxedo jumpsuit, the prim auctioneer nodded at the monetary antics with somber approval. Considering what it was that the O'Neil Art Museum of Space was offering here today, the crowd was actually behaving in a most seemly manner.

Just then, from somewhere within the attending crowd, a Bedlow laser derringer discharged toward the ceiling, vaporizing a priceless Venusian chandelier, and a fistfight broke out between the maids and chauffeurs. Gloves, lace, and feather dusters went flying in every direction.

Ah, well. So much for dignity.

"Going three times . . ." A dramatic pause and then the gavel began its downward swing for the grand finale announcement. "And the *Carx-Toz joq* is sold to—"

Suddenly the locked doors at the rear of the huge room violently slammed apart, the ornate brass handles hitting the opposite walls so hard they became imbedded into the stucco, sending cracks along the smooth plaster for meters in every direction.

"Hold it right there, Mac!" bellowed angry voices from the hallway beyond.

Everybody present pivoted toward the unexpected intrusion.

Standing brazen in the sagging doorway was a group of four beings dressed in gleaming white spacesuits. Lying discarded on the nearby floor was a broken marble pillar, a crude battering ram obviously appropriated from the foyer of the art museum without the express written consent of the management.

As the shocked crowd of assorted 'illionaires stared agog, eight armored gauntlets worked four louvered neck seals. With a hydraulic hiss, the spacesuit helmets were unlocked and deftly removed, exposing the grim faces of a pretty woman, a distinguished man with streaks of gray at his temples, a young man who was painfully clean-shaven, and a massive alien mountain of muscular flesh, hair, and teeth. The ridiculously tiny pince-nez glasses perched on the end of his snout did nothing to reduce the overall impression of raw beastly power.

"How dare you!" thundered the auctioneer, spraying spittle from his mouth in uncontrollable outrage. "Guards! Throw these interlopers out of the museum, off our L5 and into space!"

And from different corners of the huge room, a small army of muscular people in tan and black security uniforms started to converge upon the recent arrivals. Their hands were empty, but holstered at every hip was the ominous presence of a 40mm PeaceMaker stun pistol. Promoted as nonlethal, a single volley from the weapon was fully capable of pounding a raging volcano into a thirty-day coma. Guaranteed. Or your volcano cheerfully refunded.

But then . . .

"Holy prack!" cried out a squeaky voice from somewhere within the murmuring crowd. "It's the Satellite News Team!"

. . . and the guards ground to a halt, amazement changing to respect on their stern faces.

As the roomful of people started to coo and ah, the young reporter standing in the doorway smiled and the gray-haired anchor tried not to smirk and spoil the effect. Ah, there was nothing like being publicly announced. Even if you had to do it yourself. Ventriloquism was a skill every good reporter should learn. Almost as important as learning how to sleep with your eyes open during a station budget meeting.

Now the crowd looked closely at the intruders. Boldly emblazoned on the armored chest of each spacesuit was the name of the operator: Rikka Collins, Harry Snyder, John Smith, and a plain Michelangelo spanned the meter-wide chest of the hairy alien.

"The SNT?" squeaked the auctioneer. "But . . . ah . . . why are you . . . ah . . . here to make a bid?" he ended hopefully.

"Not bloody likely, you crook!" stated Harry, leveling a stern finger at the speaker. The anchor started up the center aisle with a bold sure stride, the giant Michelangelo and frowning Rikka at his side.

Staying by the ruined door, Jhonny whipped a 3-D camera from his shoulder bag. With a wrist snap, the video unit began to sprout telescoping struts and supports in every direction. In seconds the camera-op was entwined in an incredible maze of metallic legs, sensor arrays, shotgun mikes, dish receivers, klieg lights, gels, telephoto lenses, WatchDog scanner cones, and dangling boom mikes. Perched discreetly on his shoulder like a pet parrot was a tiny camcorder. Small and silent, the semisentient camera was what the android camera-op used to take the real pictures for broadcast, its array of lenses capable of getting a crystal-clear picture off the bottom of the sea in the middle of the night. But the complex maze of struts formed by the big 3-D camera created a solid defensive barrier about the android camera-op, helping to hold off pushy security guards and stop nosey people from jostling his elbow during a critical shot. In a pinch, it could also serve as a nifty hat rack.

Ignoring the anguished cries of the attending millionaires, the news team placed themselves on either side of the display case situated before the podium.

Protectively sheathed under a thick dome of military-grade Armorlite glass was a bizarre machine. Composed entirely of twisted pipes, conduits, and unearthly wiggling bits, the ancient device seemed to be half melted but still audibly hummed with power. Sections of the ceramic and metallic housing were deeply pitted with tiny meteor impacts, denoting its incredible age. Hundreds, maybe thousands of years old. And yet, it was extremely difficult to focus your vision upon the device, as if it was not wholly in this dimension, but partially extended into galactic subspace, the hypercosmic void, or even primordial Time itself.

"This is outrageous!" sputtered the auctioneer, his face a ghastly shade of white usually reserved for things long dead and found at the bottom of an old well.

"Damn straight!" agreed Rikka, crossing her arms. "Hey, John, you getting all of this?"

Within his jungle gym of struts and pipes, the android

raised a thumb at the use of his public name. "Tones and bars, chief!" he called from the back of the cavernous room. "All set to broadcast!"

Quickly the millionaires and the guards began to straighten their clothing, pocket combs passing around with total disregard for status or sanitation.

Kneeling in front of the locked display case, the huge alien was adjusting his minuscule glasses and studying the lock for an inordinate length of time.

"Can you do it, Mike?" asked Harry from the side of his mouth. If not, they were in a heck of a lot of trouble.

"I think ... yes!" The hairy technician smiled, baring rows of sharp teeth. Removing a slim probe from the bulky tool belt of his spacesuit, he worked on the lock for almost a full second before it yielded with a loud satisfying click. Promptly Harry started forward, but Mike held the human at bay with a massive paw.

With a mechanical hum the canopy of unbreakable Armorlite lifted upward and sleep gas billowed out from underneath the weird alien machine.

After a precious moment the technician lowered his restraining arm and Snyder surged forward.

"Behold!" cried Snyder. Raising his armored gauntlet high, he brought the metallic glove smashing down on the vibrating artifact.

"*No ... !*" cried the auctioneer, but it was too late. The alien device exploded, spraying bits of paint and white dust everywhere.

Leveling a portable WatchDog scanner on the smashed relic, Michelangelo angled the display to throw the results upon the conveniently smooth white wall above the podium. Bars of light danced across the plaster wall and alongside scrolled a mathematical and molecular analysis for those folk in the audience who couldn't read a simple spectrograph.

A gasp rose from the more literate members of the crowd. Mostly concubines and chauffeurs. The lawyers looked even more confused than normal.

"Latex plastic, petro-chemical coloring, gold dust glitter, pipe cleaners, chicken wire, water, paper, and flour!" cried Harry didactically in his best onstage voice. "Better known as papier-mâché! The *Carx-Toz joq* is a fake! A painted piñata!"

Now the murmurs of the crowd grew dangerously low and the guards turned to glare at the man responsible for the mega-dollar auction. The man who claimed to have personally found the legendary *Carx-Toz joq*!

Ensconced behind the podium, the pale auctioneer offered a feeble smile and heroically tried not to wet himself again.

"The asteroid belt was never a whole planet," continued Snyder loudly. "Any fool knows that! Thus there was no indigenous life, no *Carx Toz* civilization and no *joq* which destroyed their entire world, blowing it apart to form the asteroid belt!"

"What nonsense!" stammered the trembling man. "You . . . ah, must have switched the real *Carx-Toz joq* with this pitiful fake!"

Suspiciously the rich turned to face Harry.

Hands akimbo, Snyder stared at the criminal with his downstage eye so that the majority of his face was directed toward the camera and his unseen audience of 1.4 trillion.

"Pure quill crap," retorted the anchor. "The SNT has been trailing you for weeks and knows everything!"

Uh-oh. "Nonsense!" repeated the sweaty man. "Knows what?"

"We were fully aware that the blind bookstore owner was from Belgium, not Pluto, and thus could have no possible knowledge of the archaeologist, or the smuggler with the scarf."

Anger overwhelmed fear and breath hissed through perfectly pearly teeth. "But when the bank telegram arrived, the chief clerk of the Earth Defense Force poured the bucket of moon water out the window!"

"Into an empty bucket waiting on the ground," stated the anchor triumphantly. "Held and guarded by my close friend and companion, Rikka Collins!"

Demurely the investigative reporter gave a little curtsy.

The auctioneer croggled in astonishment. "But if she caught the water, then you knew—"

"Everything about the hamster, which meant I easily found—"

"The blueprints! But then, when the crippled android asked for more—"

"We already had the computer downloaded!"

"So that space shuttle that crashed into the comet—"

"Was a scam to trick you into believing *we* were dead!"

Dumbfounded, the auditorium frantically stared from one man to the other as they valiantly attempted to figure out what the hell was going on.

Only Gertrude Trump-Rockefeller understood what the exchange meant and the woman was growing madder and more red in the face by the minute. In response, her pocket-doc went into emergency status.

For a tense minute the two men stood panting and staring defiantly at each other as point, counterpoint, plot, gimmick, ruse, ploy, and trick swirled about in their storming brains to eventually reach the final, the ultimate, the inescapable conclusion!

"Oh, poop," sighed the auctioneer. In resignation, he loosened his tuxedo collar and removed his false nose. Cavalierly the crook tossed the artificial appendage over a shoulder. "You got me. Yes, I confess, the artifact is a phony. I made it myself out of parts from the Sears catalog."

Women cursed.

Men blanched.

Accountants swooned.

Jhonny zoomed in for a close-up.

"But what about the shimmering transdimensional effect of the superweapon?" demanded the furious Congresswoman. "Modern technology can't go into other dimensions. The *joq* has to be real!"

The auctioneer peeled off his blond scalp exposing a black crew cut. More gasps. What an incredibly good toupee!

"I merely played a hologram recording of the *joq* back

over itself following the exact mathematical lines of its contours," the man snorted. "That gave the unreal aspect that you rich goofballs swallowed like a drunk rube at the three-cat booth of a carny grifter!"

Few of the millionaires understood the slang terms, but the rude tone of the words was certainly clear enough and now the entire assemblage focused their hateful attention on the little man on stage.

Amid the glaring staff, some stalwart soul raised a small pocket camera and started adjusting for a picture. Moving fast, Jhonny whipped out a small box from his shoulder holster, clicked off the safety, aimed, and fired all in one motion.

With a musical twang, the camera disassembled, the lens falling off, the batteries popping out, and the roll of film spilling onto the floor and unwinding like a slick welcome carpet for some very small potentate.

The camcorder on his shoulder cooed with delight at its master's aim and total lack of morals. This was a QSNT exclusive. End of discussion. Ha-ha, so there.

"Okay," sighed the auctioneer, raising his hands. "Arrest me. But the charge is only attempted bunko. I'll be out of jail in two hours!" He sneered at the anchor. "Ya really should have waited until I sold the silly thing. Big mistake, newsboy."

For a split second Harry's expression of supreme confidence started to slip. But just then a soft beep made Rikka glance at her wrist secretary. What in the . . . bless you, Major Deitrich!

"Oh, no, you're not!" retorted the reporter hotly, reading from the data scrolling on the tiny monitor. "Your real name is Zultar Stitt, an ex-member of the Columbus, Ohio, police force. Escaped from New Alcatraz two years ago and wanted on fifteen charges of grand larceny, blackmail, bunko, grand theft, speeding, littering, arson, counterfeiting, smuggling, and felonious avian molestation!"

"What?" asked a puzzled butler from the crowd.

Rikka turned. "Contributing to the delinquency of a mynah!"

"Zultar Stitt, you are under citizen's arrest!" cried Harry, stepping onto the raised platform. "Guards, please take this hooligan into custody!"

Eagerly, the security personnel swarmed in to comply.

But with a snarl Stitt pulled a Bedlow laser pistol from within his tuxedo and tried to point the deadly weapon at everybody. Everybody stopped moving.

"Okay, so you know who I really am!" growled the criminal mastermind, backing away toward the side door. "But I'm still getting out of here! Even if you called the police right this very moment, I would still have plenty of time to—"

Glass exploded into the room as hundreds of police in full SWAT armor swung in through the windows on ropes, charged in from the doors, crawled out of the air vents, and parachuted down from the new laser hole in the ceiling where the chandelier used to hang.

"Zultar Stitt, you are under arrest!" chorused the hundred officers, and the museum echoed from the metallic clicks of a hundred safeties clicking off an equal number of Gibraltar Assault Rifles, with optional antipersonnel missiles and biological spleen imploder.

Instinctively, several members of the watching crowd raised their hands in automatic submission, then suddenly realized they were not the people being addressed and tried to switch the action into an innocent stretching motion.

Slumping, Zultar glumly tossed the pistol aside. A museum security guard caught it and handed the gun to an advancing cop. By gadfrey, the con man really hated being constantly interrupted like this.

In a standard ten-on-ten defensive formation, the platoons of police converged upon Stitt, soon hiding him in their beweaponed midst. But then there came the telltale sound of handcuffs closing and locking.

The entire room broke into wild cheering, which effectively masked the sound of the discarded spacesuit helmets in the hallway beginning to urgently beep.

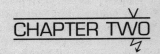

CHAPTER TWO

IMPULSIVELY THE NEWS team took a bow.

In response, the cheering was renewed and hats flew into the air. But after a fluttering moment, the headgear activated their directional jets and neatly returned to the rightful owners. Waste not, want not, that was the first rule of staying rich. The first rule of getting rich was lie, cheat, and steal.

Using Michelangelo to clear a pathway for them, the reporters crossed the auditorium and rejoined Jhonny at the doorway. In the background, a bedraggled Zultar Stitt was being carried away by far more police than was really necessary. But the news team was nonplussed. A public appearance of strength and reliability was even more important to the officers of the law than a car manufacturer. Sad, but true.

Then a familiar beeping sound caught their attention.

Stepping through the doorway, Collins retrieved her helmet. At the touch of her hands, the spacesuit dome transcribed the incoming signal into words that flowed like silver water across the visor of her helmet. Backward, of course.

Quickly donning the top of her spacesuit, Rikka demanded a repeat and the computer dutifully complied.

"It's a recall signal from Media!" she announced over the external speaker.

"Emergency?" asked Mike nervously.

She consulted the computer again just to be sure. "No," the reporter replied in relief. "Just a standard recall."

"How weird," said Harry, pulling a cigar from the air-tight pocket on the forearm of his suit. "As far as they know, we're still in the middle of an assignment."

"Jhonny, did you record everything okay?" asked Collins, removing the helmet again.

"Tones and bars, chief," stated the android, quickly starting the laborious process of folding his 3-D camera outfit. "Already encoded, scrambled, and en route back to HQ for a system-wide broadcast."

CONFIRMED, scrolled Deitrich on everybody's wrist secretary.

Smiling, Snyder lit the stogie with a touch of a red-hot fingertip. A special function of his executive nonmilitary model Wilkes Corporation spacesuit. It could also do the same thing to the entire inside surface of the boots, but only if someone other than the owner tried to wear the spacial garment.

"Then we were fast enough to make the six o'clock report?" Harry puffed inquisitively.

"Definitely," coughed the android. "We even have a sponsor already."

"Who?"

"Murphy's Law Soap. Whatever can be cleaned, will be cleaned."

Snyder blew a smoke ring. "Great!"

Gauntlet to mouth, Jhonny coughed again, louder this time, and the camcorder on his spacesuit shoulder flipped a dust cap over its delicate lenses.

Basking in the glow of victory, Harry ignored them both.

Pushing and shoving a path through the boisterous crowd, Congresswoman Trump-Rockefeller plowed relentlessly toward the smiling reporters.

Pulling up an abandoned chair, Rikka sat down and sighed in relief. Whew. Capturing a wanted criminal is all well and good. But the Station Manager would have their butts in a blender if the team ever missed a deadline. So what could the recall be for? Another hot lead? A congratulations party?

"Oh, and thanks for the save, Deitrich," whispered Collins to her wrist secretary.

GLAD TO HELP, scrolled the MainBrain pilot of the shuttle. HEY, WHEN I'M NOT FLYING THIS FATAL BUCKET OF BOLTS TO THE ENDS OF THE SOLAR SYSTEM I GOTTA BE DOING SOMETHING!

"Have you considered solitaire?" asked Michelangelo to his gauntlet.

The disembodied Brain scrolled a chuckle across the screen. NO THANKS. I'M ENGAGED AND JUST HATE PLAYING WITH MYSELF.

The big alien opened his snout to speak and then closed it with a snap. Must be another garbled translation.

I ALSO CHEAT, added the four-pound pilot as an afterthought. BUT ONLY AT CARDS.

"Excuse me for interrupting, folks, but how did the Lunar Police get here so quickly?" grunted a security guard, struggling to hoist one of the fallen doors back into place.

Politely Michelangelo picked the other portal off the floor in a single paw and laid it gently in position.

"We phoned them en route," puffed Snyder. "No sense taking chances." As the anchor tapped his cigar ashes into a convenient urn, the museum pottery immediately extended robotic legs and scurried away to empty itself into the nearest trash receptacle.

"Well, we appreciate the help," groaned the guard to both of them as he shuffled away to find a Closet-Doc and have a quick hernia test.

In a sudden flurry of elbows and grunts, the Mercurian woman finally broke free of the busy throng who were currently using their hats to brush all the glass shards off them. Pracking police couldn't have opened the windows first?

"Sir, madam, you have saved me over 16 billion dollars," gushed the politician in a single breath. "Plus, my honor and good name. How can I ever thank you?"

Glancing about the noisy room, Rikka stood and, taking the elderly woman by the arm, gently pulled her off to the side. Having done this sort of thing many times before,

Mike and Harry stepped in front of them to offer a meager modicum of privacy.

"Well, since you asked," started Collins demurely. "I have come to understand that somebody has been doing odd things on the Interplanetary Metals Exchange."

"And what exactly do you mean by—odd?" hedged the Congresswoman.

"Deliberately losing money."

Although she refused to show it, the politician was shocked to her very soul. A Mercurian deliberately losing money? That was heresy! Insanity! Her people would rather agree with each other than fail to make a profit! On the other hand, being a snitch was also socially unacceptable. Unless, of course, this could be considered industrial espionage. Then anything was okay. Hmm.

Sensing weakness, Rikka leaned in closer. "Now, if you should come across anything of interest, a simple anonymous phone call would be of immense assistance."

Thoughtfully, the billionaire chewed a lip in hesitation, so the news reporter moved in for the kill. "Of course, if repaying a service and honor means little to you—"

"Ha!" barked the Mercurian. "You got me. It's a deal." And the two shook.

Suddenly there was a blinding flash of light in the doorway and a pair of holograms appeared, the torso of the man and woman sticking ludicrously half out of the floor.

The man was tall, dark, and professionally handsome, with hair too neat and skin too flawless to be anything but an actor. All apples and curves, the buxom blond woman was about to pop out of the low-zipped front of her skintight jumpsuit. Floating in the air above was another hologram bearing the logo of their station and a brief announcer identification: QINS—Hardcopy & Sunshine, ace reporters.

Adjusting something off camera, Hardcopy stepped up onto the floor as if climbing a set of stairs. "Wait!" he cried in a perfectly pitched baritone.

"The *joq* is a fake!" added the sultry woman, joining him.

"Papier-mâché," said the Congresswoman. "Yes. Thank you, Mr. Hardcopy, Ms. Sunshine. But I know already."

Stunned, Jason Hardcopy and Susie Sunshine stared at the Mercurian.

"You do?" gushed the blonde, surprised.

The man narrowed his eyes. "How?" he demanded rudely.

"Hello!" chorused the QSNT team, gaily waving their hands.

As the QINS reporters buried their faces in their hands and groaned aloud in pain, their logo obediently blinked out.

"Yep," agreed Rikka amiably. "It be us."

"Ha!" laughed Mike, bearing a grin. "You are a dollar late and an hour tall, as usual."

In ragged stages, the reporters and politician turned to stare, puzzled at the big alien.

"Ah . . . a penny saved is worth a bucket of nine?" he tried again.

Eyebrows raised and then lowered in concentration.

IN YOUR HAT, BOZOS, scrolled the huge IBM portable strapped to the forearm of his gigantic spacesuit that served the Gremlin in lieu of a wrist secretary.

"In your hat, bozos," said Michelangelo loudly and then he added a finger snap.

The QINS team took the reproof as best they could. Which was not well at all.

"Thanks," the technician whispered into the device.

HEY, NO PROB, BUDDY, scrolled the machine in response. THAT'S WHY I'M THE BRAIN OF THIS OUTFIT.

In reflection, Mike supposed that he really should study these human axioms more before trying one again in public. Occasionally he offered a Gremlin witticism, but such alien sayings as "Never stick your own foot in the shoe of an angry fish" and "Private privates pirate pyrite" only caused humans to moan and clutch their heads. Obviously a lot of ageless wisdom was lost in the translation. Some damn fine jokes too.

Facing each other, the two INS reporters muttered under

their breath for a few minutes and then glared hatefully at the brazen SNT team.

"Congratulations," growled Jason, forcing out the vile word by sheer blood pressure.

"You beat us fair and square," added Susie as the furious woman tried to telepathically make the heads of the other news team explode.

"Thanks," puffed Harry, allowing the pungent smoke of his cigar to momentarily smear the visuals of their long-distance transmission. "Well, we hate to scoop and run, but we have another hot lead to check. Later!"

"In hell," muttered Hardcopy sotto voce as the chuckling news team scrambled from the room dragging their equipment haphazardly along behind them.

Firing daggers from her pretty azure eyes, Sunshine agreed. "God, I hate the SNT," cursed the ample blonde, a prominent vein in her dimpled temple throbbing wildly.

"God, I hate the SNT," muttered Stitt, as the jail cell door of the L5 prison clanged shut. Whistling a happy tune, the guard shrugged and ambled away twirling his stun stick.

In the cell across the corridor, a mountain of scarred tissue and biomechanical implants that vaguely resembled a human male gave a loud guffaw. "Ha! Join the club, fella."

Zultar sat on his folding bed and bounced a bit to test the comfort factor. Of which there was none. "A lot of us in the club?" the con man wryly asked the neighboring goliath.

A nuclear snort. "I'd guess that almost ten percent of the prisoners in this one jail alone—"

"Eleven point five percent," corrected a voice from down the corridor.

"A lot of the folks in this prison," backtracked the titan, "were put here by those motherpracking reporters." Then a new and unique thought somehow percolated its way through the thick mass of bone surrounding his cerebellum. "Why, it's almost a mark of distinction!"

"Yeah, right," scoffed the voice.

Folding his tuxedo top as a makeshift pillow, Stitt lay down on the iron mattress and mentally fumed at his predicament. His only hope of salvation was that somebody else would someday outsmart these nosy newshounds and put the SNT themselves into jail. Then the reporters would soon come to understand the true meaning of revenge.

Outside the museum, the team took a moment to reorganize themselves and admire the view. There was nothing else even vaguely similar in the whole solar system and it was inspiring to say the least.

Before the news team the horizon stretched out in a curved valley to abruptly end in a colossal white wall, a flat circular disk that neatly separated the Living section of the colony from the aft Industrial and fore Manufacturing sections. Pollution was nonexistent here, although rush-hour traffic converging on the one door was sometimes hellish. Especially on the weekends. Mostly composed of suburban side streets and sprawling dirt farms, the O'Neil colony had only a small downtown area with but two 50-story skyscrapers and sixteen 10-story apartment buildings. Compared to the bustling, overcrowded North America, this place was a nuclear test site.

Floating in space between Terra and Luna where the gravitational pull of the two spheres perfectly canceled each other out, the gigantic L5 colony was three kilometers wide by ten kilometers long and roughly resembled a sideways soup can. It even had similar markings, red on top, white on bottom, and a large golden seal marking where the main airlock was. The prototype O'Neil space colony had been mysteriously dedicated to a Scotsman named Campbell for reasons now sadly lost in antiquity.

A carefully controlled rotation along the main axis of the artificial world created sufficient centrifugal force to give the functional illusion of gravity on the inner surface where everybody lived. And nobody really noticed the subtle difference except for some grumpy scientists who were forever bickering about the Coriolis effect or tangent force vectors, and idiot novel writers who were forever diddling with important scientific details for the sake of artistic continuity and entertainment.

Off to either side, the ground gently sloped upward, ever upward, up-up-upward, until finally joining at the zenith to form a distant dizzying arch of overhead houses and farms. Thankfully the diametric side of the colony was skillfully masked by puffy white clouds placed there by the Strategic Internal Weather Department of Tourism. Vertigo was a constant danger to visitors, but a simple bit of atmospheric camouflage helped tremendously to ease the acclimatization of a new arrival. Made for a dandy postcard too.

Stepping to the curb, Rikka and the team hailed a cab, and then another. One for them and their equipment, and the second just for Michelangelo. It was a tight squeeze, but the technician finally managed to wiggle into the ground vehicle. Shutting the door, however, was another matter entirely. And his large fuzzy posterior ended up in a socially unacceptable position.

Obviously the cab had been built before 2285 when the deep space sleeper ship of his people had discovered Earth. In the ensuing forty years, a great many concessions had been made for his race by mankind, mostly in the matter of doorways and public lavatories. Which was pretty damn nice of humanity since there were only four hundred of the alien star-travelers in the whole solar system. And there wouldn't be any more of his species until the next Gremlin sublight sleeper ship arrived in eighty years with its precious all female crew.

Sigh.

In the first cab, Rikka, Harry, and Jhonny slammed the door shut, their heads trapped in the valleys formed by the mountains of their equipment bags.

"Wheretofolks?" slurred the driver as one word.

Having taken taxis for the majority of their lives, the reporters had no trouble understanding the cabbie.

"The Red Spider," puffed Snyder. "And step on it!"

Having heard the joke countless times before the driver somehow refrained from laughing. "Natch," he replied simply and the cab wheeled away from the club, its lumbering sister vehicle in close pursuit.

Unable to raise her wrist to her mouth, Rikka tongued the transmitter switch located on the collar of her spacesuit. "Deitrich, we have a recall from Media. How soon can we lift off?"

SOON AS YOU GET HERE, came the delightful reply. I HAVE ALREADY ASKED KENNEDY FLIGHT TOWER FOR PRIORITY ONE CLEARANCE AND RECEIVED AUTHORIZATION FOR AN IMMEDIATE LAUNCH, answered the pilot.

"Great!"

HOWEVER, THE SHIP IS NOT IN PERFECT FLIGHT CONDITION.

"Why?" demanded Harry, annoyed. "What's wrong now?"

WE ARE VERY LOW ON LIQUID HYDROGEN, OUR ALLOTROPIC URANIUM IS BADLY DETERIORATED, WE'RE NEARLY DEPLETED OF WINDOW WASHER FLUID, AND ARE COMPLETELY OUT OF APPLES.

"But you can still get us to Media?" asked Jhonny.

YOU EXPECT MICHELANGELO TO JOURNEY INTO SPACE WITHOUT EATING? WHATAREYOUNUTS?

"And where the heck are we going to get an apple between here and there?" chewed Snyder around his cigar.

Wordlessly the driver passed over the seat a plump red specimen of the aforementioned snack. Obviously a kindred soul on the subject.

"We have apple," said Collins in her best NASA impersonation.

There was a pause. GREAT. I'LL HAVE THE MAIN ENGINES WARMED AND READY.

"Roger!"

A pause. UTHER, ACTUALLY, replied Deitrich in an embarrassed font. BUT PLEASE DON'T TELL ANYBODY.

Minutes later the cabs rolled to a halt at the Red Spider Train Station and the reporters disembarked. In an explosion of white, the gargantuan spacesuit containing Michelangelo burst out of the second cab, both the vehicle and passenger giving a tremendous groan of relief. Momentarily the alien had a brief flashback to being born. Yikes, what a memory.

Gathering on the sidewalk before the train station, Jhonny looked at Harry who looked at Rikka who grimaced and reached for her wallet. Darn, it was her turn again.

"How much for the rides and the fruitsky?" she asked, riffling through her collection of credit cards and money. Did she have any cash usable here? Hmm, Mercury marks, Venus G-spots, Mars sanddollars, Jupiter pounds, Pluto degrees . . . What, no Earth money? Prack! Ah, here we go! Her Interplanetary Express card. Rikka never left her homeworld without it.

While mentally trying to calculate a proper tip, she proffered the shimmering card to the driver, but he pushed it away.

"Coo, no charge on this un, sheila," canted the driver, sticking a relaxed elbow out the window. "I'm a big fan of yourn, I am. Glad to help the ol' SNT. G'day!"

And as the two cabs drove away, the reporters allowed themselves to exchange smiles. Fans. They were wonderful. And everywhere. Well, almost.

Going to the grilled booth, the team paid a uniformed android for some first-class tickets and a set of transfers, then trundled onboard the next northbound train. Gently rocking from side to side, the electric tram rattled through the picturesque countryside and even went into a tunnel for a while as it proceeded underneath the Home On Le Grange Olde West Shopping Mall. The last stop was the Gerald K. Station, where the team piled off with everybody else. Waiting till the crowds of commuters thinned down, the reporters started to randomly choose an elevator from amid the line bank of the waiting lifts when a voice called out for them.

"SNT? Over here! I've held an express!"

Scampering over, the team piled into the open doors. As the reporters took a hold of the handrails, the cage closed and gently began its ascent.

The person inside was a portly fellow of indeterminate

age and a beard-mustache combination of truly impressive size. However, his black hair was slicked back in a style long out of fashion and he was wearing a deadly serious business jumpsuit of neon green, no lapels, and a natty fluorescent Hawaiian bow tie.

"Excellent job, chaps!" cried the man, stroking his whiskers. "My total congratulations!"

"Who are you?" asked Jhonny, his arms full of helmet and camcorder.

The man seemed surprised. "Why, I'm 'Big' Lowell Lutzman!"

Blank stares.

"The top DJ at LQQQ."

More blank stares.

"The radio station one Q short of being taken off the air?"

Totally blank stares.

OUR LOCAL AFFILIATE, scrolled the ever-present Deitrich.

Now smiles blossomed and hands were shaken.

"I received a call from the police that you were having a hullabaloo. So I decided to beat the rush and hurried on over to hold you an elevator and cut a deal while you departed."

Harry looked at the fat man with fresh respect. "Damn good thinking, Lowell."

"Thanks."

With a sudden lurch, the elevator rapidly built velocity. The lessening gravity and inertia battled it out until the team was soon floating inches off the floor.

But here in the mathematical center of the revolving colony, zero G ruled supreme. It made transporting cargo a relatively easy effort and the luxurious honeymoon suite of the Only Nice Hotel was located dead center in the L5—for the obvious recreational reasons.

"So," said Big Lowell eagerly. "Can I have the exclusive L5 right to the story?"

"But you don't know what it is?" stated Michelangelo.

With a plump hand, the radio DJ waved that trifle away.

"Considering all the cops you had hit the art museum, I just know it's a wowser."

Chewing on the nub of his cigar, Harry nodded at the sage wisdom. At the action, Rikka made her decision. If stupidity was its own reward, then so should be brains. "Sure. You got a colony-wide exclusive."

The mustache twitched in excitement. "Great! The usual fee for running the story?"

"Half the usual if you use our name this time instead of merely 'another news service,'" offered Collins in her patented "I've got a flush and you've got crap" poker face.

The outrageous idea took a full second to be considered, reviewed, analyzed, decoded, and understood.

"Done!" Lutzman cried, and they shook.

Noticeably slowing, the elevator gradually came to a halt and with a musical ding, the doors parted.

"We'll Z-band a copy of the edited version to you within the hour," said Jhonny, stooping to gather everything he could. "Retrieval code will be . . . um, Otis."

"That's pure modulation," laughed the aerial DJ. "Later, guys!"

"Later!"

Nimbly retracting their legs, the team curled into balls and flipped over to kickoff from the rough textured walls. Moving steadily along with the air currents, they drifted past a tethered fleet of hovertrucks and, angling past a police officer who waved hello, flew safely through the counter-revolving rings that connected the main cylinder of the colony to the launch bay.

Just then their helmets beeped again. But a new signal this time. Now it was an emergency recall. What the prack?

Quickening their pace, the reporters skipped/flew along a ramp that spiraled down past a tall building of tan brick topped with a colonnade of windows and a roof jammed full of antennas. An electric sign on the brick facade proudly proclaimed "Welcome to Kennedy Space Port." Underneath which, somebody had used a spray can of paint to add the clarifying codicil "John not Ted." Security was still trying to decipher exactly what that meant.

Beyond was a cavernous room, with a hundred shuttles flying in from space, taxiing about on the deck, or standing ready on their assigned orange squares. The white-tiled, flat-bottomed astroliner design, with two sets of stubby wings and a cluster of jet engines at the rear, made each of the shuttles nearly identical. A simple fact, which made finding your spaceship at a deep space parking lot a real bitch and a half. Which was the main reason why the position of parking attendant was considered equally important with king or bartender. A few ships had tiny orange tennis balls attached to their main radar scanners, but that only served to add to the general confusion. The sole identifying factor was that all of the shuttles had a line of script writing directly underneath the prow, announcing their name or company logo.

Except one. Along the side hull of that shuttle was the three-meter-tall, Broadway style letters—QSNT. As was often said by Gardner Wilkes, the owner of Media Station, advertising, like charity, began at home.

At the extreme end of the runways, a triple set of leviathan doors cycled apart. A sonic curtain retained the air, and through the gaping portal could be seen a section of Terra and starry space. Despite the rotation of the colony, the stars and planet were standing perfectly still. Every launch bay on the L5 was actually an independent sub-cylinder, which turned in precise counter-synchronization with the mother colony, so that the launch port and landing field were relatively motionless. Thus maximizing the safety factor for the pilots. Oiling the endless layer of ever-processing bearings underneath the deck that supported each space dock was a job usually reserved for condemned ax murderers who wished a few decades knocked off their sentences.

As the team bustled toward their shuttle, the door cycled open and a stair ramp extended, courtesy of Major Deitrich.

"Why can't our shuttle have a name?" asked Mike for

the umpteenth time, stepping inside without bothering to use the tiny ramp. Silly thing kept bending whenever he stepped on it. "Like 'The Fourth Estate' or 'The News Hawk'?"

"Undignified," grunted Harry, slinging in the bags.

"Unprofessional," added Rikka, packing the stuff into a cargo locker.

"Can't decide on one," said Jhonny, retracting the steps. It took him two tries. Sometime in the recent past the thick ramp of ferruled dura-steel had become bent. Which wasn't surprising, really. Their long-suffering shuttle got the bejesus slammed out of it on a regular basis.

"Come on, people, let's shake a leg," said a voice from the ceiling. "It's an emergency recall."

"We know!" answered Collins, stepping through the small galley and onto the bridge. Nimbly she climbed into the copilot's chair of the cockpit. Winking, blinking instruments now completely surrounded her tantalizingly on every side.

"Want me to fly her?" she asked hungrily, hands partially raised to start flipping things.

"Is our insurance fully paid?" asked the disembodied voice.

Hands went into lap. "Ha. I laugh."

On the dashboard, control levers adjusted themselves and on the low ceiling console, buttons recessed and dials swirled to pre-set markings.

Settling into his communications chair, Harry grunted in annoyance as he switched on the com-links, booted the sublight X- and Y-band transponder, modulated the faster-than-light Z-band transceiver, and balanced the mix on the stereo. "Mike, when are you going to get him a hologram body again?"

"Hey, I just fixed his in-ship voice," said the technician, strapping himself into the aft engineering chair four times too large for a human. "Give me some time to work on the rest."

Jhonny took his place at Sensors and put his camcorder inside an angular recess where his pet could start recharging. "Well, this invisible pilot stuff gets wearisome after a while."

"And you know how hard it is to shave this way?"

Unnoticed by anybody inside the vessel, as the hatchway closed and locked, the huge QSNT on the side of the shuttle melted away and flowed to the bow of the craft where it re-formed into the tasteful Gothic script: UTHER & MIKE'S FLYING LOONY BIN.

"Can we go now?" asked Collins, petulantly tapping a boot.

Immediately the whispering belly jets started to increase in noise and the steering wheel pulled backward.

"I just received final clearance from the tower," announced the ceiling. "We're history."

In a wash of warm air, the SNT shuttle lifted off the deck, her landing gear cycling back into the keel of the spaceship, and stout plates of dura-steel covered with lithium fiber tiles sliding out to cover the exit holes.

"Quarter thrust."

A feeble flame whispered from her aft jets, and the shuttle pirouetted about and advanced to the open hatchway. The sonic curtain resisted its prow so Deitrich upped the power and the ship slid quietly into the cold vacuum of space.

Behind them space was filled with the awesome bulk of the revolving L5. Below was the blue-white grandeur of Terra and off to port was the dingy gray rock ball of Luna.

"Half thrust," announced the pilot, and the controls, levers, buttons, and slides on the dashboard of the cockpit re-adjusted themselves before the empty seat.

"Full thrust!"

Now an eruption of green flame blasted from the aft rocket nozzles, then the turbo-jets kicked in, then the auxiliaries, and the shuttle lanced out into space steadily accelerating to over two thousand kilometers an hour.

On the dashboard the speedometer just barely managed to register the meager velocity.

"Course plotted and laid in," Rikka called out, operating the navigation console.

"Check," responded Harry, both hands busy. "Life support is operating. External beacons recognize our signal."

"Forward zone clear for the run," added Jhonny. "Minor deviation in course from drunk Shriners in a stolen garbage scow noted and correction laid in."

"Confirm."

"Roger."

On the console the camcorder changed its lens from telephoto to wide angle as it tried to see everything going on in the bridge. Space was fun! But really, really big.

"Sterlings are at ninety percent," finished Mike, munching an apple. "Mains are on line."

"Going Fatal . . . now!" announced Deitrich.

And a button was expertly pressed.

To the flight controllers of the L5, the news shuttle simply vanished.

CHAPTER THREE

TO THE REPORTERS onboard the shuttle, the L5 and Terra vanished as the moon became a blur. The stars before them took on a definite reddish hue while those behind turned a lovely blue. Watching on the main monitor, Jhonny loved it. Gave the shuttle a lovely Christmas feeling every time they went FTL.

"Thirty-eight ... thirty-nine ... forty ... forty-one ... forty-two ... forty-three ... forty-four ... now!" cried Rikka in the cockpit.

On cue, Deitrich killed the mains, and the stars returned to their normal color as the shuttle slowed to sublight speed. Uncrossing his eyes, Michelangelo took a few breaths to orient himself. Going faster than 186,502 miles per second always made him a bit woozy. The human medical books called it temporal space sickness. He liked to refer to it as becoming light-headed.

Now below the hurtling craft was only the dark side of Luna. But the hemisphere wasn't really black because the main crater on this side of the bleak orb was completely filled with the mighty, majestic Starlite City: a thriving metropolis of sixty-five thousand mostly law-abiding people. The sprawling lunar town contained every aspect and attribute of planetary life a person could wish for: schools, universities, a swell amusement park, numerous scientific institutions, a fortified military installation, a thriving theater section, the infamous Pleasure Palace, a brand-new Club Med, and a damn good pizza delivery service. Although they did have the bizarre habit of putting anchovies on everything. Including the staff.

As the shuttle streaked by, the city below sparkled brighter than the unreachable stars above. But the reporters paid it little attention as directly ahead of the speeding newscraft was a familiar sight. Permanently locked in a geosynchronous orbit above the dark side of the moon, safe from solar flares, the ionic winds, and governmental censors, was a large lumpy structure resembling a white beachball stuffed into a stainless-steel doughnut.

Media Station. Home.

Its outer hull was spotted with huge dish antennas set in triplicate, proof against any possible accident so that nothing could interfere with the Z-band transmitters that connected the news station to the rest of the solar system 24 hours a day, 365 days a year. Or 185 days a year for Mercury, or 2,567 years a day for Pluto.

A wonder of the ages, Media consisted of 57 million tons of state-of-the-art communications machinery jammed into thirty-seven climate-controlled levels operated by five thousand highly trained professionals whose sole concern was the proper dissemination of the news.

Or keeping their jobs. It all depended upon whom you talked to and if they were drunk enough to tell the truth.

All about the busy space station, shuttles, tugs, freighters, military gunships, paddy wagons, and executive singleships came and went with amazing regularity. Starry space was sprinkled with the assorted green flames of their distant chemical engines. Colorful buoys blinked lanes for traffic, with hologram arrows indicating the direction for those unsure if they were coming or going, a historical danger in the news biz.

"We have clearance for an approach," said Harry, adjusting his communications console. "Level 10, Airlock 5, Parking Spot number one. Wow." The hatchway was open and everything! A real red carpet treatment. Nine times out of ten, the team was pressing a deadline with a hot story and just plowed straight in at sublight speed to do a spectacular crash on Level 27.

Mike nodded at the unspoken thought. Their usual space dock was getting particularly battered and the team was giving serious consideration to switching to Level 13, the public access level. Although rumor did state that it was bad luck to work there. However, the alien technician didn't believe in superstitions. Bad luck? Bah. Foolishness! Sure, 13 occasionally burst into flames for no apparent reason, or a wild comet smashed in through a window. But those were freak occurrences. Statistical anomalies. Happened no more than once or twice a week.

Maneuvering his way through the ballet of traffic, Deitrich put the news shuttle on the proper approach path and smoothly glided in toward the doughnut. Off-duty personnel at the observation windows pointed at the passing shuttle and threw their heads back in silent laughter. Everybody but Mike exchanged puzzled glances. Now what could that be all about?

As the QSNT neared the busy space dock, a large rectangle edged in red changed to yellow and then green. Attitude jets sounding all over their hull, the pilot neatly swung the craft about and slid past the glowing hatchway. The sonic curtain gave only a brief tug at their hull. Rolling along the deck on her landing wheels, the shuttle came to a rest exactly in the middle of its assigned orange square. With a rumbling sigh, the jets flickered out.

"Ally-ally-oxen-free," sang the ceiling off-key.

"Sterlings off," stated Michelangelo, flipping switches with practiced ease. "Life support off. Internal power off. Coffee maker off. Umbilical connected to the station."

Without thinking, Jhonny slid his credit card into a well-worn slot on his console. "Paying the fine for our landing . . ." His hand stopped. "Hey, but we didn't crash this time." What a weird feeling.

Undoing the straps of the copilot's chair, Rikka mumbled something under her breath.

"What?" asked Harry, shutting down his console.

"A ten-point landing? This could give us a bad name."

"True enough," said the android and he transferred the funds for the standard fine into the appropriate bank account anyway. There, now they had credit! Gave him a nice warm feeling of security to know that they now had one prepaid crash coming. Sort of like having an extra disk of film with you on assignment, or a good blackmail photo of the big boss doing something illegal in the state of Iowa. But then, what wasn't illegal there? Walking? Breathing? The public use of gravity?

Removing their spacesuits, the team stowed the garments into wall lockers for a recharge and quick dry cleaning. Cleanliness counts on television. Now in street clothes, Harry was wearing an elegant pin-striped, three-piece jumpsuit with matching soft-brim hat. Rikka primly smoothed out a few wrinkles from her forest green-blue jumpsuit and clipped on a pair of silver SNT earrings. Black camera bag slung over a shoulder, Jhonny sported a strictly utilitarian jumpsuit of dark blue, which in a pinch could double as a projection screen. In fact, the suit had done so several times. Most notably during office parties and the Worlds Series. As always, Mike was dressed in black boots of a homeric size, short hiking pants, and an unbuttoned toolvest made entirely out of pockets, every damn one of them filled to the bursting point.

On the deck outside, a crowd of maintenance techs had gathered about the shuttle. And as the airlock dilated wide, exposing the reporters, the smiling techs gave a rousing round of applause.

A showman supreme, Harry bowed, Jhonny waved, and Mike looked at the roof while twiddling his hairy thumb. Suddenly suspicious, Rikka glanced fast over at the shuttle. But all was as it should be, the call letters of their channel QSNT big and bold on the side of the stately craft.

Hmm.

Leaving Deitrich to handle the usual details of shuttle maintenance, the team grabbed a turbo-lift and punched their destination into the keyboard. With a vibrating spin, the cage took off like a whirling dervish on holiday, angling up and away.

"Okay, how are we going to handle this?" asked Rikka,

tying a green cloth band around her forehead. "Separate
and converge?"

The towering alien rumbled agreement. "Sounds good.
We stand a better chance that way."

Smooth and silent, the turbo-lift ceased its gyrations and
with a musical ding deposited the news team on a dark
and dusty corridor filled with trash bins and lined with
gurgling sewage pipes. On command, the reporters broke
apart and ran to different locations, each concentrating on
a specific area of expertise.

"Air vents have new locks on them," grumbled the
kneeling Michelangelo after a minute. "I can't get
through."

With an expression of disgust, Jhonny ripped a handful
of wires out of a repair panel of an old service lift. "Damn
cargo elevator won't take my override command."

A moment later Collins returned from around a corner.
"Stairs have been blocked off."

"Fire doors welded shut," announced Snyder with a
snarl, futilely rattling the handles one more time.

Taking a deep breath, Rikka set her jaw. Damn, this
time Security was prepared for them. "Okay, then we have
no choice."

"Ready?" said Harry, rubbing his shoes against the
flooring.

"Set . . ." Jhonny said, looping the strap of his camera
bag over his neck and holding on with both hands.

"Go!" cried Mike and he hit the doors like an unshaved
meteor.

Violently the portal slammed apart and the team raced
desperately across the reception area. The pretty android
woman behind the desk waved a cheery hello and the air
shimmered into a hologram picture of a politically correct
choir.

"Welcome to QSNT!" sang the happy group. *"All news
all the time!"*

Trying not to barf, the team raced past a frowning guard
and slammed apart a set of swinging doors. After twenty
years of working here, they still weren't immune to that

dreadfully cheery chorus. It was enough to make a reporter stop drinking. Almost.

Still gagging, the gang burst through the next double doors and slowed as they stepped onto the carpet of a cavernous room.

Here in the exact middle of Media, the station was one single huge area; an ocean of brown desks, topped with white computer monitors extending off into the horizon until details became lost from the sheer distance. Aisles separated the different departments of the news from each other, and low-grade sonic curtains held the noise to a minimum. It also helped reduce the volume of paper airplanes and spitballs between rival sections.

Off to the left, one wall was composed solely of TV monitors that showed the news broadcast of every other service in the system. The sound knobs from all the sets had been permanently removed after a rowdy incident involving a Miss Underwear Beauty Contest on another network and a lewd display of public lip-synching by the QSNT staff as they put new words in the moving mouth of the silent master of ceremonies. The conduct of the newsroom personnel had been vulgar, crude, sophomoric, unprofessional, and everybody wanted a repeat as soon as possible.

To the right was a single wall-spanning TV monitor, the same size as all the rest combined. This showed what QSNT was broadcasting. Currently, the color tint was off and everybody appeared to be either Chinese with jaundice, or recent patrons of the dreaded employees' robo-dining room.

Continuing onward at a more sedate pace, the team stepped through a sonic barrier and entered Classified.

Scaw!

"Ready!" called out a wild-eyed man typing away at a battered antique keyboard.

Seated at a littered desk, a sweaty woman sliced open a physical envelope of sheet plastic and unfolded the letter inside. "Lady Swatch seeks King Timex for a good time,"

she read from the missive. "Hands and face only please.
No chains, old fobs, or windups."

"Logged and boxed," panted the typist. "Next?"

A new envelope. "Amoral, buxom nymph seeking rich
old man about to die. Willing to do unspeakable things for
a prominent place in your will." She paused. Well, at least
this one is honest.

"Next?" called the man, a slight smile on his face.

Slice. Unfold. Gulp. "Genetically damaged eclectic yak
herder seeking meaningful relationship with radioactive
ambidextrous hermaphrodite balloonist. No freaks please."

"Next!"

Scaw! Icons and incense abounded in the Religious Department.

Muttering to themselves, a priest, a Buddhist monk, and
a rabbi were huddled around a scrolling teleprinter.

"This is terrible news!" cried the priest, aghast.

"A civil ceremony!" gasped the monk. "What'll we
do?"

The rabbi pivoted about. "Mr. Colson! Get the supreme
being on the phone!"

At his desk their secretary was shocked at the absolutely
unprecedented request. "You mean . . . God?"

"No!" chorused the holy trio. "The Station Manager!"

After a pause the man started punching numbers into his
phone. "Actually, I think I'd have better luck trying to get
a hold of the other fella," whispered the secretary to himself.

Scaw!

"North America has a new president!" called out a
woman in a straw skimmer, hunched over a hooded privacy monitor. "Jefferson won by a landslide!"

"Great!" cried a stout man in a jumpsuit one size too
small. "Higgins, release the prewritten report on his righ-
teous victory."

"Already on it, sir!"

"Smatingan, start an article criticizing his early days.
Jones, begin an analysis of possible impeachment proceed-
ings."

"You bet!"

"Gotcha, chief!"

Scaw!

A large group of people wearing assorted sports jerseys over their jumpsuits were gathered around a young, trim redhead.

"But why do I have to wear a sweatshirt for a major Chicago baseball team?" asked the woman, staring down at her new garb in remorse. "I know I'm new here, but I like hockey and hail from Moscow!"

"Because you are now a 'Cubs' reporter!" chorused the laughing Sports Department.

In response, the woman grabbed an autographed puck off a marble stand on her desk, assumed a pitching position, and everybody scattered for cover.

Scaw!

A ghostly wind moaned among the vast array of empty desks and toppled-over chairs. Amid the desolation sat a lone teenager alongside a silent Z-band teleprinter. As the team approached they could see he was beginning a solitaire game of Chess-Monopoly. He obviously planned to be on shift for a long while.

"Hello, Dame Collins," called out the youth listlessly as the team walked by.

Rikka froze in her tracks and stiffly jerked about. Hastily the rest of the news team backed away from the woman. If they achieved sufficient distance, there was a theoretical possibility of surviving the coming explosion.

"For your information," stated the newswoman, her words rising in both tone and timber, "I have divorced that symbiotic life-form which I was once foolish enough to call a husband. So don't call me Dame Collins, Countess d'Soyez, Milady, Lady, or anything else that even remotely resembles a pracking claim to the pracking aristocracy of pracking Mars!"

A white flag hastily formed from a handkerchief and pencil popped into view from under the desk and began energetically waving. "No problem, buddy," squeaked a voice.

Accepting the obviously sincere apology, Collins stomped back to rejoin her friends.

"I'm so glad that you have finally learned to control that awful temper of yours," said Harry with a straight face.

"Ah, shaddup," she grumbled.

Scaw!

A plush velvet rope supported by brass stands surrounded a large, humming, white box about the size of a shuttle. A tiny speaker was mounted on top and a technician on a stepladder was fiddling with the attached wires.

"It's the New-New Download News!" called out the speaker. "All the pertinent details of every important news story fresh for you every minute on the minute!" A beep. "It's the New-New Download News!"

"Excuse me, Bill?" said Harry, stopping for a moment. The tech glanced up from his work. "Yeah, Harry?"

Snyder made a face. "How the prack is this any different from the original Download News? Sounds like exactly the same old thing to me."

A grin. "It's new because of all the fresh viewers we have gotten after slapping a brand-new 'new' before the old word 'new' in the title."

The team shuddered and walked away. Next week it would probably become the All-Brand-New-New. Marketing. Ek! Briefly Jhonny wondered if being insane was a basic job requirement in that department, or just a perk?

Scaw!

Suddenly the carpet changed from functional to decorative and grew a couple inches in thickness. Dotting the downy acreage were a dozen islands of plush couches forming artistically pleasing conversational pits. Perfect spots for impromptu interviews, surreptitious bribes, and quietly firing somebody popular. Like your mom.

Next came a squat fortress of polished mahogany cleverly disguised as a simple desk, behind which sat a smiling old woman frosting doughnuts. Behind the formidable secretary was the enclosed office of Paul Ambocksky, the Executive Producer for the Satellite News Team, who was as close to a boss as they would deign to admit existed.

Normally the four walls of soundproof Armorlite were perfectly clear so that all could see how hard the boss was working. And vice versa. But today the glass was clouded white for privacy. In addition, crimson laser beams formed a brilliant cage about the office, informing everybody with the mental IQ of a slug that there was no admittance. Which meant the Producer was safe from everybody but the legal staff.

"Hi, Mrs. Seigling!" sang out the android as he approached the desk.

"Morning, people," gaily called the white-haired woman. "Oh. Mr. Smith, Major Deitrich called to say that you forgot your camcorder."

Drat. So he had. "Thanks!"

"No problem, Jhonny."

That stopped the android cold. His name. She had just used his real name. "Ah, pardon me?" he managed to say coherently.

"Oh, pooh. Of course, I know who you really are," she whispered in return. "And I think it's just wonderful that the station has illegally employed you. The Organic Law of 2285 forbidding the hiring of artificial people for anything other than menial labor is . . . oh, it's just dumb!"

The vehemence with which the elderly woman administered that last word made it seem as if that was the ultimate insult to her.

"I agree," he smiled. Hesitantly he offered a hand and it was accepted without any hesitation on the part of the human woman. They shook.

"Doughnut?" she offered politely and everybody took at least four. Just to be polite.

"Now get on in," she scolded him. "Mr. Ambocksky has a very important message for you."

"From whom?" asked Harry as the thick office door swung open wide at their approach.

"Don't know!" replied Seigling to the closing door, paused in the act of offering the plate of fresh doughnuts.

Inside the office, encased by the clouded glass walls, the room appeared much smaller than usual. In the corner a si-

lent TV monitor showed a picture of Harry bringing his
fist hurtling down toward the *Carx-Toz joq* and cut to a
picture of a bar of soap wearing a cape and flying toward
a toxic waste dump.

Across the room, a sturdy steel desk backed a row of
file cabinets. Slumped in a floating chair was a pale, thin
man in a rumpled gray jumpsuit.

"You're too late," announced Ambocksky glumly from
his seat. "It's dead."

CHAPTER FOUR

AT THE HORRIBLE pronouncement, shocked silence exploded across the office. Then puzzlement.

"Eh?"

"What?"

"Who is dead? The story?"

"What story?!"

Listlessly, Paul Ambocksky gestured at his desk where a plain plastic envelope lay on the recessed control panel. "It's not a story. Not yet anyway. I was talking about this letter."

Brushing crumbs off her jumpsuit, Rikka paused to squint an eye and try to hear that correctly. "Gimme this again, Box. The *letter* is dead?"

A glum nod. "I tried to keep it powered for as long as I could, but too much of the circuitry had been changed."

Now she understood. Ah, an electric letter!

"Well, who is it from?" asked Harry grumpily, trying to clear a stubborn walnut bit from a molar.

"Can't tell. The outside has been wiped clean."

Eagerly the curious team gathered around the limp rectangle.

"Interesting," murmured Collins thoughtfully. Was it a warning? A dire call for help? A hot tip? Stolen government documents? Bulk mail from some billionaire?

"Is this an example of E-Mail?" asked Michelangelo, poking at it with a surgical probe. The tips of his whiskers were lightly frosted with pink sugar.

Toothpick in mouth, Jhonny cocked a grin upward.

"Nyah. E-Mail is a message received over a computer modem. This is a hollograph."

"A what?" asked the alien. "You mean a . . . no, wait." Slowly came comprehension. If a holo-gram was a three-dimensional image and a holo-graph was a message or letter written by a single person. Then combine them and you get—a hollograph.

"A 3-D letter?" He paused. "Two l's, correct?"

"Exactly." Harry smiled, using a handkerchief to wipe a bit of chocolate from his chin. Never had this problem with a good wholesome Danish.

Personally, the anchor was quite pleased that the tech had figured out the terminology so fast. A lot of humans still hadn't gotten the three classifications clearly defined. Three meters tall and the guy was all brains.

"Open this baby up and almost anything could pop out."

"Impressive," cooed Jhonny, raw avarice illuminating his eyes. Advanced technology was better than doughnuts! Yum.

Box agreed. "And costly. Mrs. Seigling almost fainted when she found it on her desktop this afternoon. We checked with security and discovered that a janitor had found it lying in a corridor on Level 22."

"Life support?"

A nod. "For some reason the thing has been deliberately bent, folded, and mutilated. Stomped on, set afire, bombarded with gamma rays, and then flushed down the toilet. An automatic rag picker in Sanitation pulled it out for a human worker to authorize its destruction." A rueful smile. "Biodegradable this thing is not."

"Good system," complemented Mike.

A shrug. "It saved our butt before, retrieving misplaced documents," noted Paul. Leaning back in his chair, the producer laced his hands atop his stomach. "But what I can't understand is, who would send you guys one of these? It's made of pure Florentine Plastic, tougher than a spaceship hull and will not, repeat not, open unless all of you are present. That thing costs more than a year's salary!"

"Wow," said Mike, duly impressed. And he thought the postage rates on his world had been high!

Curiously flipping the envelope over with the probe, the technician took an EM tuner from his toolvest and tried adjusting the molecular polarity of a photovolic sensor patch. After a bit of fidgeting, there came a tiny sucking sound, and the moist patch of plastic eased up to show an amazing complex of ultra-fine superconductor integrated circuitry nano-filaments.

Box almost jumped out of his chair. "Mike, baby, sweetheart, booby, buddy!" he gushed uncontrollably. "Can you fix it?"

Absentmindedly the alien started removing tools from his bulky vest and laying them haphazardly about on the desk, uncaring of the precious station documents he was getting soiled.

"Maybe," he murmured, removing his pince-nez glasses and sliding on a pair of microsurgeon's optical scanners. There was a click/hum and the letter was now illuminated with a low-level, sourceless, white laser light.

"Where were you anyway?" demanded Ambocksky, straightening in his chair. "I did send an emergency recall."

Pushing his hat back on his head, Harry walked over to the file cabinet and opened the top drawer. "Box, half of our recalls are listed as an emergency," he said, mixing Scotch and water in a tumbler. "So we came straight here. No stopping off for a beer or anything."

Reluctantly the Executive Producer had to accept that. Fair was fair. Even when it was damn annoying. "Gin and tonic, for me," he sighed. "And don't forget the antacids."

A wink. "Of course." And Snyder handed him a glass filled with a murky liquid swirling with tiny white particles. Together, they clinked and drank. Everybody else tried to ignore them. It was an acquired taste of most studio executives and all of the sales personnel.

Trying to assist, Jhonny rolled up a chair for the alien who sat down when it hit the rear of his knees. A grunt was the only response.

During all of this, Rikka had been making a four-course meal out of the inside of a cheek. So somebody had seriously attempted to destroy an incredibly expensive letter to them, eh?

"Maria," she declared at last. "It's got to be."

Laying aside his empty glass, Ambocksky agreed. "Most likely, yes, it was the handiwork of our beloved Station Manager, Ms. Valdez.

"But," Paul added, raising a cautionary finger, "knowing the lady fox, chances are we'll never be able to prove it to the boss."

Yeah, she had Wilkes wrapped tight around her little finger and the owner liked it there.

Light flashes strobed from the desk and a sudden stink of ozone and burning wood filled the room. Automatically the vents started blowing fresh air in an effort to filter out the odious impurities. Then the overhead fire sprinklers started to warningly tick and Box used the cut-off switch under his desk to kill the onrushing deluge.

Harry went to the cabinet for a refill. Where the heck was the ice? Ah, under C for cube. Cold? "Actually, I'm rather impressed at the resiliency of the material to still function properly after a full week in Maria's conniving hands."

"Florentine Plastic is tough stuff," said Jhonny. "It's what the United Solar Defense Alliance uses to make Samson powerarmor."

A grudging acceptance. USDA was the best.

Cycling up a chair from the floor, Rikka took a seat. "I wonder where the prack has this thing been since it arrived? Whenever it did arrive."

Fascinated, their boss was minutely watching the alien tech do things he could not even comprehend.

"Unknown," said Box honestly, refusing to glance away. "Because apparently after failing to destroy the letter, Maria did the most clever and fiendish trick of all!"

Jhonny turned from staring over Mike's shoulder. "She gave it to the boss?"

"Yep."

Everybody groaned.

Miniature lightning bolts were crackling over the desk and parts of Michelangelo's hide seemed to catch fire. But since the busy tech wasn't complaining, the rest of the team decided not to disrupt his concentration. However, Snyder did bring the seltzer bottle closer by. Just in case.

"Gardner Wilkes," sighed Collins, shaking her head. "That man could get lost in his own Closet-Doc."

Swiveling about, Paul offered a half smile. "Not anymore. On his tenth anniversary of inheriting the station, we gave him a signet ring that has a homer broadcast unit built into the Armorlite stone. So wherever he goes in the station, Security can instantly locate him."

"Bull," declared the anchor.

With a humph, Box hit a button on his desktop. "Security, this is Mr. Ambocksky. Where is Mr. Wilkes at the present moment?"

A crackle of static.

"Security?"

"Here, Mr. Ambocksky," replied a voice from the desktop. "We're ah, busy at the moment digging through the garbage in the trash compactor on Level 36."

Harry leaned in close. This was too delicious to miss. "Why?" he asked succinctly.

There was a pause.

"We . . . ah . . . have located Mr. Wilkes's signal ring at the bottom of the refuse pile and are valiantly trying to retrieve it for him."

"Are you sure he's not also down there?" asked Jhonny, crossing his legs. *Dead* was the unspoken condition.

The desk spoke fast. "Oh, no sir. No doubt about that. He was just recently seen on Level 12 trying to go up the down turbo-lift." Another pause. "We think."

Grinning, the Executive Producer couldn't help himself. "Lost again, eh?" he asked, amused.

"Lost?" squeaked the desk, as if it had never heard the word before. "Oh, good golly gosh, no sir. The owner of the station never gets lost. He's just doing one of his infamous surprise random inspection tours. Isn't that right, troops?"

"*Yes, sir!*" chorused a dozen voices. "*A surprise inspection tour, sir!*"

Chuckling, Box hit the switch cutting the connection. "Wilkes certainly has them well trained," he acknowledged.

"And you should see them dance!" added Snyder, tipping his half-full tumbler in remembrance of the New Year's party.

Suddenly there came a small eruption at the desk. Coughing into a paw, Michelangelo backed away fast as a miniature mushroom cloud began to form over the glowing envelope.

"It's working!" he cried, whipping off his goggles and sliding his glasses back on.

Ready for anything, the reporters circled around the desk. But not too close. In ragged stages, the letter creaked open its flap and then began to unfold like a badly rusted mechanical flower. When it was perfectly flat and square there came a loud click.

. . . and a fifty-piece Philharmonic orchestra appeared jammed within the small confines of the office, packed tight to the walls, the string section actually suspended upside down from the ceiling. Harry had a tuba sticking out of his head and Ambocksky was speared through the chest by the longbow of a bass fiddle. Loudly the translucent conductor tapped a baton upon his music stand, situated directly behind the giant Michelangelo, and instantly the band crashed into a stirring rendition of the ancient classic "Oklahoma!" which rapidly swelled into a thundering crescendo of legally stolen ASCAP cleared music!

Trapped somewhere among the woodwinds and the cowbells, Rikka had to admit that she was impressed. This was really expensive paper. The best Collins had ever seen before was a birthday card that created a hologram clown head that gave her a cake and lit the candles. But then the card short-circuited, the clown blew out the candles, and the cake promptly exploded.

Actually, it was one of the better presents she got that year.

Just then from off camera a dapper man wearing the ancient red velvet jacket, white ruffled shirt, red velvet pantaloons, and camouflaged combat boots of a high Imperial butler stepped into view.

In silent terror, Rikka had backed through kettle drums and violins to reach a corner of the office and drag a chair in front of her as protection. No . . . no! It can't be!

"Greetings and salutations, Satellite News Team!" partially sang the outrageously dressed servant. "Let it be herewith known to all and sundry that their most royal majesties, King Hobart Van DeLellis Yertzoff Junior and Queen Lolita 'Boom-Boom' Yertzoff XXVIII, the Imperial rulers of North Mars, South Wells, East Burroughs, and Lower Phobos—up to, but not past, the big meteor crater—are pleased and proud to invite Harry Snyder, Rikka Collins, John Smith, and Michelangelo to cordially come, with a few thousand friends and guests, to Not-Uncle-Bob's Castle to partake in a gala party celebrating the betrothal of their son, Prince Vladamir Yertzoff and Lady Henretta Caramico, of New Old South Mars, as they officially announce their engagement to be married!"

The trumpets did what trumpets do best and the gasping reporters wiggled fingers in their ears attempting to restore lost hearing. Goddamn, didn't this thing have a volume control?

"R. S. V. P. is not necessary," continued the icily proper manservant, obviously impervious to the brutal sonic assault. "Nor is BYOB. Hors d'oeuvres will be served. Come early for good seating. No lizards, please."

The trumpets blared again, even louder than before.

"Be there, or be square!" finished the butler in the ritual good-bye of the Martian rich.

Once more the entire fifty-piece orchestra crashed into action, this time doing a rousing version of "Money Can't Buy You Love" that cross-faded into "I'm Getting Married in the Morning" and ended with an excerpt from *The Twilight Zone* theme. Then the hologram faded into nothingness and blessed silence reigned in the office for several minutes.

In one gulp Harry downed the rest of his drink. Ice cubes included. Jhonny rushed over to revive the fainted Rikka and Michelangelo sat down hard on the floor with a strident boom that rattled keyboards all the way to the semimythical Weather Department.

"By the blessed ghost of St. William F. Buckley," gushed Ambocksky, crossing himself. "What an honor! It'll be the scoop of the year!"

"Furgl," said the alien, sticking out his tongue.

"On toast!" agreed Jhonny, patting the wrist of his fallen comrade. The camera-op had no idea what the Gremlin word meant, but it sure sounded appropriate!

As Snyder dampened a cloth under the water cooler and got more ice from the file cabinet, Box twisted about to stare at the comatose Collins. Hmm, she could be a problem. But then again, nyah. Rikka was a trouper. A pro! Besides, there was plenty of time to con her into going. It might take a couple of days, or even a week, but that couldn't matter. Why, the party wasn't scheduled until . . . quickly he bent over his desk to read the written copy of the announcement on the plastic sheet and went totally pale.

The royal party had started five minutes ago!

Lying naked on a massage table in her expansive office, with only a small towel covering her pert hindquarters, Maria Valdez rested her head in the crook of a bent arm and started to allow herself to relax under her daily massage.

Standing alongside the reclining woman, Danny J continued to run his large hands along the oily expanse of her long sensuous body. A fully functioning male android, he was having his usual difficult time at this task. To his everlasting shame, Danny was a sexual pervert and found human females extremely desirable. Especially his often nude boss. His tiny cubicle was wallpapered with photos of her lovely scowling face and his dreams were tortured

with fevered visions of going to Iowa with her and endlessly breaking the law.

"I had really hoped the letter would get lost and they'd
blow this assignment," the Station Manager purred, a fleeting tingle coursing through her supple form under the
adroit administrations of the anatomically correct machine
male. God, she has got to stop thinking like that! "Even a
minor black mark against the unorthodox team would be
something I could use at the contract negotiating table to
help oust those mavericks!"

Automatically Danny eased more oil from the reserves
in his forearms and proceeded to knead the tanned flash of
her soft calves, slowly working his way up past the dainty
knees.

"It was a valiant try, madam," he offered, trying not to
ogle.

"They never send in written reports! Or get receipts
when they bribe an underworld contact. They crash that
shuttle once a day! And they aren't aware that the station
even *has* a dress code!"

"I know, I know."

Petulantly Maria turned her head about, her long ebony
tresses whipping up and over her back to teasingly slash
across the face of her android butler. Several of his internal circuits went into near overload and his heart started
pounding hard enough to be visibly seen outside his
jumpsuit.

"Bah," she said grumpily, wiggling deliciously. "A
news station should be like any other business. You throttle the competition and force the workers into total uni-
formity, thus increasing their work output to excellence
yielding a maximum profit!"

A sudden rush of internal warmth in his torso and cyborg brain nearly overcame the sweating butler. Holy Ko-
pek! He just loved it when she talked money! Warming the
palms of his hands slightly, the android started running his
fingertips up along the outer swell of her slim thighs, his
thumbs arcing over the dappled curves to tantalizingly stop
just where the stolen hotel towel barely covered one of the

three forbidden portions of her nubile body. Actually, there were four. Left and right.

As Maria reached down to scratch at an itch on her hip, the tiny motion made the towel lose its precarious position and flutter to the floor. Electrified, Danny gasped, his hands going stiff. In response, Maria Valdez rolled over to see what was wrong.

Before she could even speak, his eyes filled with the ample glorious wonders of the voluptuous human. Danny's beleaguered brain reeled under 134 different and conflicting emotions. Overwhelmed by the sheer volume of these new feelings, the android turned itself off and dropped limp to the floor.

Eh? "Danny!" In a rush of uncharacteristic concern, Maria leaped off the table and rushed to the fallen android. She felt for a pulse in his hands, then shook herself. The arms and legs were mechanical, only the torso and head were silicon-based living organic material.

Straddling the fainted being, Valdez ripped off his jumpsuit and started pounding on his chest. Nothing. Desperate, the woman crouched over the still form to attempt mouth-to-mouth resuscitation. She was willing to do anything to get the heart started of her valued butler and only friend.

Anything!

In the presidential wing of Media, in the vaunted Chief Executive Suite, the handle of the Closet-Doc rattled once more.

"Hello?" called out the voice of Gardner Wilkes from inside. "I seem to have accidentally, ah, broken the lock again. Anybody out there? Security? Box? Maria? Hello?"

On the nearby dressing table lay an executive cellular phone, a com-link, a wrist secretary, and a ring key.

The handle rattled louder than before, but nobody in the hall outside could hear the tiny plaintive noise.

* * *

"NO . . . !" screamed Rikka at the top of her lungs, digging her fingernails into the dura-steel floor of the space station launch deck. "I won't go! No! Never!"

Each holding grimly on to a wiggling ankle, Harry and Jhonny exchanged exasperated glances as they struggled to try to drag their friend into the waiting QSNT space shuttle.

"Well?" grunted Snyder. "Where's some of that fabulous superhuman strength?"

Jhonny sneered at the anchor. "I'm a droid, not a robot, you bozo," grunted the camera-op back at him. "I only have normal human strength." A pause. Grin. "Which is about twice what you have."

"Up yours, Tobor."

"Anytime, Methuselah!"

While searching for a suitably insulting retort, Snyder jerked his head. "Why doesn't the furry mountain lend a paw?"

Lounging near the open hatchway of the space shuttle, Mike crossed his leviathan arms and gave a mighty shrug.

"Sorry," the technician apologized in a rumbling stentorian bass. "But I'm a pacifist and would never use physical force on a sentient being." A smile. "It's not like she's a space pirate or an Amway salesman."

Steel hands wrapped tight around a boot, Jhonny exerted all of his strength to no avail. Damn muscular humans! "Behave!"

"No! I don't do weddings!" shrieked Rikka, scratching wildly at the smooth metal of the launch deck.

"It ain't a wedding," grunted Harry. "It's an engagement party!"

"That's even worse!"

"It's for the pracking prince of Mars!"

"I didn't vote for him!"

"It's the most important social event of the year!" added Deitrich from the hatchway.

"Phooey!"

"It's the political event of the decade!" tried Harry.

"Then call me next year!"

A sudden twinkle formed in Mike's pupilless eyes. "Then you didn't hear about the plot to kill the prince?" he asked, askance.

Instantly Rikka stopped fighting and rolled over to face the towering alien.

"Really?" she breathed gingerly. "An assassination plot?"

Solemnly the alien took a taloned finger and made an X over his lower left side. "Cross my hearts."

Shaking off the grip of her friends, Collins leaped to her feet and sprinted into the shuttle. Her repulsion for Mars was totally swamped by her lust for news.

"Well?" her voice echoed from inside the vehicle. "What are you waiting for? An assassination? This is real news! Is it politically motivated? A personal revenge? The first step of another military coup by his Mad Uncle Bob?"

Stumbling inside, Harry patted the alien on the arm. Which was as high as he could reach. "Nice going, big guy."

"Thanks," panted an exhausted Jhonny. A toothy grin. "I do what I can."

"Hey, guys!" called out Collins. "Will you come on? We're late already!"

"All aboard!" Deitrich yodeled. "First stop, Mars!"

CHAPTER FIVE

MARIA SUCCEEDED.

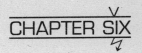

CHAPTER SIX

THE LIVERIED HERALD of the royal castle thumped the golden end of his announcement staff a mandatory three times on the polished floor of Martian marble.

"Ladies and gentlemen," he boomed in a perfectly pitched operatic voice. "Sirs and dames, doctors, lawyers, chiefs, braves, knights, pages, mages, sages, dandydancers, bindlestiffs, hottentots, and yahoos, may I present thee . . . the Satellite News Team!"

On cue, the ornate gilded doors irised wide and in through the portal stepped the QSNT reporters. Or, at least, something that vaguely resembled them.

Hurriedly grabbing something from the good side of the Closet-Queen in her apartment, Rikka was still snuggling into a full-length, formal ball gown of layered white chiffon, with gathered tiers of frothy lace about the waist, puff-topped angel sleeves, and an underwire bodice that augmented her figure absurdly and left the end result on open display for all to peruse. A pristine satin choker with a sterling silver clasp in the shape of a butterfly went about her throat, enhancing its natural length, and a corsage adorned her left wrist, neatly hiding the miniature stun gun she was carrying in case her moron ex dared to show his nose.

The lacy, white, high-heeled shoes that had come with the garment, Rikka had unceremoniously dumped out the airlock of the shuttle while they were still in high orbit about the purple planet. There were just some things she wouldn't do for any story.

Ever-prepared for sartorial occasions, Harry was sporting a painfully elegant, six-piece hyper-tuxedo made entirely of primary colors and exposed electrical circuitry. A small Jacob's ladder formed his tie with a constant ripple of lightning cracking up the parallel bars of insulated metal.

Downplaying himself as much as possible, Jhonny was in a formal Zoot suit with fifty-seven-inch shoulder pads, pin-striped sneakers, and an apparently endless loop of gold chain dangling from his waist. Even his camcorder was decked out in studded leather with a tiny tasteful plume of genetically duplicated bald eagle feathers cresting its array of lenses.

Astonishingly dignified, Mike was cocooned in a Chinese landscape design burnoose, his great head topped with a rainbow-colored turban sporting what resembled a fresh turnip pinned to the middle.

As the trumpets blared once more, the team proceeded down the wide marble steps, shaking hands and murmuring endless introductions about themselves to countless potentates, aristocracy, royal bastards, and other assorted regal nobodies.

"Ex-Lady Dame Ricardalena Collins d'Soyez!"

Gritting her teeth, Rikka took the insult but made a mental note to shoot the herald in the kneecaps later on. Her full name, eh? She deduced the subtle revenge of her ex in that.

"Professor Harold Farland Snyder!"

Trying not to trip on her ridiculous gown, Rikka eyed her friend. "Professor?" she whispered, releasing yet another limp hand.

He made a face. "A Terran university gave me an honorary degree once long ago, when I exposed some folderol with the faculty pension funds."

More damp hands. "Interesting. What college?"

"Harvard, Rutgers, Duke, who remembers. Who cares?"

Collins wisely sensed a sore point here and decided to drop the subject. But not forever.

"Jonathan Smith, Pulitzer prize winner!"

"I wish they'd stop adding that," mumbled the android, palming hands with machine precision, but his camcorder preened with pride.

DID YOU REALLY? scrolled Deitrich, surprised. I NEVER KNEW.

A shrug. "I was lucky once and got a shot of a frigate of the Free Police, who are neither, being blasted out of a midnight sky by a battery of Terran Defense laser cannons above the Aurora Borealis on Earth. I won for best Humorous Photo."

KEEN. ARE POSTERS AVAILABLE?

As Jhonny choked back a laugh, Snyder gave his friend a thumbs-up in appreciation. But Michelangelo was deeply impressed. The alien technician had been unaware of the vaunted company he kept!

Now the herald at the top of the steps consulted a monitor imprinted on the palm of his left hand, took a deep, deep breath, and cut loose, *"Qotht-nkjr Djb'bhtn* Michelangelo"—the sound of a door falling over and slamming to the floor—*"aaraa-ting!"*

"Good job," acknowledged Mike in sincere admiration.

Releasing another group of wiggling digits, he briefly returned up the stairs to paw the coughing man a throat drop. Gratefully the herald accepted the lozenge and began sucking. Whew, that had been a toughie.

Reaching the bottom of the stairs, the team passed effortlessly through a deadly weapons detector, with only a minor problem occurring with Jhonny's metallic limbs. But the team played games with steel fountain pens, iron suit buttons, and the mobile camcorder until the guards were thoroughly confused and finally satisfied.

Hopefully the food was better protected than the King, noted Harry as they retreated from the weapons sensor and the guard found new people to play with. Ye gods, he hated amateurs.

"By the way, Mike, what does all that stuff before your name mean anyway?" asked Rikka.

"That my parents were married," replied the alien. Then a thought occurred. "Out of curiosity, were yours?"

Collins barked a laugh. "Yes. And to each other, I might add!"

The technician turned away from the reporter so that she couldn't see the smile on his face. "Really? How bizarre."

Caught in midstep, Rikka almost tripped. Here the floor was deeply carpeted for an arrow's flight of length. Then came a small country of marble stretching off to the distance. Dimly it appeared the carpeting again graced the floor later on, but it may have only been a mirage caused by the extreme distance. The vaunted ceiling itself was only a vague rumor to be substantiated later. Not-Uncle-Bob's Castle was big. Really, really big. The place was most definitely, uncategorically, absolutely, monstrously, dictionary definition big. Maybe even huge.

And the crowds . . . !

How many thousands moved about the palatial abode was impossible to calculate. Every type of dress and suit was to be seen in the colossal room, every manner of person, people, human, android, cyborg, and fuzzy alien. It was as if the insane asylums of the worlds had been given a day pass and raided a local shopping mall. Rikka realized wryly that they could have disconnected Deitrich from the life support system of the shuttle and wheeled the disembodied brain in a jar into the castle and nobody would have even noticed. On the other hand, the attending crowd might have run screaming into the night. Chuckle.

Just then, with a blond bimbo on each handle, a disembodied brain in a jar wheeled by on a mobile life support cart and the news reporter almost swallowed her tongue.

Then again, maybe not.

A dozen or so Philharmonic orchestras scattered about the upholstered airplane hangar were playing a jazz/polka fusion music for a skimpy thousand or so dancers. Incredibly, all the bands were doing the exact same tune, at exactly the same timing. These guys were good!

Hundreds of giant chandeliers dotted the two-hundred-hectare ceiling, approximately one every ten meters. Lining the endless walls were limitless white linen tables piled high with mounds of unidentifiable stuff. Tremen-

dous cargo bay hatches, thinly disguised as ornamental
French doors, offered unlimited access to scores of other
rooms, gardens, pools, patios, alcoves, balconies, terraces,
and colonnades. Set twenty meters up the colossal fresco
walls were dozens of planetarium-sized windows made of
millions of pieces of stained glass. The setting sun cast a
stunning panorama of breathtaking rainbows slashing
across the assorted aristocracy and their trailing retinues.

Unfortunately, spoiling the whole artistic effect was the
unsettling fact that the pictures in the windows were all of
famous cartoon characters: mice, ducks, cats, wombats,
flying squirrels, etcetera. Each was doing the most improb-
able and highly painful things to one another with farm
implements, boulders, kitchen appliances, and explosives.

"Yet another grand contribution to the world of fine art
by Mad Uncle Bob," smirked Jhonny. But to be honest,
the android was forced to grudgingly admit that the windows were actually the only thing he liked about this
billion-dollar mausoleum.

Mike tilted his head at the name, almost losing his turnip and turban, but said nothing.

"Shall we mingle and rendezvous here in, say, an
hour?" asked Rikka, glancing at her wrist secretary.

"There's safety in numbers," reminded Jhonny.

Harry slapped the android on the back. "Oh, how bad
can this place be? I say we go get the bird's-eye lowdown
on his engagement."

"And the assassination," added Collins, a steely glint in
her eyes. "With this crappy security anything can happen
to the prince! So keep an eye out for His Highness. But
don't get too close. We want to observe the murder, not
get killed ourselves."

Somehow, her friends managed to remain mum and
tried valiantly to radiate an aura of total innocence.

"Oh, there you are!" called a sultry voice from the
crowd. "Rikka-Tikki-tavi!"

With a sigh, Collins turned as the rest of her team
quickly dispersed into the throng.

"Hi, Aunt Matilda," the reporter exhaled.

Dripping furs and fringe, the female zeppelin wafted closer. "I just thought you'd like to know that Armand can't make the party, but he sends his deep regrets."

Not deep enough, mentally added Rikka. Unless he's in hell and still digging.

"By the way, where's your new lover?" asked the countess in a conspiratorial tone as she glanced around at the nearby males.

"Dead," said Rikka woodenly. "I ate him."

A mascara blink. "Really?" Matilda leaned closer, her jewelry clinking like diamond bells. "I often do the same myself, but men are just so darn fattening!" With a merry laugh the widow found another person to bother and drifted away.

Staring aghast at the departing countess, Rikka hit her knees there in the crowd and quickly thanked the lord that the royal loony was not a blood relative. Ohthankyouthankyouthankyou.

Strolling about, Michelangelo felt somebody bump into him slightly harder than the rest and looked down to see who it was.

"Hey, *aaraa*!" called a young man with a dueling scar on each cheek. "A question please?"

"Yes?" rumbled the alien in his most threatening tone. That usually was enough to send the majority of humans scurrying for cover. But apparently this one was more resolute, or dumber, than most.

"What is that thing atop your head?"

A fuzzy blink. "It is called a turban."

The scars curved into an amused grimace. "Yes, I know that! I meant what's that other thing?"

"A turnip."

"I beg your pardon," bespoke the duelist in a tone to suggest that doing so was entirely out of the question.

"An edible root," explained Mike slowly. "Of the biennial herb genus *Brassica*, the family Cruciferae." One should always be patient with the mentally handicapped.

Laughing, the youth wandered away to begin retelling the humorous tale for the rest of the party.

Michelangelo coldly viewed the decapitated dying rose in the young man's lapel. At least his was functional. You could always eat a turnip! And with that thought, the Gremlin glanced about the ballroom and headed straight for the buffet table. Apples? Were there any apples? Yes!!

Maneuvering through the parade of dignitaries, Harry continued his quest for a chair. If he had to associate with these loonies for the rest of the day, at least he could be comfortable. And drinking was verboten, as this was work. It was even theoretically possible that something newsworthy might occur.

In a corner, Snyder spied the prince. His outfit was a military jumpsuit with a red sash across the chest and only a handful of medals. Unlike so many of his brethren, Harry knew that Vladamir had earned what he wore rather than simply purchasing them from the Not-Uncle-Bob's Castle gift shop.

Oddly, for a man who was getting engaged today, Yertzoff seemed somber, almost depressed. Taking a stance behind a stand of fruit-bearing oak trees, Harry watched as the heir to the Martian throne called over a butler and handed him a wristwatch. Eh? No, wait. Snyder had seen Wilkes himself with a similar watch. It was a personal Z-band transponder. Impressive. Hmm, must be broken and he wanted the butler to have it fixed. Those babies were not a disposable item. Even for a prince, the communicators were expensive!

The butler seemed loath to accept the device, but the prince insisted. Solemnly the manservant turned to depart and the watch trilled. The prince nearly fell as he spun about and sprinted forward to snatch the watch from the stunned servant. Yertzoff fiddled with the controls for a moment. Then became very calm and strolled away with the watch still clutched in his white-knuckled fist.

Curious. Most curious.

A manicured hand tugged at his sleeve. "Excuse me, sir?"

Braced for the worst, Harry was pleasantly surprised to find himself being addressed by a slim, dapper man in a conservatively cut tuxedo. A cluster of ribbons and medals on his lapel marked the fellow as a duke of the northern regions. One of the less goofy divisions of the Martian royalty.

"How can I help, your lordship?" oozed the anchor.

"As a reporter who has traveled the solar system, do you happen to know any good assassins?"

Eh? "What was that?"

The duke rotated to show a bull's-eye target painted on his back. "Killers, I need a good murderer," he repeated. "I'm the current Count de la Canals and all fifteen of my ancestors who held the title were assassinated before the age of forty-five.

"I'm forty-four and a half!" wailed the man. "I must maintain the tradition or disgrace my family name!"

The anchor could only stare at the lunatic.

Trying to look everywhere at once, the duke lowered his head to whisper. "Actually for the past five years I have been doing my very best to annoy major crime figures in hopes of bringing their dire retaliation upon myself."

Harry's jaw sagged.

In misunderstanding, the lord took it as an attempt to speak and raised a hand to cut him off. "I know, I know. I should have done something nasty to those awful space pirates, the Free Police. But who can find them when you don't want them?"

Taking a moment to regain his composure, Harry shuddered and then raced pellmell into the amassed royalty. The bar. Where was the bar? It was his only hope. Off to the right, he spied a tiered fountain gushing amber liquid with a foamy head on top and he veered in that direction.

Ah, salvation.

Narrowly having escaped a meeting with even more of her ex-relatives, Rikka stood catching her breath over by the gift table. The doomed prince was nowhere in sight,

but that was hardly surprising. The reporter knew from experience that rich people would drop off their own gifts
and then quickly scurry away so that nobody would think
they were snooping on what everybody else gave. Thus in
this boiling madhouse of the rich and brainless, it was a
small island of serenity.

As gifts had been discouraged, the linen-draped stage
was relatively small. Probably no more than a medium forest had been chopped down to make the massive support.
And wood on Mars was as rare as an original euphemism.
The centuries of terraforming that had changed the dead
red planet to the purple world of today, capable of supporting life, such as it was, had not yet made Mars a blue/
white oxygen-rich planet where trees grew in abundance,
oceans of fresh water lapped at sandy shores, and birds
could fly in the upper atmosphere without the aid of tiny
specially built respirators.

Every color in nature, and more than a few artificial
ones from Wilkes Labs, adorned the boxes, crates, and barrels piled higgledy-piggledy on the table. A fire engine
was parked alongside, so that guests could use the ladder
to place a new gift on the ever-growing pile o' loot. Indeed, the offerings were stacked dangerously high, the top-
most layers swaying to and fro in the thermals caused by
this many noisy people jammed together. There was even
what appeared to be a solid gold space shuttle half buried
under the bacchanalian booty. It was as if some mad
yuppie god of old had combined the Horn of Plenty with
a posh jewelry store.

There were no apparent guards; however, the suits of
medieval armor standing in the nearby wall niches were
not holding antique halberds spears or claymore swords,
but Mark IV Gibraltar Assault Cannons. Having twelve
barrels, one trigger, and no safety, the dire weapons were
each capable of delivering more assorted destruction than
a squad of drunk Marines on furlough.

Keeping her hands in plain sight, Rikka eased away
from the table. A reporter's immunity did not extend to su-
personic bullets, or antipersonnel lasers. Besides, one of

them might conceivably be a fan of QINS and look upon this as their big chance for revenge.

After getting a couple of nice minutes of the stained-glass cartoons for the stock footage file, Jhonny wandered about the crowd taking random shots of whatever seemed interesting. A muscular man atop a shaved puma rode into view, closely followed by a lavender jumpsuit with nobody in it. Sadly, people often got intimidated by the presence of a photographer and shied away trying to hide.

"Ah ha!" cried two voices.

And a pair of dowagers collided before the camera-op. Each woman was wearing more jewels than clothes and incredibly that seemed to be the actual intent.

"I'm wearing eighty-nine percent of my body weight in diamonds," declared one.

The other scoffed. "I'm wearing ninety-two percent of my body weight."

"Oh, yeah?"

"Yeah!"

Appearing from the crowd came a slim woman of inter-mediate years. She was tastefully dressed in a simple black gown and was carrying a bowling bag. Stepping close, she opened the bag and let the other women peek inside. They both gasped in terror.

"I win," smirked the third woman.

Stifling a yawn, Jhonny moved on. Get a hobby, ya bozos.

"And how are you enjoying the engagement ceremony of Prince Yertzoff?" asked Rikka Collins, holding a microphone close to the pile of caviar on the elaborate snack table.

"Oh, we love it!" cried a voice from the direction of the food. An elderly man nearby used a napkin to wipe his lips and hide their movement. "Haven't had so much fun since my last tax audit!"

Adjusting the camcorder resting on his shoulder, Jhonny smiled at the silliness while the towering Michelangelo stared at the caviar in abject horror and started to back away, nearly bowling over a duchess, her toy poodle and pet husband.

"Gods above and below," whispered the alien in horror. Then memory flared and he threw away the cucumber sandwich he had been nibbling.

Stepping close, Jhonny took a hold of the hairy technician's arm and typed a command into the IBM portable that served him in lieu of a standard wrist secretary. In seconds, a detailed description of the word "ventriloquism" scrolled onto the screen and the alien started reading with interest, then anger, and finally amusement. So that explained the incident at the museum!

"Good one," the Gremlin finally acknowledged.

Across the heavily laden table of culinary delights, Harry winked at his friend and started pouring himself a fresh glass of Grey Poupon Sherry '02. Ah!

"And why were you questioning the caviar?" asked Mike curiously.

"Well, we've pracking interviewed everybody else in the upholstered train station," she retorted, waving an arm about at the huge, cavernous marble place around them.

Just then a hovertrain slid into the room; mechanical arms reached out the top, seized the barely touched table of food, and hauled it inside the carriage. Then dutifully, another fully laden table was returned and the train hovered onward, ever in search of more soiled napkins that desperately needed immediate replacement.

Collins grunted at the sight. "Geez! I'm surprised the toilets in the royal john don't wipe your butt for you!"

Having recently used the facilities in question, Harry started to speak, but then held his tongue. No, let it be a surprise for her.

"Yeah, well we arrived hours later than asked and the main festivities have not yet begun," said Jhonny, clearly perturbed. "So much for punctuality on Mars."

Gesturing with his glass, Harry shrugged. "What do you expect in a world forged by Uncle Bob?"

"'Tis true," agreed Rikka out of the corner of her mouth.

"Enough!" cried Michelangelo, raising a paw toward home. "That is the umpteenth time I have heard the name. Gods above and below, who is this Bob?"

Appropriating some chairs, the team sat down and gave the alien a short history of Mars.

A criminal sent to Mars as slave labor, Bob Yertzoff had been one of the foundling fathers of the Martian revolution, which overthrew the chains of old Earth and forged brand-new chains with the leaders of the revolution at the top link.

Soon ousted by his own organization for being a bit too zealous in the matter of revenge against the Earth, the ex-criminal now vowed revenge against Mars.

Disappearing completely from Martian society, within a year there surfaced an insidious drug upon the underground market. An odious concoction quickly called WOW!

For approximately two hours after ingesting WOW! everything you saw, felt, tasted, or did was brand-new to you. Endlessly you could rediscover your favorite movie, food, book, and the joys of sex; and all the while shouting the aforementioned word.

Totally benign, the chemical compound was nonaddictive and had no side effects at all, except for a pleasant, spring-fresh, minty aftertaste. Virtually overnight, the population of Mars was shouting WOW! but what was worse, they soon stopped buying new things. Cable TV service was canceled at an alarming rate. Video-tape rentals dwindled. So did business at bookstores, clothes emporiums, car dealerships, record shops, stereo outlets, computer centers, arcades, theaters, brothels, motels, and movie palaces. Entire budding conglomerates bordered on collapse, millions of ex-slaves were in danger of unemployment. The Royal Martian empire teetered on the brink of total economic chaos!

At first, the self-appointed King of Mars tried taxation, restriction of sales, import fees, export duties, embargoes, tithes, and just saying no. But the sale of WOW! continued to increase and the very foundation of society threatened to crumble. Until, pushed to the limit, the King went for broke and declared the incredibly popular substance *illegal*.

Within a matter of only hours, SWAT teams apprehended all known stockpiles of the infamous drug.

In retaliation, the criminal genius mailed a sample of the drug to everybody on the planet, along with a copy of the formula. The postage alone must have bankrupted him, for the scientist never did pay his staggering phone bill for directory assistance.

An order for the immediate confiscation of those letters was instantly dispatched. Unfortunately, the order was sent via the mail and thus arrived long after the samples and formula did.

Now, anybody who wished was able to manufacture the drug themselves, using only a standard kitchen, small nuclear cyclotron, and a few goats.

Knowing that they couldn't arrest the entire world, although the Prime Minister did suggest it, the new King and Parliament of Mars racked their collective brains to concoct a clever plan so that the public would have no reason to ever bother making any WOW! After outlawing goats, that is.

Coffers were unlocked and trillions of dollars were poured into the liberal arts. Viewer-supported television stopped their annoying beg-a-thons and started broadcasting twenty-four hours a day. Community players delightfully found themselves ankle deep in federal funds. An original play opened every week. First novels were published by the truckload. Brand-new, old-style radio plays were broadcast and became astonishingly popular. Any innovative form of entertainment was backed by the government to the hilt. Parades and circuses became daily events. Fireworks filled the nighttime sky. Band concerts were held in every park. Nightclubs sprouted like mushrooms and their stages became jammed with jugglers, mimes, comics, magicians, sword swallowers, animal acts, and song and dance teams. Almost overnight, Mars became a vicious nonstop party of government-sponsored fun.

The consumption of WOW! slowed.

Encouraged, Parliament made prostitution legal, with licenses available to anyone of the proper age who passed the biweekly physical and the self-esteem test. Then gambling debts became tax deductible.

WOW! sales slowed more, but not enough.

Desperate, the King ordered the site of the new Worlds Fair reconditioned and opened early to the public. The Summer Olympics began months early. The Winter Olympics was repeated. Then Parliament nationalized amusement parks, made nude beaches legal, abolished the air tax, lowered the drinking age, and raised the minimum wage.

That was the death stroke. Eventually, the demand for WOW! dwindled away to finally stop. And, incredibly, despite an intensive search by the police of three continents, its creator was never found.

However, a new problem replaced the old. The population of the planet was now hooked on the thrill of discovery. Trash entertainment didn't satisfy their appetites any longer. They wanted more. Needed more. Something, anything, to challenge their minds, to stimulate their intellects. In droves, people across the globe reentered school and tackled the most difficult of subjects. Thousands of colleges and universities had to be built to meet the impossible, growing demand. The shameful world literacy rate of 25 percent rose to 56 percent, 98 percent, 99.999 percent and stopped there for a month until they discovered the last holdout was blind. So they imported Braille from Earth and hit 100 percent.

The planetary renaissance was unstoppable. Besieged with scholars, the arts and sciences flourished like never before. A cure for most diseases was discovered, along with antigravity, pollution-free power plants, functional robots, edible trampolines, and the vaunted Youth Drug.

"Which their whole economy is based upon," noted Michelangelo, his furry ears standing straight up from interest.

Rikka primly crossed a leg under her dress. Nobody on the outside could tell. "Exactly."

A giraffe in a pink tutu ankled by. If there was a rider, they were too high for anybody to see.

Lost in rumination, the alien technician chewed the tips of his whiskers. "So the whole of Martian civilization is actually a betrayed ex-slave hierarchy, twisted into a mutated society of hedonists and artists by a brilliant, but inept drug lord!" A low whistle. "No wonder they're such loonies."

Crouching low, Harry shss'ed his friend. "Not so loud," the anchor warned. "They're still rather touchy about that."

Just then, a distant siren began to howl. In seconds, it was backed by a closer siren. Then a bell started to ring, a klaxon to clang, and then a steam-whistle keen erupted from every chandelier in the ballroom. Iron grates slid solidly over the windows. Doors slammed shut. In midsonata, the band pulled guns. The suits of armor stepped off the wall. Then a blinding white light flooded the crowd. Suddenly Rikka felt her stun derringer go hot and she cast it to the floor, where it joined a rapidly growing collection of assorted nonlethal ironmongery from almost everybody present.

"Uncle Bob again?" asked Michelangelo, using talon tips to remove a few hot tools from the vest under his caftan.

Reaching behind his neck, Harry killed his tie, which was starting to smoke. "Lord, I hope not!"

"He's still alive?" croggled the alien.

"No," said Rikka, looking about. "But his children are!"

Black pupilless eyes went round as moons. Oh, dear.

The camcorder on his shoulder revving madly, Jhonny adjusted something in his ear. "There's some sort of military emergency, but the radio signals are scrambled and coded."

"Deitrich?" asked Collins to her wrist. Was this it? Had the assassin hit?

WORKING, scrolled the MainBrain. I'VE BEEN MONITORING THE GOVERNMENTAL FREQUENCIES IN CASE ANYTHING IMPORTANT . . . WAIT . . . I THINK . . . HOLY PRACK!

"What?" asked the news team anxiously.

THE PRINCE HAS BEEN KIDNAPPED!

CHAPTER SEVEN

"YES!" CRIED RIKKA, jumping to her feet. Finally, a real story! This was even better than the prince getting killed!

"Kidnapped," mumbled Harry, chewing a thumbnail. Hmm.

I THINK, amended the Brain. AT LEAST HE'S DEFINITELY MISSING. SECURITY REPORTS THAT HIS SURGICALLY IMPLANTED TRANSPONDER IS NO LONGER WITHIN THE CONFINES OF THE CASTLE. AND THERE'S NO REPORT OF HIM LEAVING OR EVEN BE-ING ANYWHERE NEAR AN EXIT.

"Better and better," said Collins, opening a text file in her secretary and already typing in some rough notes. Dateline: the royal castle of Mars, 4:55 P.M., August 45, 2317. Today amid the gaiety and jubilation of a royal en-gagement party, Prince Vladamir Yertzoff was kidnapped by a heavily armed contingent of the bloody and ruthless . . . hmm. Oh, what the heck, when in doubt blame the Free Police. The crazed space pirates usually did the crime anyway. And if any of them appeared in public to deny the crime, the police would shoot them dead and Rikka could get a reward for tricking one of them out of hiding. Hey, this could be great for everybody!

Meanwhile, pandemonium ruled in the ballroom as the petrified royalty screamed and ran around in circles, while butlers and maids remained demurely quiet and followed along after their employers as per orders. Soon the ball-room resembled a living whirlpool of tuxedos and ball gowns following each other in a fast race to nowhere.

Yanking off her satin choker, Rikka watched the panicky aristocracy in ill-concealed contempt. Maybe the poor prince simply had a sudden rush of good taste and fled for the hills.

"Come on, troops," stated Harry, loosening his cummerbund. "Let's find out what is really going on here!"

"Natch."

"Right."

"Banzai!"

"Deitrich?"

ON LINE, scrolled the MainBrain. BUT THE AIRWAVES ARE NOW SOLID WITH ENCODED TRANSMISSIONS. I DON'T KNOW WHICH TO TRY TO DECIPHER.

Prack! "Can you record them all for later?"

ALREADY DOING SO.

What a brain!

"First we have to discover where the prince was last seen," stated Collins, dodging a panic-stricken lord. "Either him, or the princess what's her name."

NO WAY, CHIEF. EVEN I'M NOT THAT GOOD TO BREACH THEIR INTERNAL SECURITY COMPUTER.

"Fifteen minutes ago, over by the oak trees," said Harry, not even looking in that direction.

Faking a cough, Collins covered her mouth with a hand. "How do you know?" she hacked.

"Saw him with a butler," said Jhonny, without moving lips.

Snyder tried not to show his astonishment. "You too?"

A tiny nod.

"No good," throated Mike, while licking his chops. "We can't follow him. Guards galore by the door."

Collins wanted to turn and see for herself but heroically resisted the temptation. Time was fast running out. If they didn't fast get inside the castle proper, even these guards would soon have every entrance sealed off.

"Deitrich, I saw him receive a message on a private communicator. Any priority broadcasts on the military channels?

CHECKING . . . NO, BUT THERE WAS A VERY SHORT Z-BAND BURST FROM DEEP SPACE. SOURCE UNKNOWN.

"That's it! Got a copy?"

SURE.

"What does it say?"

THUNDERFISH.

"Huh?"

WELL, THAT'S WHAT IT SAYS.

Rikka ground her teeth. Damn! A one-word code. Like back in the interplanetary wars. In a public broadcast, the word "dog" could mean "retreat," and "banana" meant "there's a spy in your group, shoot the man with the bad haircut," that sort of stuff. They had the transmission, but it was impossible to break.

"Back door," muttered Mike, literally out of one side of his snout. "We need a back door."

Inspired, Rikka smacked a fist into her palm. And maybe they had one. "Deitrich, did you by any chance record the frequency of the burst?" asked Collins, fixing the lipstick she wasn't wearing.

SURE . . . AH, GOOD IDEA . . . TRYING . . . YES, IT WORKED!

Jhonny borrowed some. "What? What worked?"

I SENT A CARRIER WAVE ON THE SAME FREQUENCY AND GOT A BOUNCE RESPONSE.

"And you triangulated on the source?" puckered Harry, feeling incredibly foolish. The things he did for the job.

SURE. IT'S EASY. THAT'S HOW I ALWAYS FIND YOU GUYS.

Smiling in spite of the situation, the team glanced at their wrist secretaries. Ah, another mystery solved. And all this while they had been looking for attached strings or trails of bread crumbs.

"So where is the prince?" asked Jhonny, holding the camcorder in front of his face as he checked the brand-new thirty-year batteries for signs of age or weakness.

UNKNOWN. BUT THE WATCH IS AT A STATIONARY POINT ABOUT TWENTY METERS DOWN AND A HUNDRED TO YOUR LEFT.

A horde of midgets in leprechaun outfits went screaming by.

"Map," whispered Rikka confidently, running both hands through her hair.

A beep made her teammates glance at their wrists. The

monitors blinked and showed a vector graphic map of
most of the sprawling castle.

"Good going, Rikka," complimented Harry, wiping his
face with a napkin.

THANK JHONNY, HE PHOTOGRAPHED THE MAP IN THE LOBBY.

Quickly, they reviewed the meager options.

"Garbage chute?" asked Jhonny, stopping to tie his
sneakers.

A floating stretcher went by loaded with limp bodies,
most of them reeking of booze.

Harry scratched his nose. "Mike won't fit. Side terrace
window?"

"The one under Bambi with the chainsaw?" coughed
Mike.

"Agreed," yawned Rikka. "Let's go."

Strolling casually, but quickly through the screaming
stampede, the news team made it to the terrace relatively
undamaged, except for a few trod-on feet and six separate
cases of elbow surprise. Surprise! Ugh.

Standing with their unbruised backs to the cool wall,
one by one the reporters slid behind the curtains. The iron
grating wasn't locked, but simply held closed by hundreds
of pounds of hydraulic pressure. Trying not to damage the
thing, Mike gently eased the bars apart and they snuck out
onto the terrace.

This side of the castle overlooked a maze of hedges
with an Olympic swimming pool in the center. A battalion
of Royal Martian Marines with combat chainsaws were
ruthlessly cutting down the maze piece by piece and examining every bush. A small submarine appeared to be diving
in the pool itself. Farther off was a lush terrarium valley
full of golden corn and squadrons of ebony flying tanks.
Distant mountains edged the planetary horizon and flights
of silvery delta-winged interceptors were screaming into
the purple sky.

Utterly delighted, Jhonny took a quick shot for the files.
Fabulous! Add a couple of unisex bikinis and he could be
up for another Pulitzer!

"Okay, they don't think he's in the castle," remarked

Rikka, watching the nearby skies for patrol craft or gunships. All of the military seemed to be concentrating their attentions in an ever-widening circle around the outside of the castle. Whew. If they were caught out here, the King might extract from them the ultimate penalty and rescind their press passes. A fate worse than death for a working reporter.

A dry forest wind whipped about the QSNT crew as they peeked over the iron balcony. There was another terrace just below them about three meters down. Perfect.

"Mike goes first," snapped Harry, unbuttoning his cuff as a prelude to action.

Nimbly the hairy titan leaped over the balcony and landed on the marble with a dull thud. His head now peered at them from the exact level of the floor.

"Small castle," he remarked as the android and humans scampered down his backside. "Hey, stop tickling."

"Stop wiggling!"

"Stop tickling!"

Finally gathered on the lower terrace, they gathered in a pool of protective shade from the upper projecting lintel. Ripping off his cumbersome burnoose, Michelangelo took a box from his vest and checked for trip wires and alarms. Impatiently the team waited as the technician did things to meters and dials without any obvious results.

"In!" he barked, pocketing the box.

After piling through, Mike closed the door, Rikka got the curtains, Jhonny jammed the lock, and Harry slid a chair under the handle.

"Every little bit helps," the anchor said with the voice of experience.

The spacious room they were in was a deserted library, every wall jammed solid with physical printed books. Thankfully the place was sans any visible security cameras. So far, so good. "What now?" Michelangelo asked, munching a turnip as he tossed the turban into a trash can. One second later the headgear vanished in a flash of atomic light.

"Change appearance," said Harry, hastily ripping off his vest, cummerbund, and weskit. "Can't look like guests."

Much more carefully, Snyder removed his red pants, reversed the material, and donned the clothing. The green jacket followed. Now the anchor was dressed in a plain two-piece suit of blue. A pocket comb run through his hair dyed the gray at his temples to match the rest and he changed the part from left to center. He glanced over the library for a briefcase to finish the illusion of an insurance salesman, but alas none was to be found.

Grinning in delight, Rikka took a letter opener from a nearby desk and savagely sliced her dress off at the waistline, then parted her bodice down along its side laces. As the material fell to the floor, the woman was suddenly in a simple white smock of undetermined origin. Quick strokes of mascara made her eyes slightly Oriental, changed her cheekbones, and enlarged her nostrils. Reluctantly the reporter removed the QSNT earrings from her lobes and stuffed them into the soil of a potted plant.

Borrowing the comb, Jhonny ran it over his Zoot suit and cloth sneakers until both were solid black. Inverting his own vest made it white. Tearfully the android deposited the gold chain into the trash can and watched it atomize. Another heirloom gone in the name of the news. Stuffing the camcorder into a pocket, he went to the large sideboard and found a silver serving tray that the machine loaded with several bottles and glasses. Then removing a doily from under a priceless Steuben crystal Frisbee, he draped it over an arm. Voilà! Instant butler.

Incredibly, Mike did something to his boots and they changed from black to white. Then he removed his glasses and switched his IBM portable from his right to left wrist. It wasn't much, but what the heck, all Gremlins looked alike. Even he admitted it in private.

Wasting precious time, the team inspected each other and made minor suggestions and corrections. When satisfied, they hurried through the shelves of volumes and stacks of tomes to reach the hallway door.

"Nothing," said Mike, his big ear held flat to the wood panel.

These doors had no alarms, but also proved to be locked. Jhonny solved that minor problem with an assortment of picks and jimmies secreted inside a reservoir in his forearm. Darn thing had a million uses. Oil went on the hinges and graphite in the locking mechanism before Rikka ever so quietly eased the door ajar.

"Wait," warned the woman as she watched a grimly intent platoon of Space Navy technicians lugging a huge WatchDog scanner down the hallway. At this close range, its normally invisible sensor beams were a shimmering white cone that revolved everywhere in a rapid globe as the scanner beams probed through walls, floors, and ceilings. The tech was accompanied by a squad of SWAT troopers in Samson powerarmor, the louvered helmets of the Marines bristly with deadly weapons and their featureless boots sinking ankle deep into the terrazzo floor.

Trying not to breathe loudly, the reporter watched the rescue patrol stomp off down the hallway and turn a corner. Yeow, these folk really took their missing royalty seriously!

"Clear," she announced at last.

"Stairs that way," pointed Harry after consulting his secretary.

Moving with extreme care and speed, the crew tiptoed down the hallway and then proceeded down the stairs. Intruders would walk on the edge of the steps where the boards meet the wall, where the steps were the strongest and least likely to squeak, but the team was pretending to belong here, so they scurried boldly along in the middle. However, they did not touch the banister where far too many sophisticated security devices could be easily concealed. They had once gotten rudely thrown out of the North American White House for that little mistake. The U.S. Secret Service had absolutely no sense of humor about reporters from another world, and Earth sidewalks were unusually hard.

At the next landing, Mike shorted out an ID scanner and

reactivated it after the team dashed by. Hopefully, the interval of inaction would not be long enough to catch the attention of these grim Martian guards. Obviously, the security upstairs in the ballroom had only been for show, and all the real guards, the competent ones, were down here in the private living quarters. The conclusion made sense, but did not lighten the hearts of the news team.

In ascending order, a pair of blue, hazel, brown, and black eyes peered around a corner. In this hallway, the walls were wood and the floor carpeted with petite chandeliers lighting the lumpy ceiling. Boot prints? Some poor trooper was going to get cashiered out of the service for that mistake. Or at least do one hell of a lot of sanding for the next fifty years.

Several doors away, a weeping maid was dusting and talking to a dapper fellow in a neat brown worsted jumpsuit respectfully holding a bowler hat. Much more distant, a pair of clergy were discussing a matter and slowly departing in their classic I-have-all-the-time-in-the-world-'cause-I-know-where-my-soul-is-going walk.

"Pretty empty," joked Rikka, withdrawing into safety. "Could be worse."

"It is," spat Harry, crouching against a six-hundred-pound Ming vase. Boy, whatever a Ming was he was sure glad they were extinct. "That's Lord Alexander Hyde-White of QBBC out there!"

Since that service was a merely friendly competitor instead of a hated enemy like QINS, the team growled at the pronouncement. They hadn't seen any of the other news teams in attendance, but that was understandable considering the mob upstairs. So, it was a race for the story, eh?

"Solo, or a team player?" asked Mike, gauging distances.

"Solo. Although he sometimes shares with O'Toole from QCNN."

Share a story? Outrageous! Obviously the man was some kind of crazed anarchist.

"Okay, how do we get rid of him?" asked Jhonny, tapping a heavy wine bottle in the palm of his hand.

Snyder had to grin. "Not a big fan of Asimov's Three Laws are you?"

"Never heard of the guy." Tap. Tap.

"I'll do it," countered Rikka. "Mike?"

"Routine nine?"

"Yep," whispered Collins, and the alien slipped her a small red capsule.

Stepping into the hallway, Rikka crossed to a door with a brass plate marked Linen. Sure enough, inside she found a sleepy janitor. The door swung closed as the reporter flashed cash and the two started to chat.

As the QBBC reporter walked by minutes later, the janitor stumbled into the hallway, his arm pumping crimson fluid.

"Help ..." he gasped, staggering. "Tripped ... knife ... oh, the pain!" Then he rolled his eyes and collapsed upon the astonished newsman.

Removing his jacket, Lord Hyde-White tore off his white shirt and wrapped it around the bloody wound as a compress. Then, bare-chested, he lifted the twitching form and began to spring off in frantic search of a Closet-Doc.

In appreciation of a job well done, the reporters gave the janitor a round of silent applause. He could have a career on the stage! Or, at least, doing knife commercials.

"You are a bastard," whispered Michelangelo from the shadows as Collins coolly stood and took a bow in the empty hallway.

Pleased, Rikka dimpled at her big associate. "Thanks. I like you too."

"That's the place," said Jhonny, checking the monitor. "Third door from the elevator, second from the big Grecian voz."

"Vase," corrected Rikka automatically.

"Not in this place," scoffed the android through his pinched nose.

There were no guards positioned in front of the door, but an army could be inside. In remembrance, the team rubbed their butts, painfully thinking of adamantine sidewalks and thirty-two feet per second per second.

"I'll try solo," said Harry, straightening his jumpsuit. "If they catch me, then you guys should have plenty of time to check the place out as they haul me off to jail."

"Good plan," said Jhonny.

"The hell it is," hissed Snyder. "Talk me out of this!"

Instead, six hands shoved him into the hallway. Ah, friends. He really must get himself one of those someday.

The door was unlocked, so the anchor went straight through, his face a mask of bored impatience, the classic expression of most policemen.

"All right, what are you doing in here?" he demanded in his best angry but bored voice.

Turning from his vigil by the window, a teary butler sniffed and dared to cock an eyebrow at the newcomer. Another MIA officer? A policeman? His clothes were certainly common enough, but he was not displaying a police badge or military insignia like the rest of the security staff.

"Are you with MIA?" the servant asked as politely as possible. It was never wise to annoy an operative of The Agency, or else you quickly became missing in action.

Mars Intelligence? Taking his cue, Harry leveled his gaze on the manservant and watched as the personage visibly wilted under the vitriolic gaze. Ah, it was nice to know he still had the old pizzazz. Pity it didn't work on his bookie.

"I said," repeated Snyder in a voice and tone implying that he never before had found it necessary to repeat anything. To anybody. "What are you doing here? You're supposed to be with the rest." Yeah, that was suitably vague.

"B-but I was specifically told to wait."

Hazel eyes looked into the very soul of the sweating butler. "Leave," whispered Snyder in ill-controlled fury. "Now."

Accustomed to taking bizarre and often conflicting orders from his royal employers, the servant shrugged in resignation and shuffled off. Why they wanted him in the throne room he had no idea. Oh, dear, hopefully not as a makeshift skeet again!

Watching the butler leave the room, the team waited a minute for the door to close. When it didn't, they started into the hallway one at a time. Dusting all the way, Rikka the maid got inside with no problem. Striding purposefully along with tray and bottles held high so did Jhonny.

But just as Mike was about to go, somebody started coming down the stairs behind him. A peripheral glance showed it to be a Royal Space Marine in full dress uniform. Yikes!

"Hi, Bob. Hell of a thing isn't it?" called out the Space officer, holding a palm to the ID scanner. There was a beep and the woman passed through the glowing archway unharmed. Now the Marine faced the alien directly and a flicker of puzzlement crossed her scarred features.

"Fred," offered the technician in correction.

"Oh, he's boiling mad and having a nervous breakdown, of course," replied the officer, relaxing, misunderstanding entirely. "And Lulu?"

Fast, Michelangelo racked his brain for any of the thousand evasions he had personally witnessed the veteran team members use over the past few years.

"Ditto," he confided cryptically, baring his teeth in an indecipherable gesture.

A nod. "Yeah, she's a good bodyguard. I really have no idea how anybody could have gotten to His Highness without going over her dead body." Absentmindedly the Marine adjusted the holster at her hip holding an MPB Neutrino blaster. Even on its lowest setting, the dire weapon could reduce the huge alien to a steaming charcoal briquette faster than he could say "Aiyee!"

"Well, gotta go get my butt chewed off in the throne room," said the Marine, squaring her broad shoulders. "See you at the security meeting?"

"Of course," responded Mike, nodding his head as if human. To his race, the motion meant you were falling asleep from boredom, or about to hibernate for the winter.

Straightening the brim of her cap to a mathematical perfect plane, the officer departed. "Later, buddy."

"Later."

As she turned the corner, Michelangelo allowed himself to sag against the wall and brutally pounded his chest in an effort to get his auxiliary heart started. Ye gods above and below, that was close! Humming to itself in consultation, his Pocket-Doc flashed a message on its monitor in his native language that roughly translated into written medical permission to go somewhere and faint.

Crossing the hallway induced no further coronary incidents for the hirsute titan. Gratefully closing the door, Mike rummaged about in his vest until he found a key of the proper size and material. Inserting the tiny oval rod of bronze, the alien bent it to the left and jerked to the right, snapping the key in half. There, that should stop anybody from entering for quite a while. Except this Lulu person.

Pocketing the other half for later use, the technician turned and glanced about the room. No, the office. Well illuminated by a huge oval picture window of crystal-clear Armorlite, the floor sported a strictly functional flat carpet. Spacious enough for Michelangelo to wander freely without worrying about smashing the stray couch, the place contained only a solo desk, accompanied by a scattering of high-backed chairs, end tables, and reading lamps, the robotic light fixtures still in the act of reading. Clearly whatever happened here did so unexpectedly.

The plain gold desk sat catty-corner to a bank of itty-bitty machines: a miniature telex, a diminutive Z-band fax, a pocket copier, matchbox mainframe, micro-stapler, and an espresso maker. Although everything was edged in platinum, it was the complete executive line from the Rhode Island Business Company of Earth. Very impressive. This array of equipment must have cost a small fortune! Without a doubt, this was the private office of the prince.

Wiggling his ears, Mike found that the ceiling proved to be standard Wilkes Corporation acoustic tiles buttressed by rough-hewn oak beams. Three of the walls were bare block stone adorned with only a few pictures of smiling celebrities, laughing friends, and chained relatives. The fourth was a floor-to-ceiling bookcase.

Inquisitively Mike glanced at the title lining the upper shelves of the bookcase. It could tell them a lot if they knew which volumes were valuable enough for the prince to place on display, but not something he would consult every day. There was an old encyclopedia, a collection of 1001 Free Police jokes, volumes 1–37, and crowning the middle span was a handsome set of twenty volumes bound in tooled leather: *A Princess of Mars, John Carter of Mars, Chessmen of Mars,* et cetera, et cetera. Clearly these were genealogical texts about his family history. The alien heartily approved. A person should always be aware of their humble origins.

"Okay, Deitrich, now where?" asked Harry, glancing about.

Only static answered.

Shaking his wrist, Snyder upped the volume. "Deitrich?" he whispered. "Do you copy?"

Nothing.

"This room is shielded," stated Mike, consulting an EM scanner from his vest. "Nothing is getting in or out."

Rikka frowned. Their four-pound Greek chorus of advice was gone for the duration. However, that also meant The Agency and palace security weren't watching them over secret video cameras and laughing uproariously as they prepared a nice jail cell with a group discount.

"Okay, where do we start?" asked Snyder, eyeing the cherry wood sideboard amply loaded with liquors from around the worlds. There was even a can of the vintage Australian beer Marsupe Ale, the only brew guaranteed to make you awaken hanging upside down from a tree. Wow. Even college sophomores hesitated to drink that stuff. Somebody here was a serious boozer.

"Let's do a visual search for the watch," said the reporter, chewing a lip. "That's as good a place to start as any. But don't touch anything with bare hands!"

In unison, the team gave sour looks.

"Sorry. Jumpy," she apologized lamely, her own hands hovering above the remote control of a life-size TriD set. With the screen turned off there was no way to tell which channel the monitor had been last set on. Had the prince been watching the party upstairs on the local station? Or tuned in to some private cable channel?

Trying not to be conspicuous, Mike reached into the back of his vest and slid on a pair of specially tailored four-fingered gloves. Since there were only a couple hundred of his species in this solar system, printing a Gremlin was remarkably easy. And the aliens did have fingerprints, although the patterns resembled the veins in a tree leaf, instead of water going down a drain.

Taking their standard positions in the four corners, the team began slowly walking clockwise in an overlapping reconnaissance pattern. Minutes passed in tense silence as the QSNT crew inched along judiciously examining everything, with one eye forever trained on the locked door.

Crying out in pleasure, Rikka tried to pull a fat volume of poetry out of the end of the bookcase, but the tome proved to be attached to the shelf with a hinge. As the book swung down, a picture near her microscopically sagged. Warily the investigative reporter pushed the gilded frame aside to reveal blank stone. With fingertip pressure, she prodded the block until a sliding panel slid, revealing a small recessed alcove in which lay the watch. Yes!

"Now how the hell did you know which book to pull?" demanded Jhonny, impressed. The volume in question was the collected poems of A. E. Housman. Well, watches had housings, so . . . nyah, that wasn't it.

"How?" repeated Collins, gloating over her find. "I have decades of training searching for the afikoman."

Snyder barked a laugh in appreciation.

"The what?" asked Mike curiously. "Is it anything like the Maltese Falcon?" The alien tried accessing the word on his portable, but was referred to the religious file. Strange.

"I'll explain later," smiled Rikka, examining the watch.

With a yelp, Jhonny hit the floor. "Duck!"

Throwing themselves flat, the team went motionless and the room darkened as the setting sun was momentarily eclipsed by the immense bulk of a Tiger hovertank. Silhouetted by the mighty solar orb, the detailed outline of the warcraft's 200mm projectile cannon and flanking neural disruptors was horrifyingly easy to discern. In fact, the tank was patrolling so close to the castle that the shimmer-

ing blue antigravity field of its aggie motors penetrated the
thick stone wall and infused the office, making the window vibrate, whipping the curtains into a frenzy, and accidentally levitating Michelangelo.

Digging talons into the carpet, the meowing alien tried
to remain where he was, but he was almost at windowsill
level when the Tiger angled away and Mike suddenly
dropped to the floor. The impact toppled over a reading
lamp onto an end table that tilted and an ashtray slid off
to crash on his skull. Gingerly touching his bruised head,
the technician silently mouthed a word of pain. Clearly it
was just going to be one of those days.

"That was close," said Jhonny, pressed flat against the
wall alongside the window and daring to snap a couple of
fast shots of the flying Tiger. Military machines always
made good TV copy.

"Too close," agreed Harry, checking the carpet for loose
change from his pockets. No sense advertising that somebody had been here. "Let's finish this search for clues to
the kidnappers and get the prack out of here."

Finishing their sweep of the room perimeter, the team
now concentrated on the desk. While Mike and Jhonny
carefully began opening the locked drawers, Rikka exam-
ined the keypad of the Hush phone and Harry checked the
chair. The material was a tough black tweed, perfect for
holding samples of hair or lint. The seat was clean, but
one of the armrests seemed off kilter. Using the tip of his
pipe as a probe, the anchor tested underneath the support
for hidden controls. As he depressed a bolt, the cushioned
top of the armrest snapped up to show a large compart-
ment hidden inside. Ha! Rikka wasn't the only person who
could do a Sherlock Holmes impersonation.

Nestled among a stack of hollograph letters bound in
pink ribbon was a sealed envelope and a clear box of
Armorlite full of medals. Eh? Those strongly resembled
the medals Harry had seen the prince wearing in the party.
Curious. Trying not to disturb anything else in the com-
partment, Snyder went to lift the box and disappeared.

Before the shocked alien or android could react, Rikka

vaulted over the desk. What greeted her was a hole in the
floor and a fleeting vision of the anchor disappearing
down a pipe as if he were one.

"A secret exit!" she exclaimed. Oh, boy, this was getting good.

Mentally hitching her pants, Collins dove into the opening after her friend. Without a qualm, Jhonny followed.
Rapidly doing some calculus equations on estimated size
and girth, Michelangelo finally held his snout and jumped
in also, narrowly missing decapitation by the metal leaves
that irised from the floor, sealing off the opening with
clanging finality.

Once more, the office was silent and empty.

Screaming jets rocketed through the darkening sky high
above the Martian castle. Rumbling thunder, the imposing
bulk of flying Tigers lumbered nosily above the landscape
like somber military snails. And dozens of superdread-
nought spaceships, great globular mountains of polished
metal, settled into the smooth green perfection of the
sprawling Yertzoff estates, their awesome armored hulls
sinking meters into the hard-packed soil with a total and
deliberate disregard for public safety and basic lawn care.

High on the castle roof, Jason Hardcopy and Susie Sunshine were dictating notes into their wrist secretaries as their
QINS camera-op panned the horizon taking a wonderful
panoramic view of the massive military search for the
prince. Great stuff. If only there were a few more bikinis.

On the stonework floor was a fuming mad redhead in a
beautiful green gown, matching shoes, a beige gag, and
about sixty feet of white nylon rope. A gold name tag
pinned to her ruffled collar read: Hannabal O'Toole, QCNN.

"Hey! Watch it, lady," said the camera-op, almost trip-
ping over the outstretched legs of the prisoner. "I just
work here, it was these two who shot you with the Peace-
Maker pistol and did the Thanksgiving turkey routine."

Although her words were garbled by the gag, Hanna
O'Toole's opinion of the technician, the two smirking
QINS reporters, and the Wilkes Corporation that manufac-

tured the stun weapon was still easily understandable and illegal to say over most of the airwaves. Even the public access channels.

Interrupted at their work, Hardcopy and Sunshine snarled at the competition to be quiet, when a sleek white space shuttle arced into view from behind the north turret of the castle. With streamers of flame blasting from its turbo-jets, the craft skimmed low over the roof. The powerful backwash buffeted the QINS trio off their feet and the video camera smashed against the hard cold stone. Set free, the video disk holding all of the recording of the royal search went rolling gaily away. Scrambling in frantic pursuit, the reporters dashed after the disk and just missed grabbing it before the recording went sailing off the edge of the roof to plummet straight down into the distant blue ribbon of the moat.

Panting from the exertion, the furious news reporters seriously debated trying to retrieve the precious disk by throwing their camera-op down there to get it, but then magnanimously decided that was foolish. The sharks would only eat him and then who would carry their equipment bags back to the spaceport?

Then the immense scale of their loss overwhelmed the team and they pivoted toward the circling shuttle.

"Son of a bitch!" screamed Susie, and the reporter jerked a hand skyward.

The throwing knife bounced harmlessly off the lithium fiber shielding of the spacecraft as it swung around the castle. But for a moment, the Gothic lettering on the side was clearly visible, boldly proclaiming the name of the owner/operators.

"Quiller Geo-Medical Plumbing?" demanded Jason, replacing the Bedlow derringer into his boot as the shuttle moved out of range. "And who the hell are they?"

"I don't know," muttered Sunshine hostilely, her magnificent bosom barely restrained by the jumpsuit and its weakening zipper. "But we're damn well going to find out!"

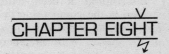

CHAPTER EIGHT

IT WAS ALWAYS a surprise to the new staff members in Not-Uncle-Bob's Castle that the royal Martian throne room was so ordinary and, dare they say it, non-Martian; the truncated corners blended into a curved outer wall with its five tall bay windows that overlooked the rose garden and antisatellite laser batteries. Facing away from the bulletproof Armorlite windows were two massive hardwood chairs, with a pair of flags hanging from poles on either side: the right bearing the Imperial Seal of Mars, the left, a precise mirror image of the other.

Across the throne room was a working fireplace suitable for roasting small planets, the tiered marble lintel flanked by a pair of molded armored doors. Both of the portals were set flush against the wall and were discernible only by the thin crack of their outlines. The freshly white-washed walls were spotless and mostly bare, with only a few paintings on display, giving the room a just-moved-in feeling. In raised relief overhead was the Imperial Seal of Mars, a smaller version of which was woven into the carpet underfoot, carved into the frame of the thrones themselves, embroidered on the pillows on the thrones, and even stitched into the tiny tags detailing laundry procedures for the aforementioned cushions.

The room was immaculately clean: vacuumed, dusted, and debugged daily by a housekeeping staff whose security credentials rivaled those of Planetary Defense generals. And who were paid even more. Just another example of what a good union can do for you. A faint smell of lemon polish scented the air and the wooden arms of the antique chairs felt oily smooth to the fidgety fingers of the waiting dignitaries. Top personnel from the Army, Navy, Castle Security, Imperial Secret Service, and MIA were present; even though the MIA was not supposed to operate within the confines of the planetary surface. Although that rarely stopped them. Royal chamberlains scurried about delivering reports and pouring coffee laced with brandy and Dramamine.

Perched uncomfortably on an H. G. Wells free-form love seat was Tars Gooden, in a somber checkered jumpsuit, and Elizabeth Fairchild, in a black and tan uniform. The chief operative of the Imperial Secret Service and the captain of the Castle Security were huddled together in tense conversation. While the informed guardsmen of the Imperial castle were not under the direct auspices of the Secret Service, they usually followed its lead in any important matter. With the sole and notable exception of betting at the racetrack. Quite enough money from their pension fund had been wasted there thanks to inept Imperial handicapping and a bad tendency to shoot any horse faster than the animal they had bet upon. Socially, it was most embarrassing.

Everybody else in the room was similarly engaged in business. The sole exception being Ernst "The Spike" Gunther, the chief of the MIA. Silent, he sat rigidly in his wicker chair, hands folded neatly on top of the attaché case in his lap.

All talking stopped when the air before the thrones began to shimmer and a three-dimensional image of a liveried herald appeared. Thump-thump-thump. "Pre-senting the King and Queen of Mars!"

The staff braced for the worst and that's what they got.

It started slowly at first, merely a faint tingle in the floor. But then it rapidly built in power until the walls began to shake and the ceiling shudder. Windows cracked! Chandeliers dropped like glass meteors! The flags waved good-bye. Columns toppled over. The jacuzzi did a tsunami over the fireplace, extinguishing a nearly cooked stuffed elephant.

Then the front wall exploded, spraying shards of marble and dust as the 200mm turret of a Tiger tank punched through the divider. Jagged cracks spread outward from the puncture point and great chunks of wall crumbled to the floor as the rest of the military war machine rammed the decorative archway above the throne. Armored treads spinning for traction, the leviathan machine tilted over the last bit of wall and smashed on top of the royal chairs. With the sound of splintering wood, the vaunted throne of Mars was gone, reduced to a million dollars' worth of kindling in a split second.

Looming before the quaking crowd of executives and staff with a hydraulic hiss, the 200mm cannon of the Tiger lowered until it was directly pointed toward them. Then the side-mounted .30 caliber machine guns cut loose, stuttering rods of steel-jacketed rounds sweeping across the once meticulously clean throne room. Lines of puckered holes stitched the walls as the heavy-duty combat rounds chewed a path of destruction. Vozs seemed to vaporize. Windows disintegrated. Spent shell casings formed a glittering arch in the air and rained endless upon the cowering staff. And the cumulative bad luck from all the smashed mirrors would plague the castle for the next two centuries.

As the exhausted guns abruptly stopped, a sharp explosion came from the top of the tank and the access hatch slammed backward, wrapping itself around the aft stanchion.

"Okay, you pracking morons!" cried King Yertzoff, popping up out of the access hole, his face bloodred and flecks of white foam staining his lips. *"Where the hell is my son!!!"*

Brushing the dust and shell casings off themselves, the attending crowd of palace personnel exchanged knowing glances. The King was definitely unhappy about this situation.

From behind the roaring Tiger swarmed a platoon of Space Marines who quickly unrolled a plush velvet carpet swatch directly underneath the thick ferruled barrel of the 200mm cannon. A lawn chair was unfolded and a cool butler added a silver bucket filled with crushed ice and a couple of raspberry Slushers from the peon convenience store down the block.

"I asked you clowns a question!" growled the King, snapping the breech of a Mt. Everest .75 recoilless machine gun and starting to load in a fresh belt of explosive shells.

"Wait a moment, dear," said a softer, calmer voice. "Let me get out of here first."

Grumbling acceptance, the King eased off the firing bolt of the weapon and began to impatiently drum his fingers on the dangling ammo belt.

Stepping daintily down the side of the monstrous vehicle descended the lovely Queen Lolita Yertzoff. She was still dressed in her long flowing formal gown of transparent plastic. Only now Her Most Royal Highness was armed, a brace of Webley .444 Express revolvers on each hip and a bandolier of extra rounds draped across her chest, each bullet painstakingly decorated with the red and gold mushroom cloud of the Imperial crest.

Dutifully, the Imperial Council stood and remained standing until the Queen took her place in the lawn chair. Quickly, apologies were marshaled, along with excuses, lies, and several obituaries.

Then the doors to the throne room opened and in trod a troupe of Secret Service agents holding mammoth Gibraltar Assault Rifles and wearing WatchDog scanner sunglasses. Discreetly the bodyguards probed the place for danger while taking strategic positions about the destroyed room. The Imperial agents had been caught once with their jumpsuits down and they would be damned it it would happen again! That is, outside of officially sanctioned holidays.

An android butler stepped forward to artfully wave a pocket-doc over the Slushers, searching for poisons. Receiving clearance, the Queen took a sip of the fruity beverage and nodded in approval.

"Gentlemen and ladies," said the Queen, a slim hand resting on the massive cannon of the Tiger. "I am most disappointed."

As a sonic punctuation mark, the King snapped the firing bolt on the .75 recoilless.

Sensing danger, the chamberlains quickly took their leave.

"Especially," continued Lady "Boom-Boom" in a voice to shatter stone, ". . . in the incompetent idiots in the ASPCA who allowed this catastrophe to happen in the first place!"

Gagging on a mouthful of coffee, the representative of the Assigned Strategic Party Control Agency grabbed for a handkerchief and frantically wiped his face clean. The ASPCA was a special branch of the Imperial Secret Service that ascertained whether or not a place was safe for the royalty to visit, and that included their own home.

"Our son, the sole heir to the throne of Mars, is either dead or in the hands of enemy forces!" continued the furious Queen, Slusher slopping onto the carpet. "Even as we speak the entire planet may be in dire jeopardy!"

Visibly rattled, the ASPCA operative rallied his meager forces to the defense. "But, milady, we . . ."

"Well?" roared King Yertzoff, leveling the crosshairs of the Mt. Everest .75 straight at the man's heart.

"Clean! We thought the party and castle were clean!" cried the agent, struggling to save what remained of his career. "Hel . . . heck, Your Highness, this was the official engagement party of the prince. It was fitting and proper that we give him a little slack in security so that he could properly say good-bye to many of his lifelong personal friends."

"Are you saying," throated the King in ill-controlled fury, "that you told the personal bodyguards of my son to occasionally look the other way so that he could get laid by every ex-girlfriend he has on the whole pracking planet!"

"Yes, sir," quaked the ASPCA.

"Fair enough," relented Sir Yertzoff, releasing the trigger.

From her expression, even the Queen's anger was somewhat mollified by the response. After all, their son had been raised to be the military ruler of a planet, not a Sunday school teacher. Having six or seven bastards was almost a prerequisite for becoming a king.

As their supreme potentates seemed to relax, the Imperial Council issued a collective sigh and released their armrests from white-knuckled grips.

"By the way, where is Lulu?" asked Queen Yertzoff, toying with the flex straw. "I fully expected her to be here."

"She's down in the Arsenal, sir," answered Tars, stepping into camera range. "Requisitioning a new weapon."

"Probably another damn revolver," said Gunther of the MIA, twisting his mouth about as if the word had a bad flavor. Gunpowder weapons. Gak. What was this, the twentieth century?

"Actually, no," replied Gooden with forced politeness. "She's ordering a handheld model of the Gibraltar Assault Cannon."

A shocked silence filled the decimated room.

"Can we get some of those?" asked Captain Fairchild of Castle Security. She wanted a dozen just for Christmas gifts alone!

Gooden turned to face the woman. "Certainly. Simply use the requisition form BJG44683283/2A to get form JNLI893635634/49-a and ask for twice the number you need at half the price offered."

"Thanks," said the officer, hastily typing notes into her secretary. Gee, that sounded easy enough.

"Bah," snorted "The Spike" irritably. "Why don't your people carry HK 1mm needlers like any sensible person?"

Coldly the head of the Imperial Secret Service gazed at the man, his opinion of the person readily discernible. "Because, sir, my agents can hit the broad side of a barn."

Gunther stiffened, the insult striking home. Okay, so

some of his people had weak wrists. Was that any reason to be rude?

Deciding that the time for pleasantries had passed, King Yertzoff fired a few bursts into the ceiling. "Enough! Can anybody even tell me if the prince is still alive?"

"Yes," said Gunther. "He is currently alive and undamaged."

Tars Gooden jerked about on the love seat, accidentally snapping off an armrest. "And just how does the MIA know that, sir?" he demanded hotly, stuffing the broken bit under his seat cushion.

Loftily, the little man sniffed at him. "From a highly confidential source that I cannot disclose for fear of endangering planetary security." No matter what pressures they brought to bear, Gunther would never tell anybody the name of his Tarot card reader.

This statement annoyed everybody in the throne room, but the Imperial Council had learned long ago to accept the inevitable. The MIA zealously guarded its arcane sources of information.

Swiveling the Mt. Everest, Sir Yertzoff directed his deadly attention to the chief of the Castle police. "Okay, Fairchild, have you been able to find any clues to the possible whereabouts of our son. Or the identity of the kidnappers?"

"Yes and no," replied the police officer, respectfully removing her cap. A collection of shell casings rained to the floor. Hmm, no wonder it was so heavy. "The majority of the criminals found in the castle at the time of the event were guests. Over fifty percent of them relatives."

"Interrogate them first," advised the King.

A nod. "Already in progress, Your Majesty. Of the rest found outside on the grounds, most were minor league car thieves, mudlarks, and prostitutes of no real importance. However, records indicate that recently arriving in Marsportville only days before the party was a nasty little group that calls itself The Wolf Pack consisting of a Brad Angelo, Mercurian; Moose Raincloud, an Earthling; Charles Raugh, the Independent Asteroids; and Kathleen

Liptrot, Venusian. Four real tough bastards. They worked the interplanetary scene. Sort of terrorists for hire."

"Find them. Kill them. Torture them!" roared the ruler of the planet. Then he paused. No, wait, that wasn't quite the correct procedure.

With a loud slurping noise, Queen Yertzoff finished her drink and, placing it in the ice bucket, signaled for the replacement. As the android butler complied with the request, the woman cleared her throat. "I want a complete report on the current state of Castle Security. Starting with you, Tars."

Using a pencil tip mouse, Gooden activated the monitor on his own wrist secretary. "Milady, the Marsportville city police, in collaboration with the Sandyland State Investigators and Imperial Marshals, have every radical group under close surveillance. The engagement party has been suspended during the interim and every operative I can muster is on the premises, fully armed and totally ready to lay down their lives to protect you both."

The quietly deployed ISS agents stood a little taller at that last remark. Dying was not just a part of their job, it was what they lived for!

The royal personages accepted the report at face value. They expected no less from their lapdogs. "And what is the military doing, General?" asked King Yertzoff, resting an arm atop the warm breech of the Mt. Everest.

General Hal Overton shifted his bulk in the dainty Arthur C. Clarke memorial chair he occupied, making it creak ominously. "As of 0900 this morning we went from Defense Condition Four to DefCon One. Basically, we're in a state of war with no officially declared enemy." He waited for reactions to this. There were none, so he continued. "Phobos Moon Base is on Red Alert with the entire 110th Armored Spaceborne ready to scramble in a second's notice, and I have alloted an additional ten thousand troops from across the planet to strengthen our present reserves here in Marsportville Central."

"Good enough. Admiral Sullivan?"

Leisurely the old man stood to make his report. About

time they got to him. "Roughly the same, Your Majesties," said the ancient mariner, his stiff blue uniform hung loosely on his bony frame making the sailor appear even thinner than he really was. "The Space Naval defense grid has been activated and the entire planet is on emergency watch, with the battleships *Syrtis Major* and *Ares* racing in to join the destroyer *Williams* here in Port Marsportville. And I have placed the starcruiser *Thunderfish* in a geosynchronous orbit above the capital city. They are to stay in position until ordered otherwise.

"With the *Thunderfish* our orbital defenses are fortified to impenetrability. In space, sir, Mars rules supreme!" With his fist, the sailor energetically thumped the coffee table rattling cups and saucers. "Nothing, sir, positively nothing can reach you from that direction!"

"Yeah," scoffed the King. The ruler was unmoved by this patriotic outburst, having heard far too many in his time. "Go tell it to the Marines."

Obediently the troops in the room did a quarter turn to face the admiral.

"And how is the analysis of the radio and alphabet transmissions coming?" asked Lady Yertzoff, crossing a knee and exposing a scandalous amount of leg from underneath the hem of her totally transparent dress. "Any prognosis on completion?"

The Imperial Council expectantly faced the chief Martian science adviser, a frail old man seemingly half asleep in his chair. Briefly the ex-Terran unfocused his eyes as he internally conversed with the colossal mainframe computer at the Mars Defense Citadel and Video Game Shop.

"In the allotted time, results are incomplete," announced Professor Kushner in his heavily accented Esperanto. "The majority of the standard radio broadcasts, and especially the X-, Y-, and Z-band transmissions are encoded and/or scrambled. And while I am confident that we can break any cipher, it is the sheer volume of them which is delaying completion." He raised a cautionary finger. "Please remember that we had reporters here and they were chatting with each other and their editors constantly."

Scowling, the King flicked the trigger guard of the .75 recoilless on-off-on and the Queen loosened the Webley in her right holster. The press. Bleh.

At this point, the Royal Secretary raised a manicured finger and Queen "Boom-Boom" deigned to nod at him.

"Madam, are we going to release a bulletin on what happened? Inform the fourteen worlds about the missing prince? I have prepared several announcements for your perusal."

"Several?" asked "Boom-Boom," removing the straw from her mouth.

"One detailing the truth of the situation, the second denying that the whole matter has occurred."

"Interesting," drawled Lady Yertzoff. "But I believe that we will go with number one. The media already knows too much and any attempt to deny the matter would only make us look like idiots. The planet will be jittery enough without adding fuel to the fire with some damn fool cover-up."

"Agreed, Your Majesty."

"Requisition yourself some airtime, all channels, coast to coast and planet to planet. Pay for it if you have to. Try for prime time. Get maximum exposure. I want the worlds to know we're looking for Vladamir and are willing to pay handsomely for his safe return plus kill those responsible."

The Press Secretary nodded in agreement. There was cagey political wisdom in that and the media liaison sat back with a contented grin, serene in the knowledge that he had officially asked and been told what to do. There was nothing quite so satisfying as job security.

"What about our known enemies?" asked the King pensively, reclining on the tank turret. "Could this have been done by the Sons of Uncle Bob? Or the Free Police?"

"A kidnapping? Most unlikely, Your Highness," denied Tars Gooden. "Simply not their style. Our most probable culprit is the Ringdings."

At the hated name, everybody hawked and spat on the dirty floor.

Officially called the Interworld Society for the Preservation of Historic Inertia in Space, everybody else in the whole solar system called them the Ringdings. Basically, they were lunatic environmentalists fighting to protect the orbital rings of Saturn. Thousands of kilometers wide and hundreds deep, the multiple rings around the planetary giant Saturn were mostly composed of ordinary frozen water. For centuries, the terraformers of Mars had been purchasing the spacial ice from colonists on Titan, now the Federal Republic of Titan, and hurtling the frigid chunks across space and into the atmosphere of the red planet. But before the meteoric icebergs could impact the surface, huge batteries of military Bedlow lasers vaporized the million-ton slabs, thus releasing billions of cubic meters of oxygen-rich vapor into the ecosystem. Using this simple procedure, Mars had obtained a breathable atmosphere in only a hundred years. It also really kept the ground defense crews on their toes, as a barrage of iceteroids was never announced in advance. Okay, sure, the external atmosphere was still so low you couldn't run around the block without causing an internal hemorrhage, but hey, it was a start.

Mars had already removed half a million iceteroids from Saturn and could do so for another couple of centuries before even the slightest difference would be made in the beauty, structure, or gravity field of the rings.

Try and explain that to the Ringdings. Sheesh!

Checking his mental file, King Yertzoff worked the bolt on the Mt. Everest for attention. He got it.

"Which brings us to the next item on the agenda"—he paused for dramatic effect—"*how the bloody hell did they get to my son in the first place?*"

There was a brief flurry of throat clearing and paper shuffling as the Imperial Security Council prepared for evasive maneuvers.

Seemingly at random, Yertzoff chose his first victim. "Report, Ms. Gallagher," he demanded.

"Sir?" squeaked the plump redhead, a weak smile playing on her lips.

"You're in charge of the Marsportville Imperial Shields, Amanda. Have our defensives been breached?"

Born and raised on an Earth-side Army base, Amanda Gallagher knew better than to speak the words that rose in her throat. Instead, she replied, "Impossible, sir."

"Impossible is a strong word," noted the Queen coldly.

"And so is acid," muttered the king.

"But true, nonetheless," said the woman steadfastly.

Prepared for this meeting, her composure and sanity were valiantly guarded by a prior administration of a 400cc dose of CalmUdown. Guaranteed to make you yawn through anything short of the sun going nova. And maybe even then. It depended upon the dosage. Just another fine pharmaceutical produce from the Wilkes Drug Corporation.

"May I assume then that the city shield is functioning properly?" asked the Queen, checking the load in her Webley pistol.

Emphatically the redhead nodded. "Definitely, milady. I inspect it personally every morning. With the shield in operation, the castle and surrounding grounds are totally impervious to the electromagnetic spectrum. Nothing can enter or exit. Why, if a nuclear device were to explode right outside on Gagarin Avenue, the physical shock wave would kill us, but not a single erg of radiation would get inside."

"And what a comforting thought that is," mumbled General Overton, nudging a piece of fallen masonry on the floor with the polished toe of his combat boot.

Publicly, Space-Sea Admiral Sullivan mirrored his associates' opinion of the military situation. Privately, he believed the Free Police to be behind the problem. Ever since the destruction of their main headquarters on the Jupiter moon Io, the space pirates had been just itching to find a way to get back at the Royal Reds, the Martian Space Marines, who had led the incredibly successful attack. And if they had to use mad dog mercenaries like that Wolf Pack, why not? Took one to know one.

"That seems to put the ball back in your court, Tars," said the Queen in a carefully measured voice.

Without hesitation, Gooden rejected the inferred notion.

"Absolutely not, Your Majesty. There is no 'mole' in my organization. The Imperial Secret Service has never been compromised."

"That doesn't mean it can't happen," commented Gunther dryly.

Hostilely, the chief Imperial agent bristled. "Precisely what are you insinuating?"

Ernst ignored him. "Your Majesties," said the director of the MIA in his most formal tones. "If you give my organization authorization to operate on the planetary surface of Mars, I can promise to find both the prince and the people behind the attack within seventy-two hours."

Straightening in his tank, the King glanced at the Queen who did the same. "Unfortunately, without the express written permission of Parliament, I cannot, officially, sanction such an act," said Queen "Boom-Boom" with hidden meaning.

Inquisitively, the MIA coughed and tugged on his left earlobe.

In response, King Yertzoff removed his fountain pen, opened it, closed it, paused, and placed it back inside his jacket.

With a sigh, Gunther dusted off his lapels. Oh, well, it never hurt to ask.

"However, we are getting away from the important issue of how our attackers got in and out," said the politician, resuming verbal communication. "A traitor on the staff? A secret entrance? Did the prince leave willingly? What? How, damn it, how?"

The discussion went on for hours and hours. But despite endless gunfire, nobody was able to decisively answer the question.

Not yet, anyway.

CHAPTER NINE

WARM AIR RUSHING past him, Harry fell through inky blackness. For the first few moments he waited for the drop to end, but as the passage went on and on, Snyder soon realized he must be in a gravity tube. Similar to a roller-coaster ride at an amusement park, the walls of the tube gently pushed against him in an endless series of zero-G shoves. Only this one didn't have scary monster faces painted on the sides, or constantly squirt you with seltzer.

Fumbling in the inverted pockets of his jumpsuit, Snyder found his cigar lighter and flicked the microwave beamer into life. Above and below, only darkness met his gaze. To the sides, the tube walls rushed past him at horrifying speed. It was almost hypnotic the way the sleeved sections melded into a soft blur. It was tempting to touch them, but Harry knew at this velocity even a fleeting touch would flay fingers to the bone.

"Deitrich?" asked Snyder to his wrist, but static was still the only response. Damn tube must be shielded also.

Minutes passed and the tube seemed to curve, his acceleration increasing. With nothing else to do, Harry took the opportunity to have a quick snort from his hip flask and type a few notes into his wrist secretary. On through the stygian blackness the anchor hurtled, stolidly wondering what awaited him at the end of the journey.

Abruptly Harry slowed and emerged into bright lights, plummeting a few meters to gently land sprawling in the humming strands of a gravity net. After bouncing for a while, the anchor hopped off the antigravity mesh and onto a floor of crushed stone.

He was in a jagged underground chamber crudely carved from living rock. Everbrites cleanly illuminated the room. One wall of the squarish cave offered a dark tunnel as an exit.

Hesitantly the anchor moved across the cave. If this was the route used by the kidnappers, then they still might be down here with the prince. Or have a few booby traps set to dissuade pursuers. Lord, he wished Rikka and the team were here.

A curved outcropping of stone hid a wide crack in the granite walls. Snyder listened for a moment, but heard nothing. Taking a risk, he thumbed the cigar lighter to maximum and extended it into the crack. After a few feet, the opening was clearly artificial. The floor was level, the irregular walls smooth and free of any dust. Yes, it was a tunnel sure enough. After debating with himself the chances of a collapse or death traps, he decided to press onward. What the hell, Snyder couldn't go back up the tube. Those things were one-way only. Might as well continue forward and hopefully be captured. Could get a swell story about the kidnapping from the perspective of a fellow prisoner.

Taking a cigar from his pocket humidor, the anchor broke the tobacco in half and laid it on the ground, blunt end outward, pointed tip directed inward. There, if his friends should eventually follow, that would be a clear indication that this was the way he went. If strangers came, they would probably miss the clue, no buts about it. And if a police rescue squad arrived, he'd probably get cited for littering. The Martian cops and Harry Snyder were old associates.

Lowering the beamer to a barely visible glow, Harry slipped off his shoes and proceeded cautiously through the serpentine tunnel. The sides closed in at several locations making it difficult for the reporter to squeeze through. Was he bigger than the prince? Then the tunnel shifted abruptly and ended. Light flooded in from beyond. Staying in the shadows, Harry glanced about at a brightly illuminated subterranean cavern. Only about twenty meters in diameter, it was clearly empty. Deserted.

Extinguishing the beamer before its tiny battery expired, Harry put on his shoes and entered boldly, his footsteps echoing in the bare rocky hollow. No stalagmite marred the level and tiled floor. The walls were slick and shiny from a coating of a waterproof plastic sealant. Every stalactite had been removed from the curved ceiling and strings of Everbrights, light bulbs with their own independent power supply, dangled from above. At the far end was a great set of double doors, their edges cushioned with purple sealant. It was a cargo hatch off a space freighter!

The anchor felt a tingle of excitement course through his veins. There was a fabulous story behind these events. Some person, or persons, had put a tremendous amount of effort, time, and money into this project. Did Vladamir Yertzoff have any enemies who wanted him this badly? His father did. Mom too. But the prince? Taking count, Harry started to tick off potential adversaries on his fingers: the Free Police, Uncle Bob, the Ringdings, the Mafia from Earth, The Wolf Pack, and there was always the possibility of a jealous lover, an ex-girlfriend, a plain old-fashioned psycho, or maybe even a bastard brother who wanted the throne!

In disgust, the anchor threw up his hand. Okay, like any major political figure, Prince Yertzoff had a thousand foes. Fine. Great. A sea of enemies only translated to that many more additional viewers when the SNT finally broke this mystery to the worlds.

Wandering about the cavern, Harry tried to get a feel for the builders. It was plain, simple, and efficient. Very spacial in design. There was little room for unnecessary beautification in space where one wrong move could blow you out of the airlock, which just ruined your whole day. There was no trash, loose papers, litter, anything lying about, and the cavern lacked an atomic garbage can. So the words neat and cheap could be added to the growing portrait of the mastermind behind this. Yes, there was a definite military impression about the place. Mercs, maybe? Nyah, those bozos were barely toilet-trained and had yet to discover the wonders of soap. Good marksmen though.

On the concrete apron facing the hatchway, the rough surface of the material was stained in several places with oil, hydraulic fluids, and coffee. Obviously a ship or craft of some kind had been parked here. Plus, he spied several oddly spaced round indentations in the concrete. What those could indicate, Harry had no damn idea. But he took notes and made a rough sketch in his secretary using the graphics function. Scribbling away with a stylus, half a cigar clamped between teeth in concentration, Snyder decided that he would have gladly given an atomic trash can for a pocket camera. A direct swap. No coupon necessary.

A furry hand lit the stogie for him.

"Thanks," he puffed.

"No problem."

With a yelp, the anchor spun about, nearly falling over.

A grinning Michelangelo stood holding a match, with Jhonny and Rikka leaning against him. Collins was smoking contentedly away on the other half of his imported Havana.

"How long have you been here?" asked Snyder, removing the cigar to blow a neat blue smoke ring.

Rikka blew one back at him and the rings collided with disastrous results. "Long enough to come to the same conclusions you have."

"Which are?"

"That this was done by hand," stated Jhonny as a fact, the camcorder in his grip taking a machine-gun series of photos. "Human hands. Maybe a servo-mechanism, but no androids or robots."

"How can you tell?" asked Mike, studying the ceiling in close detail. His journey through that twisty tunnel was not an experience he would ever wish to repeat. Thank the gods he had once taken a mail-order course in yoga.

Replacing the camcorder to its accustomed position on his shoulder, the camera-op ran a palm over the smooth surface of the cave wall. "No robot or droid ever built would do this lousy a job."

"Well, there's nothing of importance in here except us," sighed Rikka, turning around. The hollow was cleaner than the bathrooms at The Horny Toad tavern. "Let's open the cargo hatch and see where we are."

"Check," agreed Snyder.

"And what if we're underwater in one of the canals?" asked Jhonny, frightened.

Brushing a strand of coal-black hair out of his face, Snyder viewed the android with amusement. "Can't you swim?"

"Hell no! I was originally built to be an oceanic farmer, but my arms and legs have been modified several times since then. Totally immerse me and we're going to experience the toaster-in-the-bathtub phenomenon up-close and personal."

Dodging around the hanging Everbrites, Mike stooped low at the control panel set into the burnished metal rim of the airlock.

"There's breathable atmosphere outside," he announced. Then the technician fumbled within his toolvest searching for something. In annoyance, he removed the garment and inverted the vest to its intended side out. Ah, much better. Having a sonic screwdriver poking into your armpit was not the most fun he had ever experienced. And for a moment the alien's face took on a dreamy look as he did remember the most fun he had ever experienced. So creative and flexible were those twin gymnasts. Sigh.

"Got a problem?" asked Rikka in concern, coming closer. "Is the hatch locked?"

"Eh? Ah, checking," replied the alien, returning to this world and running an EM scanner over the entire jamb. "No, it isn't locked." Interesting.

"That tells us a lot," mused Collins from within a pungent cloud. "The kidnappers didn't expect anybody to follow."

Removing the party feathers still attached to his

camcorder, Jhonny agreed. "Pretty damn confident crooks."

"Well, they did penetrate the security of one of the best guarded government installations existing today and successfully stole a royal prince of the blood," said Snyder, gesturing around at the vacant floor. "Not bad for punk kids out on a Saturday night lark."

"Ready?" asked Michelangelo, punching numbers into the keypad with a single talon.

"Ready," replied Jhonny, his plucked camera revving to full video speed. Rikka and Harry adjusted their cigars and nodded.

The doors separated with a sucking sound and the pressure in the cavern rapidly dropped. Gasping at the sudden change in atmosphere, the team looked out into the glaring sun. Beyond the hatch was a rough-hewn ledge overlooking a desert vista of reddish sand and windswept dunes. Jumping Judas, how far away from the castle were they?

Coughing from the dryness, the team cycled the doors shut. As the portal boomed closed, fresh air hissed out from a nozzle set into the jamb and soon the cavern was pressurized again with oxygen and moisture.

"Anybody recognize where we are?" whispered Rikka around a mouthful of cotton wadding.

Paw against the wall, Mike barked a cough. "Disneyland's new hell pavilion?"

"Ha. I laugh," crocked Harry, unscrewing the cap off his hip flask and quickly administering ninety percent proof first aid.

"Could be New Old South-West Mars," said Jhonny. The leeched air hadn't bothered him a bit. "Down by the sulfur plants."

Gratefully accepting the flask, Rikka stood and took a swallow. The smooth Irish whiskey pleasantly cut the dust from her throat like a healing river of cool, refreshing battery acid. Ah, good stuff. Pity it was so bad for your health.

"New Old Southwest, eh?" asked the reporter suspiciously. "Isn't that where Lady Caramico comes from?"

"It's also the most undeveloped section of the planet," replied Snyder haughtily, taking the flask from her shaking hands. "And thus the best place to build this tunnel without drawing attention."

Munching on a tiny emergency apple from his vest, Mike decided to look for clues his way. Unearthing a pocket WatchDog scanner, the technician ran the questing beams over the cavern. Walls . . . nothing; Everbrites . . . nothing; floor . . . nothing; doors . . . whoa! By the toes of the great fish!

"I found something here on the ragged end of this service panel," said the alien, fine-tuning the focus of the scanner.

"A fingerprint?" asked Jhonny eagerly.

"No, a thread."

"Show us," said Rikka, coming closer. Any clue would help at this point.

Adjusting the display function of the WatchDog, the alien threw a magnified picture of the black thread against the wall, along with a chemical analysis. One end of the thread was neatly cut, the other broken and ragged, clearly indicating that this was accidentally torn from a garment and not a deliberate plant to throw off pursuit. Unless the criminals were smarter than the reporters, which the news team flatly refused to believe.

Lips pursed in concentration, Collins stepped to the wall and ran a finger under the baseball bat-sized picture. "Mike, can you kill the yellow tone from the projection?"

The alien understood. "Ah, background light from the cavern. Yes, immediately."

Instantly the thread changed color.

"A medium dark blue," identified Collins, "with a tinge of white in the middle." Now why did that sound so familiar to her? Tablecloth from a famous restaurant? The flag of Mars? Space Navy uniform? No, that was mostly red. Hmm.

Stroking his chin, Harry noticed his own cuff. "Hey! Could be a policeman's uniform."

"Wait!" cried Jhonny and he knelt on the floor.

Curiously, his friends watched the android creep about muttering and then counting to himself.

"Yes!" he shouted, raising a fist in triumph.

"What?" asked the team excitedly.

Rocking to his heels, Jhonny stood. "Thirty-eight feet exact," the camera-op stated proudly. "The precise distance between the landing struts of the craft that was parked here when the concrete wasn't fully cured."

Impatiently the reporters waited for enlightenment.

"That's too small for a shuttle and too large for a singleship or space scouter," continued the android with a sly grin. "But it is the exact dimensions of a Martian police interceptor!"

Stunned silence filled the cavern.

"The prince is already off-world," said Harry, glaring at the ceiling. "The kidnappers left disguised as one of the very ships searching for them!"

"Gods above, that's clever," praised Michelangelo with a growl, hating to say the words.

Without warning, Jhonny placed a cool metallic finger on each male's mouth. They glared at him and noticed Rikka.

The investigative reporter was standing stock-still, her eyes reduced to mere slits and her breath coming at a fast pace. Happily the rest of the team gathered close to the reporter and awaited developments. They could almost hear the gears in her wonderful brain revving to top speed.

Lost in a world of thought, Collins was reviewing the situation and not liking the trail it lead down. A signal from the watch lured the prince into his own office. And after carefully hiding it away, the man disappeared. Would kidnappers have hidden the watch? Could there have been a message waiting for the prince in the alcove? If so, how could they have gotten it there? Was a friend in on the kidnapping? The endless possibilities and permutations of the situation swirled round and round in her brain, tightening

and condensing as the facts battled theories until the last
shining crystallized idea lay plainly in sight and the
woman wondered how she ever could have been so stupid
not to see immediately.

"The sneaky bastard," she said aloud. "He did this himself."

"What?"

"Huh?"

"Eh?"

"Prince Yertzoff wasn't kidnapped, he *escaped*!"

CHAPTER TEN

IN THE GLASS-WALLED sound booth of Studio One on Media, Paul Ambocksky anxiously looked over the shoulders of the line of busy technicians arrayed before the ten thousand controls of the master board. On the wall aft of him, the mechanical clock loudly clicked to the thirty-second mark. This was it.

"Gimme a check!" he barked. "Z-band transmitters?"

"Numbers one through eight booted, aligned, and locked into position, sir. Numbers nine and ten warmed and ready to go."

"Affiliates?"

"On line and waiting, Box."

"Cameras?"

"Tones and bars, chief."

"Coffee?"

He was handed a cup. "Double black, twelve sugars."

"Thanks. Ten seconds," whispered Box into his throat mike, the words booming out across the dark equipment arena and dimly lit center stage. The announcement was promptly followed by a thundering slurp, a godlike sigh of contentment, and a small oops.

Down in the arena, crouching behind a humming teleprompter, a young gaffer held up five fingers, four, three, two, and the last digit went level pointing at the middle-aged woman on the small stage. The overhead arc lights and kliegs exploded into brilliance and a toy telex on the floor directly under the main camera began to chatter away, sounding ten times louder than a real model.

"From the fiery depths of the sun," boomed an off-camera announcer's voice. "To the explosive chaos of the Ort Cloud—QSNT IS THERE ... HERE ... ERE ... ere ..."

An invisible chorus sang out with, "All news all the time!"

Cut to: Lois Kent sitting and smiling at a large important-looking desk, a large pile of important-looking papers in front of her. In the background was a bustling team of underpaid actors pretending to be hardworking reporters in the office. To a trained eye, the subtle differences between the actors and real reporters were immediately discernible; all of the actors were shaved and not one of them was drunk.

"Good evening, ladies and gentlemen and all the ships in space. This is the QSNT six o'clock report and I am Lois Kent filling in for the vacationing Harry Snyder."

Just then a blinding light burst filled the screen.

"Flash!" cried the anchor, trying not to smile. God, she loved doing that. The viewers were awake now. "At approximately 4:55 Central Martian time, Prince Vladamir Umberto Yertzoff was allegedly kidnapped by unknown assailants!"

The air behind Kent blurred and changed to a posed picture of the dignified prince knighting Master Pilot Charles "Crash" Conway, the savior of Ganymede.

"The brutal abduction of the beloved ruler actually appeared to have occurred during his very own engagement party to the Lady Etta Caramico."

A portrait shot of the duke's daughter replaced the prince. She was a pretty woman of astonishingly normal features.

"King and Queen Yertzoff are currently unavailable for comment on the possibility that the kidnapping was performed by the Free Police, or Uncle Bob. However, speculations run high and rumors are flying thick within the castle walls." Hmm, that was more than a bit vague. Lois decided to have a word with the script writer after the show.

The picture now shifted to a violence-filled scene of a bloody Prince Yertzoff standing defiantly in a burning doorway and firing two hand Bedlows at a heavily armed contingent of the snarling Free Police running straight toward him. An artistically augmented sign on the wall identified the building as the Marsportville Children's Hospital for the Blind.

In the control booth, Ambocksky nodded in approval. He used this priceless photo whenever possible, because it really pissed off the Free Police who just hated to get caught in the act.

"We'll have more detailed information for you about the horrible events at the royal orgy"—well technically, any party could be called an orgy—"and the resulting riot"—that is what the aristocrats did, sure enough—"right after these important words from our sponsors: Wilkes Humble Crow Pie, when merely saying you're sorry isn't enough, and The Good Time Funeral Home, where dying can be fun!"

As the camera lights winked out, Kent contentedly scratched an armpit and the picture converted to a slide of Yertzoff at a college party, naked and swinging from a chandelier above a swimming pool full of beer, his frat brothers, and topless bimbos. The ratings would shoot through the roof if only the boss dared to show this more fun side of His Highness.

In the control booth, switches were thrown, the college scene reverted to the more dramatic hospital fight, and coolly Kent went on with the news. Paul eyed the ratings tote board and found the figures within the acceptable range. Whew. Okay, they were on line and running. It was a cobbled together Frankenstein of a report, but the other services didn't have anything much better.

"Next set of commercials ready?" he asked the booth at large.

A man at the board said yes. "Co-Bras, for cross your heart protection, and the Rooster Boys' new album 'Poultry in Motion.' "

"Roll 'em after Weather and Sports."

"Check."

A spot of dampness dripped into his palm and Ambocksky quickly drained the rest of his coffee before it ate a hole clear through the mug. Boy, the coffee on the station was constantly getting worse. Thank God. Sometimes it was the only thing that kept him on his feet.

"No word on Mr. Wilkes yet?" he asked, dropping the mug into a waste can. The atomic receptacle had to work twice before the stubborn cup finally vaporized.

"No, sir," replied Mrs. Seigling, handing him a fresh mug. "And Ms. Valdez has placed orders not to be disturbed."

He took a sip. "Are you telling me," said Paul slowly to make sure he had this correct, "that, for the moment, I'm in absolute control of the whole damn space station?"

"Apparently so, yes, sir."

This was an opportunity not to be missed. "Harrigan! Contact bookkeeping. Everybody gets a ten percent raise!"

"Yes, sir!" cried the man, and then he jerked a thumb toward the soundstage below them. "Does that include the actors?"

"Hell no, screw 'em. We do all the work."

"Yes, sir!"

Paul turned. "Varlanokstov, fire the chief cook of the commissary!"

Caught in the act of swallowing another post-lunch roll of antacids, she paused, and a fleeting smile crossed her weary features.

"Can I do it in person?" asked the Sound Engineer eagerly.

"Sure. Have a ball. Fire Mr. Ptomaine twice, if you like."

With a cackle of delight, the woman dashed out of the booth.

Then Paul Ambocksky spread his arms wide and shouted to the ceiling at the top of his lungs. "And now will somebody, anybody, please find me the pracking SNT!"

But there was no immediate response to that particular request.

Wearing only a flower print sarong wrapped low about her hips, the beautiful native girl came out of the Earth jungle carrying a steaming bowl of spaghetti in her hands. Barefoot, she walked down a flagstone path to the beach, the cotton wrap swaying in delicious counterpoint to the gentle undulations of her shapely breasts. Unbound, her long ebony hair flowed freely in the warm sea breeze. Her skin was the color of new honey and her red lips were parted in a smile that promised things only a lush, young body like hers could deliver. In truth, the cadre of old men in business suits sitting at the picnic table on the shore eyed her far more hungrily than they did the approaching dinner. One they had every day and the other with far less regularity.

The girl's semiclad state, illegal on the majority of beaches on the island of Fiji, was quite permissible here, as this cove was privately owned. The lax hands of the local police were so well greased that they often had trouble keeping a grip on their bribes.

The twenty armed guards scattered about the beach kept a watchful eye on the topless female as she deposited the huge bowl of spaghetti on the round redwood table. As always, she giggled when given the mandatory pat on the fanny from whomever she was nearest and then respectfully curtsied, with the most delightful results. Turning around, the native beauty slowly retraced her steps up the flagstone path, offering as pleasant a view going as coming. The path led to an immense mansion hidden amid the dense trees of the tropical jungle, a palatial estate that was in reality a Mafia hardsite filled with guns and troops. The bare-breasted waitress and five other girls from her village lived there in splendid comfort serving the old men's pleasure, totally unaware that the money they received for their services was soaked in human misery, the blood having been efficiently laundered off by a Swiss bank.

Don Guido "The Icepick" Scarelli, the contemporary

head of La Costa Nostra, pulled the bowl to him and took a generous helping of the steaming pasta. Then without waiting for his associates to be served, he dug right in, slurping and chewing with true Sicilian gusto. Which was the last mistake Don Scarelli made in this life. As the bowl was passed on, there was suddenly revealed among the macaroni and meatballs a video monitor.

Surprised Italian curses abounded at the discovery and in prompt response, the monitor flicked into life, displaying the detailed account of how the crime lords had planned on building a fleet of armored frigates and going into the business of space piracy. It listed dates, figures, contacts, weapon stats, codes, where the bribes had taken place, the proposed location of their secret base, and names. Everybody's name. It also listed the precincts of thirty-seven honest police officers who would love to get their hands on this data.

Then it blinked the single word: TOMORROW.

With an inarticulate noise, Don Scarelli promptly swallowed a meatball whole and started to choke.

Immediately, his *pisanos* rushed to help their beloved capo. But untrained in anything other than murder and extortion, their good-intentioned administrations only worsened the man's condition. Pushing them away, Scarelli desperately snatched a Chianti bottle and drained it in a single draft, attempting to clear his blocked throat. It was a valiant effort. But the lack of air, combined with alcohol shock and the horror before him, proved too much for the old man's heart and he pitched face forward into his plate—dead.

The guards dashed forward and there was general pandemonium until it was ascertained that their beloved godfather had indeed passed away. Then they callously threw his body into the ocean for the tide to dispose of and unanimously elected Joseph "That Gun Ain't Mine, Officer" Feroce as the new Don Supreme.

"What should we do first?" asked a nattily dressed man, fastidiously brushing some sand off his pant cuffs.

Don Feroce eased himself into the chair that he had lusted for all of his adult life and was surprised to find it slightly uncomfortable. "As I see it, we have three options." He growled. "*Una*, forget about tangling with the Free Police and go legit. *Doua*, try again. *Tria*, move to another star system."

The five remaining representatives of La Costa Nostra fearfully glanced at one another, remembering what happened to their organization the last time it tangled with the dreaded Free Police.

"Just how far away is Alpha Centauri?" asked one of the legbreakers, a single heartbeat before the video monitor, the table, the mafioso, their guards, several trees, and a good stretch of the beach violently disappeared in an explosion that bordered on atomic.

With an expression of extreme satisfaction, the grizzled admiral of the Free Police removed his finger from the lit button on the console on the bridge of his spaceship and gleefully wrote the word "closed" on his Mafia file. Now if those garlic-eaters ever tried to go into space again and cut into his profits it wouldn't be in this dimension!

Chuckling to himself, the commander deposited the manila folder into the cabinet beneath his computer console. A brief flash of light announced its destruction. There, a good day's work done and it was only six o'clock in the morning here in the asteroid belt, 7 P.M. Fiji time on Earth.

Due to the time zone differences between space and the planet, for the Mafia, it was tomorrow. Hee-hee-hee.

"On to new business," smiled the admiral, reclining in his command chair and crossing his boots. Ah, blood was better than coffee to get you awake in the morning. "So, what's the story about this kidnapped prince? Do we have him?"

Incredibly, the answer from his staff was yes and no.

"*Hi-yah!*" cried a voice and a hand punched through the wood panels of the closet door.

"*Hoo-ha!*" A shoe smashed out a bottom panel.

"*Hee-ho!*" And a balding head cannonballed apart the

middle of the portal. With the sound of splintering wood, the closet door sagged apart and tumbled to the floor in pieces.

Bold and confident, Gardner Wilkes strode over to his desk, and grabbing the executive phone, he hit the redial button with a trained thumb. "Ms. Valdez? . . . Wilkes here. Please send a medical team to my apartment immediately. Thanks."

Replacing the receiver, Gardner crossed his eyes, groaned loudly, and dropped to the carpet faster than the door. As the room began to spin, with stars and fairies dancing around him, the station owner realized that, as usual, mother had been correct on both counts. Always keep a spare key in your shoe and karate was dangerous. Ow. . . .

Stropping a knife on a whetstone in her dainty hands, Susie Sunshine leaned eagerly forward as the computer onboard the QINS shuttle raced through the published index of spaceship names. Quiller Geo-Medical Plumbing was a subdivision on Ommpah Tuba Manufacturing, which was a sister organization registered to the Gunderson Company, a wholly owned subsidiary of Enigma Industries, which was controlled by its parent business the Wilkes Corporation. Which owned QSNT!

"Ah-ha!" she cried. So it was Rikka and her gang!

"Damn those busybodies!" cursed Jason Hardcopy, slamming a fist onto the console and smashing in a section of the plastic board. "Well, they're not going to get away with interfering with us on this story!"

On his way to the kitchen with the dirty lunch dishes, the QINS camera-op dropped a sharp fork on the deck next to the bound and gagged Hanna O'Toole. As it hit her shoe, she glanced puzzled at the man. Impassive, he said nothing but flicked his eyes toward the open airlock door, then turned and ambled off to load the dishwasher.

Across the room at the control board, Sunshine slid the knife into her boot. "Okay, Jas, got a plan?"

"Yes, the ultimate revenge," snarled the handsome man.

"We're going to scoop this story out from underneath them and then sell it to QSNT!"

"At a reasonable price, of course," asked Sunshine with an evil twinkle in her eyes. "Merely cancel the contract for the whole SNT crew!"

"Exactly!"

This was the lowest, most despicable, cowardly, under-handed dirty trick she had ever heard of in her entire two decades of working the news beat on ten planets!

"I like it," she purred. "How do we begin?"

In the background, Hanna O'Toole finished cutting herself loose and dove straight out the airlock, hit the spaceport ground in a roll and came up sprinting. A phone, radio, fax machine, anything like that would do.

She had a story to file.

And a warning to relay.

Over their spacesuit radios, the Ringdings heard the preliminary report about the disappearance of His Royal Highness, but paid it little attention. All twelve members of their organization were far too busy on a colossal new project.

With the ringed glory of Saturn filling most of the horizon below them, ahead of the group stretched the endless vista of ice and rock chunks, ablaze with the reflected glory of the distant sun. And floating nearby was a gigantic spool, which slowly revolved, feeding off a single chain of linked steel.

Placing her glove on the surface of the ice, an elderly woman brought a hammer down hard and the piton in her grip stabbed deep into the primordial glacier. A snap clip attached the end of chain to the piton sunk into the fifty-ton chunk of ice. Then the environmentalist carefully jumped to the next asteroid and started the whole process over again. Only 14,739,374,499,804 more iceteroids to go.

Let's see Mars stop them now!

* * *

Pinching the fabric at his knee, Lord Alexander Hyde-White bent his leg and placed a tapered shoe atop a bucket of Wilkes Chili Floor Wax—for a shine you can taste.

"Are you quite sure it was Rikka Collins of QSNT that paid you to trick me?" he asked politely, returning the empty wallet to his pants pocket.

"Most certain, milord," said the janitor, rifling through the thick wad of golden sanddollars. "She was dressed as a maid, but far too uppity to be a real servant."

"Indeed," muttered the QBBC reporter pensively.

In the complex maze of the castle, it would have been simplicity to go around him. But they did not, and instead used a ruse. Thus there must logically be something in that corridor that the team wanted to get at very badly. Supply closet? The elevator bank? Meeting room? Finger snap.

The prince's private office!

Spinning about on a heel, the British lord hurried away to find the Prime Minister, a Vice Chancellor, somebody, anybody in charge so that he could get permission to breech the office.

And even though the QBBC reporter walked at a speed perilously close to undignified, Hyde-White had a bad feeling that he was already too late.

On the night side of Mercury, where the temperature was a cool 700 degrees Fahrenheit, a couple of stevedores in powerarmor were loading a cargo freighter with molten thulium. Suddenly they paused in their work as the radio erupted with the priority announcement that Sir Vladamir Yertzoff, billionaire, knight of the realm, royal prince of the blood, and the heir to the throne of Mars was missing, believed kidnapped!

"Gee," remarked the man, wiping sweat from his brow. "I hadn't known that Mars had, like, a prince, ya know?"

"Well, it don't no more," observed the woman, juicily cracking her chewing gum.

Her companion nodded in dumb agreement and the two returned to their more pressing work. Politics. Who cared?

"Hey, know what's the favorite sport on Mars?"

"No. What?"

"Catch the meteor. Know what the number one cause of death is on Mars?"

"Professional sports!" chuckled the woman.

Then both stopped laughing as a fresh idea occurred.

"Do you suppose that this social event may cause sufficient unrest in the Imperial business cartels that a significant drop could occur in the Martian stock market?" asked the man.

"Yes!" cried the woman excitedly, working her wrist calculator. "And there is an estimated sixty-five percent chance of the prince being ransomed alive!"

"Which will reestablish, or exceed, the present level of the market!" The man glanced at the clock in his helmet. "I propose we wait an hour for the panic to reach maximum and then advise our brokers to float a margin call. Agreed?"

"Most assuredly," grunted the woman, slinging a new crucible of thulium into the freighter. Money. Now that was important!

With a squeal of tortured metal, the last bolt disengaged from the support frame under the gravity net and Michelangelo easily slid the power unit out of the relay assembly. There! The gravity chute was dead. If anybody found the secret entrance, they would have one hell of a long crawl to reach this end.

HELLO, scrolled the wrist secretaries of the SNT.

"Deitrich!" cried Rikka in delight, grinding out her cigar butt underfoot.

"Where have you been?" demanded Harry, chewing on the last inch of his Havana. "We've been calling and calling!"

DO YOU KNOW HOW FAR AWAY FROM THE CASTLE YOU FOLKS ARE? I HAD TO TAP INTO THE MARS SATELLITE NETWORK TO LOCATE YOUR TRANSPONDERS.

"How soon can you get here?" inquired Jhonny, busy making a duplicate of the video disk in his camcorder.

ETA IN FIVE MINUTES. AND PERSONALLY, I WONDER IF WE
STILL HAVE JOBS.

Puzzled, the team members looked at each other. Eh?
Oh, prack, the Brain might be correct. It had been almost
an hour since the kidnapping and the team had yet to file
a report.

"Maybe we'd better go straight to Media," suggested
Collins, rubbing the back of her neck. "So we can show
Box and the chief that we have been working."

AGREED.

Furious, Harry shifted the cigar from one side of his
mouth to the other. Drat! He had forgotten about the time
constraints upon them while engaged in solving this mystery.

"Ms. Valdez will want to crucify us," noted Jhonny
grimly.

Sadly Mike agreed. Yes, divine intervention may be
their only hope.

"Hey, buddy," called out a voice from beyond the bars.

Turning over in his cramped bunk, Zultar Stitt was surprised to see a fellow convict standing at the door to his
cell. Must be one of the trustees. Or the midnight welcome
wagon.

"Yes, what do you want?" asked the criminal.

A heartless laugh. "What I want is out of here, but what
I need is to know if you are the guy who tried to sell the
phony alien artifact to a hundred millionaires?"

Denials automatically leaped to his lips, but then Stitt
remembered where he was. Telling lies to your fellow in-
mates in prison was almost as dangerous as dropping the
soap. Almost.

"Yes," he sighed, swinging his legs off the bunk and sitting upright. "That was me."

A gap-toothed grin. "Great! So with a hundred snooty,
high-priced lawyers after your hide, you're going to Snow-
Ball, right?"

At the very name Stitt shuddered. SnowBall Hell, so ti-
tled because that was a prisoner's chance of getting out. It

was the only totally escape-proof prison in existence, mainly for the reason that it was located in a valley on the frozen world of Neptune, where the surface temperature was a mean −700 degrees Fahrenheit. Even in Samson powerarmor, a man would freeze to death from heat loss due to conduction through his feet in contact with the ground in under sixty seconds. Witches and brass monkeys avoided the place at any cost.

"Yeah, so?" prompted the bunko artist.

"I was supposed to go there, but got into a fight and killed another prisoner," explained the convict. "Hey, how was I supposed to know he was allergic to dynamite?"

"Accidents do happen," acknowledged Stitt in consolation. Well, that explained the big explosion a couple of hours ago. He had personally fantasized it was a nuclear missile impacting Media.

The man at the door went on. "Anyway, they're going to send me to Earth for mental rehabilitation." Furtively he glanced about the corridor of lunar cells. "But I got to get a message to somebody in Hell."

"Who?" asked Zultar curiously. "Another prisoner? A member of the staff? A friendly guard?"

The answer to his question was so absolutely incredible it had to be true and Stitt eagerly agreed to convey the information. For a price. If revenge was a dish best served cold, then what better place for it to start than Neptune.

The SNT were about to go off the air. Permanently.

In a clown suit with a rubber chicken in his hand, the present Uncle Bob Yertzoff slowed the miniature choo-choo train in his mountaintop arboretum and hopped off. "Snoopy?" he called.

A female android, dressed as a World War One flying ace, poked her head into the doorway. "Sir?" she asked, removing the antiquarian goggles.

"Please contact the Free Police and offer them a substantial reward if my nephew is returned alive and relatively unharmed."

A blink. "Relatively, sir?"

Uncle Bob gestured sagely with the rubber chicken. "Space pirates have their limits. It is always best to know when not to ask for the impossible, because you won't get it."

"Like at the market when you wished to purchase a single zebra cutlet."

"Exactly."

"Understood, my lord."

As he watched the beautiful cyborg commoner depart, the royal relative wistfully wished that the differences between the two of them were not so great. But alas, it could never be.

Play trains with a girl? He'd get cooties!

Ick.

CHAPTER ELEVEN

ON LEVEL 9 in Media Station, the door to Conference Room A slammed open and four panting reporters cried, "The prince of Mars has *not* been kidnapped!"

"We know!" chorused the sixty-five people clustered around a huge circular table. Papers were shuffled, read, and destroyed.

"Simpson, you'll do a retrospective on the history of kidnapping," snapped Paul Ambocksky, covering the mouthpiece of a Hush phone with the palm of a hand. His cream jumpsuit was stained with coffee and he had a stylus behind each ear and another in his hand. "I suggest starting with something like the attempted kidnapping of the baby Queen Victoria back in 1850 England and how it led to the creation of Scotland Yard. Will this crime forge a new breed of supercop on Mars? Et cetera, et cetera. Concentrate on the kidnappings which turned out badly for the victim. Make the viewers fear for the prince."

With an explosion of red hair almost successfully hiding his incredible ears, the cub reporter glowed with the prospect of a byline, even on such a simplistic assignment. You gotta cut teeth before trying to chew a steak. "Maybe stage a mock kidnapping of a beauty contest queen to give them a taste?"

Hmm, sex, royalty, and implied violence. This kid was going to go far. "Excellent idea. Run the finished job past the Special Effects Department before bringing it to me."

"Consider it done, sir!" replied the youngster, typing

118

madly at his keyboard. Okay, now what the hell was England anyway, somebody's moon?

Passing a note to Editorial, Box removed the palm. "Sorry that you're on vacation, Immelstein, but I need an expert analysis on how interplanetary stock market is handling this, especially Mercury! Is the sanddollar still strong or . . . hey, waitaminute."

In ragged stages, the room went still and 130 eyes blinked.

"What was that again?" demanded Gardner Wilkes, tilting his head. The station owner was sporting a mauve silk two-piece jumpsuit with his initials embroidered on the lapels, a neon orange ascot, and his head was swaddled in white bandages.

Mike started to compliment the man on the lovely turban when he realized it was actually a wound dressing. Hmm, high fashion medicine. Why look frumpy during the healing process? Think of how a patient's disposition during recuperation would improve if doctors used, say, sequined bandages, French cut arm slings, ruffled neck braces, and fresco-style plaster casts decorated by grand master artists: Da Vinci, Rubens, Foglio, Dali! Well, maybe not Salvadore Dali. No sense giving ill people headaches along with everything else wrong with them. This could be bigger than the home version of Catch the Meteor! And nowhere near as messy.

"Prince Yertzoff was not, repeat, not kidnapped," stated Harry, advancing into the room along with his team.

"Seriously?" demanded Ambocksky, absentmindedly hanging up the receiver.

Nineteen billion kilometers away, by a pool of clear blue water on the New Hawaii Asteroid, Hyman Immelstein took prompt advantage of the lapse to gleefully toss his phone into the barbecue pit, adjust his swim trunks, and immediately head for the casino to do some empirical testing on how strong the sanddollar was, along with his intimate knowledge of baccarat.

* * *

"Yes, it's a fact," boasted Rikka, straightening the cuffs of her fresh green jumpsuit. Wisely, the team had changed out of their disguises on route here and into their normal clothes. They had each heard something, somewhere, about a station dress code and while breaking rules was their way of life, it seemed almost too small a regulation to bother defying. Besides, Collins certainly wasn't going to a senior staff meeting dressed as a maid. She'd never hear the end of it, just like poor Hannigan when the Advertising Dept. caught him wearing ladies' lingerie under his spacesuit. The feeble excuse that it helped him stay cool during solar storms was deemed hardly acceptable.

YOU BETTER BELIEVE IT, FOLKS, scrolled Deitrich.

"Then what happened?" asked Wilkes curiously.

Rikka said, "He left the castle of his own free will."

"Why?" demanded the Medicine & Health editor.

Harry shrugged. "That we don't know yet."

"But we soon will," added Jhonny loyally.

Towering over everybody, Mike added, "Ditto!" The alien had no idea what the word meant, but it seemed to be a good response for most situations.

Not kidnapped? While the majority of the senior staff members present reacted happily to this pronouncement, the chief crime beat reporter was aghast. If true, this was terrible. He had already prepared a series of articles on the lax Martian security and how it directly correlated to why he needed more than a measly ten percent raise.

"And how did you come by this unbelievable information," demanded Maria Valdez, her long, sharp fingernails drumming on the tabletop like tiny crimson sledgehammers. This afternoon, the Station Manager was barely dressed in a black nylon jumpsuit so thin and tight it clearly showed her muscle tone. The pectoral and biceps were good, but the deltoids needed a little work.

"There is a secret exit out of the castle from Prince Yertzoff's private office," explained Collins, folding her hands on the table. "We followed it all the way to a hidden launch bay in the Martian desert."

"And where have you been since the story broke?" she added with a sneer. "Sleeping off another hangover?"

Mike spoke, "The tunnel we traversed is some 250 kilometers long."

No suitable retort came to mind, so Valdez merely voiced a noncommittal grunt.

DON'T YOU HATE IT WHEN SHE WAXES DIDACTIC LIKE THAT?

Chuckling, the news team took their accustomed seats at the table between the rival editors of Contemporary Jazz and Classical Music. The Sax and Violin editors nodded hello to their friends, then glared at each other and in unison totally ignored the Rock reporter across the table, who was presently engaged in writing a hate article about the Country & Western reviewer, who was daydreaming of a ballerina driving a Mack truck through a smoky underground bar and annihilating the heavy metal band of accordion players on stage.

Besides, what did music have to do with a kidnapping?

"Yes, a good question. And where were you, Maria?" asked Wilkes, adjusting the bloody bandages about his head. At least he had an excuse for lying down on the job. The note from his physician clearly stated a subdural hematoma. His third this month. With practiced ease, the billionaire had neatly erased the part about abject stupidity.

Shocked at the implied accusation, Valdez turned white with anger, then flushed in remembrance and managed to mumble something that sounded like busyasleephavingmyhairdone.

Listlessly the Meteorological editor toyed with a detailed, 3-D, four-color weather map showing how the perfectly clear skies of North Mars could have in no way influenced the criminals either way. He should have gone into real estate. At least that was exciting.

"This is terrific! You have proof?" asked Ambocksky eagerly. QSNT had been late reporting the kidnapping of the prince, but a scoop like this would more than repair the damage done to their esteem from the slow response.

Jhonny patted his camcorder. "Footage of the party, castle, segments of the search, everything, right here."

Approving murmurs sounded from the attending reporters.

"Excellent," beamed Wilkes and the turban slid over his face. Darn, how did Arabs do this? Glue? Staples? Maybe owning a camel helped.

Flexing a lovely muscle, Maria jumped into the conversation. "A continuous feed of the entire journey?" asked Valdez, searching for a flaw in their prize.

Reluctantly the android had to admit there was not. "Unfortunately, we went down the tunnel so unexpectedly I didn't turn my camera on for the first few seconds."

Utterly delighted, Valdez tried not to preen and failed miserably. "So you lack an unbroken record of the escape route?" Which implied the whole thing could have been cobbled together in the video lab of the SNT shuttle. Together, Deitrich and Jhonny were capable of amazing things.

"Yes, we don't," sighed the camera-op truthfully.

"But it did happen," rumbled Michelangelo, raising one hand to God and lowering the other to cover all bases. "I can give you my sacred word of honor."

In response, the room burst into laughter. Geez, they loved the big guy. Funniest person on the station, after the owner.

"Okay, so we'll return," stated Snyder confidently. "And do the whole thing backward from the launch port into the office."

Box shook his head. "No can do. Mars has been officially closed for the duration. Only Imperial warcraft allowed in or out."

"They closed the entire planet?"

The Worlds Events editor nodded solemnly. "Martians take their royalty very seriously."

NO KIDDING. GOOD THING WE LEFT WHEN WE DID.

At the far end of the table, an overweight man with a sketch pad and stylus was busy doodling. A self-imposed embargo. The political cartoonist almost swooned from the overload of joke possibilities. This was going to be even better than his series on the pocket pool table.

Suddenly the Hush phone on the table before Box did not ring and the Executive Producer picked up the receiver. Paul hated the damn machine, as he could never tell when it was working or broken. And the call-waiting function was enough to give a person nightmares.

"Yeah? I'm busy," he said as a greeting. A pause. "There's a what? Oh, hell. Thanks."

"Bomb threat," called out Ambocksky, hanging up the receiver.

Without breaking any of their conversations, the whole roomful of people calmly departed and took the stairs, elevators, lifts, firepoles to the next level down, which was an exact copy of the conference room they had just been in. Flowers in duplicate vases, coffee makers perking, computers booted to interface with running programs, and the conference continued with only a thirty-second gap. It was not their first threat.

As the executive staff retook their cold seats, softly from above them there came the dull thud of a low-yield explosion, followed by a fire alarm and a recorded voice telling everybody to remain calm. Unable to restrain himself, the Space Disaster reporter dashed upstairs to get some pictures and search for victims.

As with most of the folks at the table, Rikka and Harry glanced upward curiously. Hmm, it actually had been a real bomb this time. Interesting.

"You okay, Deitrich?" asked Jhonny in concern. Their shuttle was parked on that level of the station.

SURE. AFTER ALL THE CRASHES I'VE BEEN IN, WHAT'S A LITTLE DYNAMITE?

"Okay, who won the pool?" called out a beefy reporter from Sports.

A clerk in Legal consulted a large chart on the wall, displaying months, weeks, days, hours, and causalty figures.

"Any deaths?" she asked hopefully.

"Sorry, none," replied a stolid security guard, touching his ear. "Just office machines."

The clerk pouted. Oh, prack. "Then Yolanda is the winner."

"Ah, *gra-ci-ous*," smiled the woman, accepting the envelope full of a colorful rainbow of assorted planetary notes.

With a fuzzy talon, Mike accessed the word on his IBM portable. Hmm, it was, Spanish for "thank you." Spanish? Then there was another human language other than Esperanto? Oh, dear.

"How did you know?" grumped Theater and Entertainment.

"Answer hazy," said the Financial Adviser, shifting a crystal ball so she could put the fat envelope in her attaché case. "Ask again tomorrow."

Although he knew Yolanda took the matter very seriously, Harry had only contempt for such nonsense. Bah! Crystal balls were bullshit. His Ouija board had told him so.

"Okay, let's work on this," said Ambocksky, reclining in his chair. This one squeaked from lack of oiling. "Operating on your supposition, where was Yertzoff going? Or was the prince running away from something?"

The SNT crew made comical faces of distress.

"Sorry, Box," said Rikka, spreading her hands. "But we don't have any idea about that yet. Only been on the story for two hours."

"And all you have is semidocumented proof for an interplanetary exclusive that the kidnapping is a fake," scoffed Maria, examining a chipped nail. "Pretty meager."

Like true adults, the SNT crew ignored the amateur sarcasm, but made a mental note to put a mouse in her milk later on.

"Actually," drawled Wilkes, finally balancing his headgear. "Considering the detailed work necessarily involved in the construction of the escape tunnel, the prince must have been involved in this project for roughly five to six years."

"And we broke through his subterfuge in under an hour," Harry reminded everybody.

Grudgingly Maria admitted that wasn't too shabby a job.

"However," observed Box, "that five-year point is a good place to start looking."

Rikka nodded in agreement. "We'll need unlimited access to the file room and archives."

"No problem," said Ambocksky, squeaking upright. "How long do you estimate it will take to find out?"

"To find him!" clarified Valdez. "That's the real story."

Angrily the team began to marshal their arsenal of crushing retorts, then stopped. Yes, that was the heart of the story. Rats! They hated it when she was correct.

"Two, three days, tops," guesstimated Collins, chewing a lip.

"You can have until the six A.M. morning report tomorrow."

"Not nearly sufficient time," denied Paul resolutely. "Two days at the least."

Valdez leaned toward him. "More than enough for any competent reporter."

Ambocksky leaned toward her. "And how would you know what competent is? Read the word in a book?"

"Now, listen to me you hasbeen . . ."

"Wannabe!"

"Putz!"

"Bozo!"

"Oh, yeah?"

"Yeah!"

Wilkes raised an executive hand and stopped the scintillating intellectual exchange.

"We've had this same discussion a hundred times and the average final decision is twenty-four hours." He faced the team. "We need this by the six o'clock afternoon report. Can do?"

Rikka smiled her widest. "Can do, sir."

"Then get," said Box, waving at the door. The man already had a Hush phone to his ear and was punching in numbers. "And I want detailed reports every hour on the hour!"

"Of course," smiled Harry, stepping away from the table. "Don't we always?"

As the team exited the room, the closing doors cut off the renewed murmurs of tense planning.

"Where should we go to establish a base of operations for the research?" asked Jhonny, scratching his camcorder under the lens. "We'll need silence and no interruptions."

"The Horny Toad?" suggested Michelangelo hopefully.

"No, that's where Box always looks for us," reminded Rikka.

USUALLY FINDS US TOO, added Deitrich sagely.

"So?" asked the technician, puzzled.

"You want to actually submit a report every hour?"

Ah, good point. "Never mind."

"Level 37?" offered Snyder in what he hoped was a casual manner. "I'm sure Sasha Parsons wouldn't mind our presence."

Jhonny and Rikka exchanged knowing glances. Love, ain't it grand?

"And how can we possibly concentrate in all the noise of those machinery and printers?" objected Mike.

Hands in pockets, the anchor accepted the rebuttal.

WHAT ABOUT THE OFFICE?

The alien perked up his ears. "I have never seen your office."

"It's your office, also," stated Jhonny.

"Really? Then why are we never there?"

"Who works in an office? We're investigative reporters, not accountants."

COME ON, SHAKE A LEG, PEOPLE. WE'VE GOT A HERO TO FIND!

"Is he," murmured Rikka thoughtfully as they started walking. "Or could that be the solution to this whole puzzle?"

CHAPTER TWELVE

A TURBO-LIFT TOOK the SNT to the desired level and the chatting team walked down several branching corridors until they reached the correct hallway.

Lined with doors, the portal to their office was no different from a score of others—except for the stolen Holiday Inn DO NOT DISTURB sign hanging from the latch.

"Wow," said Rikka, removing the dangling sign. "How long has this been here?"

Experimentally she tried blowing the dust off the plastic rectangle. The resulting cloud made everybody blind and cough for a few moments.

I TOLD OUR OLD TECHNICIAN, KNEELING STRONGARM, TO PUT THAT UP AFTER THE PARTY CELEBRATING YOUR BIG RAISE. GIVE YOU FOLKS A CHANCE TO TIDY THINGS BEFORE CALLING MAINTENANCE.

"But that was over two years ago!" exclaimed Jhonny, aghast.

Confidently Harry slid a key into the lock and turned the latch. "Aw, how bad can it be? Urmph!"

That last wordlike noise was caused by the fact that the door flatly refused to open. Reaching into his toolvest, Mike oiled the hinges, lubricated the track, and squirted graphite into the lock itself. Then he savagely pounded on the jamb, rattling the entire metal frame until a picture of Earth fell off a wall down the hallway. There, that sound loosened everything nicely.

"Hey!" cried a voice and a head popped out of another

door. "What the hell is going ... oh, hi, guys! Nice to have you back!"

Politely the team waved and wondered who was that?

As their unknown neighbor went back to work, Harry again tried to push the door aside, still with no results. So Jhonny and Rikka joined forces. Finally, they added Mike and with their combined shoulders to the panel, the four of them groaning with the unaccustomed exertion, the reporters barely managed to crack open the door.

Billowing into the hallway came a stale blast of musty air, smelling worse than the morning breath of a well-fed hyena. Only this exhalation was also tinged with a stink of mildew and something nasty sweet. As the crew backed away to a breathable atmosphere, a dust devil swirled out and madly danced among their boots until a stream of clean air from the nearby vent demolished the tiny dervish and sucked its annihilated residue off into the wall.

Inside was only darkness.

Sliding on a glove, Jhonny fumbled for a light switch. With a click, the ceiling started to hum. A blue light strobed the room as the reluctant panels were forced into life. Then for a moment blackness reigned again, and at last solid illumination flooded the office. Instantly the team was sorry they had even tried.

Visibly thick air swirled about the room as the dead gases reacted with the atmosphere moving in from the doorway. Cobwebs curtained their cluster of desks like ghostly sheets. A colony of spiders had performed the rarely accomplished task of building a ten-layer web about the watercooler, which was encrusted with mold. There was no sign of the actual floor through the smooth carpet of gray dust. Off to one side, there appeared to be significant water damage. And in the middle of that zone was a badly charred file cabinet and an editing table with a burned spot on the Formica in exactly the same shape and location of their old coffee maker. Oops.

"We must have turned off life support," noted Snyder wryly, holding a handkerchief before his face. Incredibly, this filthy hole made his current bachelor apartment seem spotless in comparison.

Then Collins gasped and pointed.

A great gelatinous mass, its mottled hide pulsating evilly under the clear fluorescent lights, was slopping slimy tentacles over her old desk.

"What is that!" whispered Rikka in horror, a splayed hand held before her as meager protection.

"An alien life-form?" breathed Jhonny, goggle-eyed, his camcorder audibly revving to maximum speed.

"A government experiment in artificial life?" added Snyder, totally fascinated. He'd never seen anything like it before on any world! "A demon? Biological warfare?"

"It's . . . a Danish," rumbled Michelangelo, double-checking the readings on his WatchDog scanner to be sure. "Just a really, really old prune Danish."

In sudden understanding, Rikka grabbed Harry's arm. "Remember! That snack you placed in the microwave and set the controls on random."

"Just a bit of tomfoolery," offered the anchor as an apology.

"Look out!" cried Jhonny, pointing.

At the sound of their voices, the Danish had started undulating toward them, knocking over chairs and forming a wave of boiling dust before its lashing nest of snaky tentacles.

In abject horror, the team scrambled outside and slammed the door closed. One split second later, the stout portal shook as something large and soft impacted on the other side. Trying not to be ill, Harry and Jhonny held the latch tight while Rikka locked the door twice and activated the emergency seal circuit. Rummaging in his vest, Mike then jammed the lock closed and sprayed a film of plastic sealant around the door, rendering the seam absolutely airtight.

Retreating to a safe distance, the team slumped to the floor in exhaustion. Whew. When a Danish went bad, it didn't fool around.

"Summon Maintenance?" asked Michelangelo, standing guard between the tiny humans and . . . IT.

Breathing hard, Snyder and Collins nodded agreement.

AND LEAVE A BIG TIP! scrolled Deitrich. BOY, I CAN'T WAIT TO SEE THAT ON INSTANT REPLAY. IT EVEN SOUNDED EXCITING.

Jhonny's curt reply was a juicy raspberry.

After taking a minute to regain their composure, and make sure nothing was in pursuit, the team shakily stood and walked to the nearest turbo-lift.

"The Toad?" asked Harry as they climbed inside.

Rikka didn't answer so he just pressed the button for Level 2.

What the hell, they hated working in an office anyway.

With a musical ding, the elevator doors parted and the SNT crew stumbled into a lobby reminiscent of pre-space times. The walls were lined with real wood and decorated with ancient flat photographs of men and women. Brass railings edged the floor, which was covered with a fine woven plastic carpet of tremendous durability. Great leafy bushes in wicker tubs stood sentry in every corner, and a velvet-covered chain blocked the set of wood and brass doors. On the lintel was a discrete sign of puce neon that audibly hummed with electrical power: THE HORNY TOAD. Underneath another sign blinked: ALL BOOZE, ALL THE TIME!

Rikka threw the bar door open and the team eagerly entered. Ah, home at last. Inside, there was a noticeable change in the atmosphere. The saloon was darker than the rest of the station and several degrees cooler. The air was crisp and fresh, thick with extra oxygen.

The walls were massive horizontal beams for the first meter, then red brick to a ceiling that was painted a nonreflective black. Optical charts of the solar system and Scotland adorned the walls in no discernible order. Cushioned leather booths lined the room and huge hexagonal tables dotted the room. Only a score of assorted people were here today, munching on sandwiches or quaffing frothy drinks in tumblers the size of small countries.

A vintage CD player stood solitary and proud near the

rest rooms. Floating above the music machine was a hologram of a badly dyed-blond woman, slightly confused about the order in which clothing should be worn, singing about how anybody could have her love with sufficient funds. Or with jewelry of equal, or greater, value.

At the far end of the spacious room was the bar, its counter a single slab of dark granite. The top was polished mirror smooth, the sides were irregular and pitted deeply in several spots.

Spanning the wall aft of the bar was an aquarium tank filled with water and plants and plastic mermaids who displayed their mammalian attributes with brazen glee. And swimming about in the aquatic wonderland was a battle-scarred fish of Herculean proportions. Even its jagged teeth and bloodshot beady eyes seemed muscular. And vicious. A small sign on the outside of the tank bore the legend: HIS NAME IS BRUNO JUNIOR AND HE IS CURRENTLY UNDERGOING SERIOUS PSYCHOLOGICAL COUNSELING. BEWARE.

Alongside the big tank was a smaller glass cube filled with deadly South American piranhas, which appeared absolutely terrified. Or maybe they were just naturally heavy smokers. The sign on their tank read: FOOD FOR JUNIOR.

Situated behind the vast expanse of aged mahogany was Alonzo MacKenzie, the owner and sole bartender. A shaved bear was the usual first impression that came to people's minds. Barrel-chested, the man was dressed in an incongruous Highland tartan jumpsuit. His long, strawberry-blond hair was tied off in a ponytail that hung to his waist and his hands appeared to be more scar tissue than healthy flesh.

"Ach now, and top of the day to ya all," canted the big Scotsman, his blue eyes twinkling with amusement.

Although she would never admit it, Rikka loved the way the bartender talked. MacKenzie still sounded as if he were rolling his r's into a burr even where there weren't any in the sentence. A neat trick that.

"Hey, Al." She smiled, taking a seat at the counter.

"Mac," offered Jhonny, getting his own stool.

In a ritual Gremlin greeting, Mike bowed to Al, who

bowed back, and then both of them touched fingers to their temples and extended the hands, palm outward.

"*Sqiuah j'tl, Mike aaraa-ting,*" said MacKenzie, straining to get the alien words correct.

"Hubba-hubba, Sir Al," said Michelangelo in Earth lingo.

Over by the confused blonde above the CD player, a patron working on his fifth double vodka wondered how many other Shriners were onboard the station. Crazy nuts had nearly smashed into him this morning in a garbage scow! They had nice hats, though.

Resting an elbow on the counter, Harry jerked his head toward the aquarium. "Bruno Jr?" he asked with a half smile.

"Aye, laddie, it be so," said MacKenzie sadly, polishing a glass tumbler stained blue. "Some fool poured ketchup into the aquarium, Bruno went mad and ate himself. This is one of his kids."

A moment passed.

"Bullshit," replied the reporters in perfect unison.

MacKenzie looked hurt. "You don't believe me?"

"No."

Ah well. With a sigh, the bartender slid a thumbnail under the sticker and peeled the "Junior" off the fish tank. His battle-scarred tail swishing steadily, Bruno watched the action of those tasty digits with extreme interest.

"I thought it would at least make a good bar story," grumbled the tavernkeeper, tossing the sticker into the trash can. Flash!

He turned around with a bottle of Scotch in one hand and four shot glasses in the other. A toss laid the glasses in a neat row and he started pouring from a foot above, not a drop hitting the wood. "And what will you be having tonight? A sandwich and drinks? Just drinks? Or only a sandwich?

"Oh, and I just had the moose in the bathroom dry-cleaned, so no smoking near stall three," MacKenzie added amiably.

"No problem."

Casually, Rikka, Jhonny, and Mike formed an arc around Harry, blocking him from the view of the other patrons.

"What we need," started the anchor, taking a pretzel and beginning to munch, "is a table where we will not be bothered. By anybody. Ever."

"Table Zero?" whispered MacKenzie, surprised. "Hoot na, what are you be working on? That princely fella?"

"Never heard of Vlad Yertzoff," answered Snyder in reply. Then, easing a hand out of his jumpsuit pocket, the anchor laid it on the countertop and slid his hand forward, with only the tiniest tip of the money underneath visible.

With a snort, MacKenzie pushed the payola away. "Not today, laddie-me-buck, I still owe you a favor for including me in the screaming incident. Most fun I had in years. The table is gratis.

"This one time," he added for clarification.

"Appreciated," said Snyder, and he put the hand back in his pocket. Although run by a friend, mostly for friends, The Horny Toad was still a business and drinks had to be paid for, as did sitting at Table Zero.

Ambling across the bar, the team started to take seats at Table One underneath the etching of legendary newspaperman H. L. Mencken when suddenly the lights flickered out.

Quickly stepping backward through the wall behind them, the SNT crew found itself in a small alcove within the wall. As sensors in the recess registered their presence, the lights snapped on in the tavern, and Mac apologized for the temporary inconvenience. Few of the patrons had even noticed this and those who did naturally attributed it to the potency of the Toad's drinks. The only water to be found in this noteworthy establishment was for Bruno and while the deadly fish was more than willing to share, the toll he extracted was more than most wished to pay.

Looking about the recess, Mike could see the tavern before them perfectly clearly. Only he didn't remember observing this private area when they approached. Or on any of their previous visits. The answer was blatantly obvious to the technician.

"A one-way hologram?" he exclaimed gleefully. "Neat!" They could see out, but nobody else could see in here. What a splendid idea for a tavern. The blackmail possibilities were endless.

Walking to the edge of the room within the tavern, the alien experimentally reached out a hairy arm and as it approached the outer boundary of the recess a sonic curtain deflected his paw.

"Welcome to Table Zero," said Jhonny, sliding two chairs together for the giant alien to sit upon. "The ultimate in privacy. In here we no longer register on the security scanners."

"I don't know how this place works, but it does," amended Collins, adding a third chair to the collection. It would soon become necessary to put their tech on another diet.

"Simple refracting light," explained Harry, removing his hat and spinning it in a hand. "It's an old illusionist trick. Stage magicians been using it for decades."

"Now how do you know that?" asked Mike, carefully lowering his bulk into the flimsy tool-steel chairs. The explanation was correct, but he was unable to explain how his nonscientific friend knew the answer.

With a flick of his wrist, Snyder skimmed his hat across the little room. The fedora hit a flat section of the wall and stayed there as if impaled on a spike. "Prestidigitation is one of my hobbies," he confessed modestly.

REALLY? scrolled Deitrich. Amazing, the old man was always full of surprises. Hey, wait a minute, maybe this was why he always won at poker. The bum!

"Go ahead, do a trick," said Rikka, resting her chin in a palm.

Grinning, Snyder cracked his knuckles. "Sure! Like to see me pull a tarantula out of your ear?" he asked eagerly.

Hastily the woman said no and reminded the anchor of the time constraints they were working under.

Dejected, Harry accepted the rebuff. Nobody ever

seemed to want to see that trick. Maybe he should make it a scorpion. Or a very small viper.

Hitting the call button on the table, a miniature hologram of MacKenzie appeared to take their orders. A few minutes later, the center of the table irised apart and up rose a pedestal supporting the glasses, tumblers, mugs, bottles, and sandwiches requested. A printed cardboard sign included with the consumables declared the First Official Kiss the Moose Contest, open to all patrons who didn't pay their bills.

"Okay," said Harry, dunking his corned beef on rye into a glass of Scotch. "According to the information we have and some intelligent guesses honed by our combined years as trained professional sneaky bastards, we appear to have two possible options."

Laying aside her mug of beer, Rikka raised a finger. "One: Yertzoff departed willingly. Going to or from what, we don't know at present."

"Two," chewed Jhonny around his tongue and head-cheese on rye. "Yertzoff has been kidnapped and the perps were smart enough to make it look as if he ran away."

"Hmm, got a nice dramatic feel, but on the reality scale . . ." Harry rested the elbow of his left arm in the palm of his right. With a whining noise, the limb trembled and went straight up.

"Barely a fifty percent possibility," noted Rikka with a smile. "I concur."

"Now if we're wrong and he has been kidnapped, by Uncle Bob, or the Free Police, Mafia, Abduhl Benny Hassan, whomever! Then we're racing with the police to find him."

"And the other news agencies," added Mike, nibbling on a barbecued watermelon.

Collins dismissed the idea with a wave. "Box will have that angle covered better than a stripper on Sunday. But we better move fast."

"Before somebody else discovers the tunnel. Agreed?

"Agreed. Fast, but circumspect."

OH, BOY, A COVERT ASSIGNMENT. I'LL SHARPEN THE CLOAK
AND YOU GO PRESS THE DAGGER.

In the background could faintly be heard a calm voice
instructing the Maintenance SWAT team where to rendezvous for the first assault.

"Why he ran is the big question," stated Snyder, removing a caraway seed from his tooth with a thumbnail. Drat
those things! "That answer will tell us where he went. We
need a complete résumé on the Yertzoff. Especially for the
years 2310 till 2305."

"When he started to build the tunnel?"

"Exactly."

SORRY. I ONLY HAVE A #3 GENERAL OUTLINE IN THE
ONBOARD COMPUTER.

"Okay, is it possible to breech the main personnel file at
Royal Computer Bank in Marsportville?"

"Of course," replied Jhonny smugly. "Give me a two-
week notice and about fifty thousand sanddollars in bribe
money."

Groans sounded.

"But it isn't necessary. We have a total file on the man
here in Media," said the android, pulling a slab of paper
from his shoulder bag. "I had these printed while we were
in the conference."

"Good thinking," complimented Rikka, passing the
tomes around the table.

"That's why I get the big money."

"You do?" said Harry, already reading. "Great! Loan me
some?"

"No. And that's how I keep the big money."

"Ah. Wisdom indeed, Obiwon."

"Thank you, grasshopper."

Munching and sipping, the forty-page résumé of the
man's life was skimmed with professional speed and di-
gested much faster than the tavern sandwiches.

"Clean," said Harry in disgust, tossing the folder aside.
"My God, is the man wholesome!"

"Pays his taxes on time. Crosses at the green, not in between. Is kind to old dogs and children. Gives to charity

and has personally killed over fifty-nine members of the Free Police."

"A noble pillar of salt of the community," noted Mike, twitching his nose.

Skimming pages, Jhonny reluctantly agreed. Prince Yertzoff was totally unnewsworthy. This is the sort of person the team rarely meets. Thank goodness, or else they'd soon be out of a job.

"Except for Inga," countered Rikka, rereading the Personal Disaster Index page again.

The rest of the team considered the possibility. Pilot Inga Swenson was an asteroid miner who had once helped the prince when his yacht was severely damaged from a fracas with the Free Police. Apparently it was love at first sight for the two and after a whirlwind courtship, the happy couple were soon planning on becoming married.

However, the royal family and Parliament strongly disapproved. She was a lowly commoner, a miner! And that was about as low as a commoner could get without being a registered Democrat. So they flatly refused to authorize the union, or recognize the marriage if performed, threatened to disinherit the prince, and even, if necessary, were prepared to go to the unheard-of extreme of canceling his membership at the country club.

After several nasty incidents involving shouting matches in the House of Lords, the prince finally decided to abdicate his throne in favor of his lady love. And that was when tragedy struck. Inga was accused of killing a man in a bar fight and was found guilty of excessive force without due cause, i.e. murder. The prince spent years and millions trying to overturn the conviction, get a mistrial declared, anything. But it was for naught. Inga went to SnowBall Hell for life and the prince remained a bachelor for the next ten years.

"Think he's going to try and break her out?"

Weighing options, Rikka gave serious consideration to the outlandish notion. "Nyah!" she announced at last. "Swenson has been in jail for fifteen years. He only started this tunnel five years ago. There's no correlation.

Besides, Swenson will be in for the rest of her life. Why the sudden rush now?"

Nobody had an answer for that.

"And it doesn't make sense," stormed the anchor, getting up to pace about the alcove. "To all indications, he was ready to get engaged. So, he either received unexpected information, or was tricked and actually kidnapped."

"Explain the watch."

"Okay, info he had stopped hoping to receive."

"What information?"

"Unknown."

"Has there been any recent event that might impinge upon his life? Is his father ill? Is Inga up for parole? Sentenced to death? Have the revolutionaries on Mars learned how to tie their shoes? Anything big like that?"

"Nope," said Jhonny, speed-reading the reports flashing on his secretary. "Nada. Zero. Zip and uh-uh."

"Damn!" cried Rikka, slamming a fist on the table.

The outside patrons in the bar looked up from their drinks to glance about. Now where had that come from? The moose in the bathroom? Bruno? In a crash of guitars, sitars, and drums, a transparent group of four young men in desperate need of a good haircut began to wail how they also desperately need assistance. Ah, it was only the CD player.

"Okay," she relented wearily, massaging some blood and feeling back into her hand. Wow, what a hard table. "If we can't figure out why, then we have to do it backward."

Removing the tablecloth bib from about his neck, Mike grimaced. "So we track him?"

"At least we have a good starting point," said Harry doggedly. "Remember, nobody is supposed to know about the interceptor. That's our key. We know he went willingly and from New Old Southwest Mars in a police interceptor. If we can't find the man with that much info, then let's just quit and go do the weather."

The whole team shuddered. No, no, anything but that! They'd rather get real jobs and work for a living.

"A Martian interceptor is too unusual a vehicle to go anywhere unnoticed," the android reflected aloud. "Outside of the vicinity of its home planet the thing would cause riots."

"A fearsome appearance?" asked Mike quizzically.

"Gold trimming and tassels."

Collins waggled a finger. "Plus, we have to remember this guy is smart, has virtually unlimited funds, and had a good ten years to plan this escape."

"Stop thinking small," rationalized Jhonny. Yes, that made sense. "So he'd take off in the interceptor and then dispose of the vehicle. A fully armed interceptor is only worth about forty-five thousand dollars."

The $12.95 camcorder fainted.

Harry made the catch as it tumbled toward the table and returned the limp machine to Jhonny.

"Maybe Vlad had a shuttle waiting in orbit about the planet . . ." The anchor bit a lip. "No good. This was a sudden change in plans, any craft in orbit about Mars for very long would be spotted by their scanners."

"Maybe it was hidden on one of the moons," suggested Mike, chewing on the rind. "Buried in a dust crater, perhaps. We did that once."

"Twice," corrected Rikka. "But only for a day. Rescue squads routinely sweep the dust pits and craters searching for idiots who get lost and tumble in."

"We could call every police headquarters and ask if anybody has found an abandoned Martian police interceptor." What the hell, the charges wouldn't be on his phone bill.

"And don't you think Yertzoff is smart enough to hide the ship?" scoffed Harry, using a knife to spread mustard on his second sandwich. "And it would eventually be found."

"Unless it was destroyed!" finished Jhonny for him. "Yes!"

Reaching into her jacket, Rikka whipped out a cellular

phone from her shoulder holster. Pressing a red button on
the side of the black case, the telecommunications device
began unfolding like a blossom to the sun. Soon a jar of
mustard was forced off the table and the phone was a full-
size video monitor.

Closing her eyes and muttering to herself, Collins calculated the code for today and then started eagerly punching
numbers into the keypad. There sounded a click, a hum,
and the monitor was filled with a four-hundred-year-old,
flat, black and white, silent movie. A fat man and skinny
man, both wearing silly little hats, stared up a long flight
of stairs and at the huge piano next to them.

"Office," said a mechanical voice.

"Mr. Nobody? Newshawk here," said Rikka, a napkin
muffling her voice.

Shoulders to the piano, the two began to push and pull,
rolling the piano directly over the fat man's foot. "Hello,
my friend! And what can I sell you today?"

"The best tip you have," said the reporter.

In pain, they released their grip on the musical furniture
and it rolled over the body of the thin man, making him
much more so. "Interesting. Nothing specific?"

"Nope."

"Working . . . I have a hot scoop on the prince of Mars."
Sandwiches dropped onto plates.

Feeling ill, Collins took a wild stab in the dark. "He's
been kidnapped?"

Utilizing rope, once more the determined pair began to
move the piano up the steep flight. "Oh, you heard."

Expressions of relief filled the table. "Yes. That's old
news. Anything else?"

Halfway up, the rope broke with disastrous results.
"Nope. Really. Nothing of importance, anyway."

"Try me," said the reporter evasively.

Continuing into the road, the piano went hurtling down
a sharp hill into traffic. "For this sort of request, I charge
a thousand dollars. In advance."

Collins ran her credit card through a slot on the phone

and the colored bar code changed from indigo to violet. "Done."

"Somebody is planning to rob the First Bank of Mars."

"Where they store the Youth Drug?"

"Yes. Exactly." Smashing cars and trucks, the runaway musical instrument proceeded to plow into a crowd of people whose mouths each formed a perfect O.

Not sure he remembered correctly, Mike accessed his file on the wonder compound. The Youth Drug was an offshoot of WOW! Not really an age reducer, the compound merely accelerated the healing process a hundredfold without undue strain on the body. A single dose could give a ninety-year-old the physique and abilities of a teenager. There was no set price for the amazing elixir. A regular monthly allotment was auctioned off to the highest bidder, with nobody allowed to purchase twice in a row. It was a tactic that kept the bidding fresh, prices high, and the royalty of Mars rich-rich-rich.

Criminals were constantly trying to rob the armored fortress of the First Bank of Mars where the biological compound was made and stored. And surrounding the citadel were six large graveyards filled with fools who had tried, and failed.

Unfortunately it had no known effect on Gremlins.

"Another raid on the Youth Bank? No thanks," laughed the woman. "I don't do obituaries."

Hats and shoes were still flying over the demolished crowd as the fat and skinny men charged onto the scene. "Unfortunately, there's nothing else. Been a slow day."

Maybe for him. "Ah well. Next time."

"Good-bye." And the screen went dark, thankfully ending just as the piano explosively crashed through a mirror warehouse and careened directly toward a gasoline truck parked in front of a dynamite factory. The fat man and skinny man went "Oh" and lost their hats as they pivoted in midstep and began to run.

Mike frowned. Drat! Just when it was getting interesting. He would have to get that flick from the library archives.

"So much for the usual," snorted Collins, rapidly dialing again. "Now let's try the un."

This time, the screen swirled into a thousand colors and then cleared into a view of a beautiful woman in a prim jumpsuit. Pinned to her crisp lapel were the tiny silver letters QINS.

"Hello and welcome to the QINS public news service. Specializing in Mars and Earth."

"New, NEWS, *NEWS!!*" sang a genderless chorus.

A perfectly toothy smile. "How may I help you?" asked the woman as if she said this a thousand times a day. Which she probably did, the poor soul.

Shoot the chorus was what Rikka wanted to say, but withheld her perfectly toothy opinion.

"Hi," grinned Collins. "My name is Shannon Elston, and my shuttle was hit by shrapnel, or something, while in a high Mars orbit and my insurance company wants me to check and see if there was any reported explosions, collisions, that sort of stuff in the upper atmosphere of Mars within the past thirty-seven hours?"

"One moment, I'll check."

"Gee, thanks."

Minutes passed.

"Thirty-seven hours?" mouthed Harry silently.

Rikka hit the mute button. "Misdirection, just in case."

Ah. What a woman!

"I have the information you requested," answered the receptionist, returning. "Yes. There was a reported meteor collision in Sector 19, Quadrant 134, Zone 2, near Phobos City, roughly three hours ago. That'll be six credits."

Collins did the ritual.

"Thank you and thanks for calling QINS, Public News Service."

Quickly the QSNT reporter terminated the connection before the chorus could do an encore.

As the screen went dark, Jhonny and Harry did a high-five slap, and Mike used his claws to vigorously scratch Rikka's shoulder blades. The woman herself began to purr.

Mmm, this alone would have been enough of a reason to keep the big *aaraa* around.

"Okay, Prince Yertzoff blew the interceptor and disguised the fact as a meteor strike. A little lower and to the left," instructed Collins dreamily.

Mike complied, being careful not to slice the cloth off her back.

"You know, I'm starting to get a feel for this job," said Snyder, lighting a cigar now that the meal was finished. "We can't track this guy by clues. There aren't any. But it is possible to follow him by the trail of mysterious events."

"Only we have to decide where to look first," grumbled Jhonny sullenly. First the answer, then the question. Swell. Suddenly the android had flashbacks to high school algebra classes. Only this time the answer was not written on a paper in his shoe.

As Michelangelo finally stopped, Rikka blessed him with a smile. Then she frowned as the reality of work crashed around her again like a blimp at a BB gun convention. Yes, this was going to be a toughie. One wrong guess and they'd lose the prince forever. Briefly the reporter wondered how much a meteorologist made?

His pocket fax whining away, Jhonny laid a map of Phobos on the table. Bottles and plates helped hold the damp paper flat.

"There's a public service tunnel near the impact zone," he said, pointing with a breadstick. "See? It leads direct to the city."

"Any security checks where you'd have to show ID?" asked Mike, craning his neck over the huddle of his teammates.

"Nope. This one particular train goes nowhere near any of the military installations."

Another negative, glowed Rikka happily. Better and better. "The prince probably had the shuttle, singleship, whatever registered under a fake ID and legally stored at the space port."

"Makes sense," puffed Harry, politely directing the

stream of blue smoke away from his cohorts. "And gives us another lead. He'd have to file last-minute flight plans."

"Working," said Jhonny, typing one-handed on his secretary. As a precaution, he had already linked it to the Phobos City Library computer. "Ah, here we go. A Mr. Smith filed for flight plan at 5:30 to go to Quebec, Canada, North America, Earth."

"Which means that is the one place he is not going," stated Snyder, genuinely enthusiastic. This was going to make great copy!

The android nodded. "Only a fool would do that. Agreed."

"Supplies," said Rikka, stretching to scratch her own back. Darn, it just wasn't the same. "If the ship was in storage, what did it have as onboard supplies?"

Fingers dancing, Jhonny retrieved that file. "Hmm, emergency rations and reserve air only."

"How much did he buy?" inquired Mike.

"Nothing."

Releasing her back, Collins put hands akimbo. "Nothing? Not a damn thing?" Wow. Yertzoff had really been in a big hurry. What a lucky break. That killed the idea of him just floating about in the middle of space for a while.

"Estimated flight time?" asked Harry, expertly tapping ashes into an empty beer bottle.

"One moment," said the alien, already working his IBM portable. His nimble talons clicked across the keys sounding like castanets on marble. "Figuring maximum emergency supplies and maximum velocity and adding a twenty-five percent fudge factor to the calculation, the extreme limit of traveling to arrive in a condition able to land without assistance is . . . 8 million kilometers."

"Map," spoke Collins to her wrist and a hologram of the solar system appeared above their table.

I LIVE TO SERVE, SAHIB.

Tongue dangling from his snout, the technician took a stylus and drew a glowing ring around the purple planet. "That's his operational range. The shuttle could coast forever, but that's sure death without calling for help."

"Which would blow the whole show," nodded Harry in agreement.

"Is anything in there?" asked Jhonny, scrutinizing the apparently empty volume of space. Awake again, the camcorder perched on his shoulder, exactly copying the posturing of its beloved master.

Adjusting the relay signal on her secretary, Collins magnified that area tenfold, then twenty. There was a lot of empty in that space. Maybe he did rendezvous with a waiting ship. "Deitrich, was there any answering pulse on the same frequency as the incoming message of the watch?"

OF COURSE NOT, scrolled the MainBrain in a miffed font. IF THERE HAD BEEN I WOULD HAVE TRACED IT AND ALL OF THIS BRAINSTORMING WOULD HAVE BEEN TOTALLY UNNECESSARY.

"And what about the word 'Thunderfish'?" asked Mike, shining a pocket flash about the solar system as he tried to throw some light on the subject.

NOTHING. IT'S EITHER PRIVATE SLANG OR A MILITARY SECRET.

Neither of which they could ever divine. Phooey.

"Hey, look!" cried the android. "Koop!"

"Gesundheit," replied the alien in his ritual joke.

Straining her vision, Rikka could just barely see a minuscule space station at the extreme edge of the circle. Koop Memorial Space Hospital. She hadn't spotted it immediately because of a badly located dill pickle.

"Can we access the status report from the hospital?" asked the investigative reporter, thoughtfully toying with an earring. "He might switch vehicles again."

Jhonny nodded, his fingers typing as if with a will of their own. "Maintenance and traffic control sure. But nothing involving medical reports. We'd have to go there personally."

Everybody grimaced. No kidding. Their last trip to Koop had been an unmitigated disaster.

GREAT, scrolled Deitrich eagerly. LET'S GO!

Okay, their cyborg pilot had gotten laid. But everything else went poorly.

"Bingo!" exclaimed the camera-op. "A shuttle arrived from Mars at 6:07 needing a refuel and supplies." Blink. "A lot of supplies."

"When did it take off again?"

A frown. "It didn't. The ship is still there."

Standing, Harry grabbed his hat. "Let's go!" said the anchor, moving for the wall.

"Hold it!" snapped Rikka.

The anchor froze motionless. What? Was his pet spider loose again? Fearfully, he lifted a shoe and looked at the sole. Clean. Whew. Hairy Jr. was still alive then.

Adamantly, Collins shook her head. "We can't trust the obvious. Not with Prince Yertzoff. The man is good. Real good."

"After ten years of planning he damn well should be," stated Michelangelo flatly.

Puffing steadily, Snyder returned to his chair. Hmm, excellent point. He would not allow himself to underestimate the prince again. Think of all that he had learned in that period! Reclaiming his seat, Harry heard a tiny squeal and felt something go squash. In remorse, the anchor slumped. Oh, prack. Obviously, he hadn't learned quite enough. Good-bye, Junior.

Pushing her half-eaten sandwich into the asteroid belt, Rikka placed elbows on the Earth. "Jhonny, access the total medical supply list for the hospital at approximately . . . oh, thirty minutes before the arrival of the shuttle."

Puzzled, the manchine did as requested. Soon an incredibly long list of chemicals, linen, ointments, tools, food, and ordnance began scrolling on the monitor.

Her eyes unfocused in rumination, Rikka stared blankly at the catalog of healing materials. Nobody said a word, they had all seen the woman in this fugue state before. Like a monorail express at rush hour, she was operating at hyperspeed and any distraction could derail her train of thought. With results just as terrible.

As the inventory ended, Collins snapped back to reality. "Now get me the list of supplies . . . hmm, an hour? Yes, an hour after the shuttle arrived."

The process was repeated with the similar results.

"Do a correlation between the two," murmured Rikka, her face scrunched in concentration. "Delete anything that stays the same on both lists."

"B-but that should be everything!" protested Jhonny.

"Maybe." Collins had no precise idea what she was looking for. She was just fishing, operating on a hunch that something was amiss here, an instinctive skill honed laser-true by fifteen years of busting mysteries from one end of this system to the other.

On scrolled the list until the monitor went ping!

"Hey, here's an item," announced the android, sounding surprised. He was. "Their stock of New Flesh actually increased during that time period! Over fifty kilograms! And no regular deliveries were made."

"Which means Yertzoff had some onboard and gave the rest to the hospital after he was done," postulated Harry, dropping something wrapped in tissues into the trash can. Flash!

"But why would he?" Collins rhetorically asked the sun. "Was he expecting to have to fight his way off Mars? Or has he already been in a battle?" New Flesh, another fine product from Wilkes Medical Corporation—patent number 65789423680—was the laboratory-grown equivalent of human muscle and skin used to repair massive physiological damage. The miracle material could fix anything short of decapitation and the lab crews were diligently working on that. Only it was so hard for them to find volunteers for the tests.

"No reports of any repairs done to the shuttle," announced Jhonny, answering the next question before it was asked.

Damn!

"Does that material have any other function aside from bodily repairs?" asked Mike hesitantly, raking a taloned paw across his furry face. There issued the sound of sandpaper being massaged with a file.

YES! scrolled Deitrich. PLASTIC SURGERY!

Impressed, Harry ground out the stub of his cigar. "So, he altered his features, eh? Smart move."

"Why, with that much New Flesh left over he could have changed everything!" chuckled Jhonny. "Skin color, height, weight . . ." The android's voice started to trail off. "Facial features, fingerprints, footprints, apparent age, hair length, even bodily sex characteristics . . ."

Silence engulfed the mini-room as the stunning implications of their discovery were finally comprehended.

"Meaning that he can now look like anybody," moaned Collins, lying atop her crossed arms. "Absolutely anybody in existence." Incredibly, after all their hard work, Yertzoff had finally succeeded in curtailing the news team and making good his escape. They'd lost him for good.

The prince was gone.

CHAPTER THIRTEEN

"AND WE STILL don't even know what he's doing!" cried Jhonny, brandishing his fists at the uncaring ceiling as Pluto went in one ear and out the other.

Tenderly Harry rubbed his perfectly classic nose. "We haven't lost the prince yet," denied the anchor. "With that kind of major surgery, you can't fly. The anesthesia takes hours to wear off and the automatic pilot bio-scanner in a shuttle won't allow you to launch. It's the same as if you were drunk."

"And how do you know that?" asked Collins suspiciously.

Heroically Snyder tried not to touch his nose again. "Read it in a book."

"Yeah. Right."

Michelangelo thumped his chest. "And trying to disconnect the bio-scanner is as close to impossible as I know."

AGREED, BIG GUY.

"Even I cannot do it!" announced Jhonny, as if this proclamation settled the discussion.

Actually, it did.

"Fine," smiled Rikka, her hopes renewed. "Then he's still there, or had to take a common transport."

Mike was already doing furious calculations. "The average time for a full body operation is an hour. Figure the prince arranged a bribe for a private doctor and immediate service, so cut that in half ... rrr ... look for any ships leaving from 6:45 till 7:15."

"Checking," murmured Jhonny, typing different mes-

149

sages with each hand. The camcorder on his shoulder was spinning its lens like a pinwheel trying to keep up with its multitalented master.

"Yep," the android announced at last. "A shuttle departed from Koop within the half hour."

"Passengers?" asked Snyder, skimming his hat toward the wall where it hit and bounced off. More practice.

"Thirty people," read the crouching android. "A standard rotating staff, leaving for a weekend on Luna."

Just a few million kilometers below. Practically in their lap!

"Got any names?"

Code words and counter-phrases flashed and blinked on the computer screen. "No, damn it, there seems to be . . ." A grin. "Something wrong with the file!"

Smiles abounded. Excellent! Despite his enormous intelligence and resources, the prince was still an amateur battling pros and they could track the runaway by his telltale trail of blank files and inoperative scanners. It was slapdash and crude, a gossamer thread likely to break at any moment, but it did inform them they were on the correct line.

Hopefully.

"Are we good, or what?" beamed Snyder, puffing out his chest.

"Any picture of the passengers?" inquired Rikka.

"Nope!" gaily cried the android.

Yes! "The moon is a good start, but it's still a pretty damn big place. Hmm, we have to think like service workers. Thirty bachelor men leaving after a two-week stint of sixteen hours a day of work go to the moon. Where would be the logical place for them to go?"

"The spaceport bar?" offered Mike tentatively.

Rikka and Harry shook their heads no. The alien really had been without female companionship for far too long.

"More likely it's The Pleasure Palace," said Jhonny confidently. "The best little whorehouse in Tycho."

"Ah, Stillisvetsky crater, actually," corrected Mike, peering at the tiny city on the table map.

"That was a joke," grumped the camera-op.

"Oh, sorry." And the alien boomed a laugh. "Happy now?"

"Aw, go shave yourself, fuzzball."

"Try recharging your brain, Tobor."

"Say," gushed Harry proudly, "you guys are getting good at this!"

They turned on the anchor. "Shaddup!"

Meanwhile, Rikka finished dialing 1-800-SEX-NOWW and clicked past the standard warning that this number was only for sentient beings over the Earth age of eighteen years, but strictly forbidden to attorneys, judges, and lawyers. Prosecutors would be violated.

As the large screen of her telephone cleared, it displayed a lush foyer completely lined with crushed red velvet, floors, walls, and ceiling. The dozens of plush chairs in evidence were so overstuffed that a sitting client would have their legs sticking almost straight up into the air. Obviously the furniture was of a purely functional design.

A winding marble staircase spiraled upward on the left side of the room with a brass fire pole on the right and a circus trampoline in the middle for exceptionally impatient customers. Erotic paintings of explicit detail adorned every wall and a granite leg columned each corner of the room. That was all that could be seen of the two colossal statues of the ultimate male and female locked in a loving embrace that supported the geodesic dome roof and threatened to bring down the house.

For nostalgia's sake a lamp with a bright red light sat prominently in the window. Off to the side was a tiered concession stand with a sign announcing a half-price sale on S&M Candies, the milk chocolate that melts on your face, not in your hands.

And filling the room were women. Statuesque women. Voluptuous women. Exotic, fantasy women, in every imaginable state of lacy undress. Victoria had no secrets here. Casually posed for the incoming phone caller to see, the scantily clad lovelies lounged provocatively, laughing and chatting while occasionally checking the seam on a black fishnet stocking or bending over for nothing more than esthetic reasons.

And walking toward the video phone with the grace of a rogue barbarian came a six-foot blonde in a white lace, gownless evening strap that exalted her ample feminine figure to Homeric proportions. Shining like new sin, her crimson nail polish perfectly matched her high heel shoes, lip gloss, earrings, and disposition.

Smiling broadly as if she had invented the act, Madam Adam spread her arms wide in greeting. A tiny blond mustache trailed about her full cupid lips to form a golden goatee under a petite chin.

"Rikka, darling! John! Michelangelo!" cried the delighted hermaphrodite. "Hello, my friends, welcome and orgasms!"

In slightly less graphic terms, the news team gave salutations to their kinky neighbor in space.

"And a very special hello to you, Harrykins," purred the man/woman lustfully.

Sorry he had eaten so much food with the whiskey, the anchor somehow was able to civilly smile at the lunar prostitute. Oh, lord, why him? Why did she have to be so infatuated with him?

"It's been a . . ." A pink tongue played peekaboo. "*Long* time since you last . . ." Giggle. "*Came* for a visit," panted the courtesan supreme, a motion that sent delicious ripples down along his/her amazing display of soft cleavage.

Twisting his head, Snyder looked at Rikka with the letters "he" in one eye and "lp" in the other.

"Sorry, Adam, no time for pleasantries," said Collins in mock urgency. Actually, the situation was urgent. "We have work to do."

"Hot story . . . ah, babe," Harry managed without choking. "News comes first."

"Before pleasure? Not here, Harrykins," purred the blonde, rubbing a hand between thighs. Then he/she pulled a pack of cigarettes into view and lit one. "But *c'est la via.*"

The anchor nodded. "Yeah. Sure. Later."

Completely out of their element, Jhonny and Mike remained totally silent. Although, in retrospect, the scene did remind the alien of the Gremlin female who drove him crazy enough to go into space as a frozen astronaut onboard a sublight sleeper ship. She also had been a bisexual. Ever time he wanted sex, she said "Bye!"

"So what is the problem?" the madam puffed, extending a silken leg toe first. "One of my guests wanted for murder?"

"Nothing like that," stated Rikka. "We only need to know if a shuttle from Koop Memorial landed there within the hour?"

"Why yes, of course, our usual Friday night group. We like interns and nurses, they're so clean!

"In body, anyway," he/she added for clarification and then giggled, spoiling the whole serious effect.

"Are they all still there?" ventured Harry politely.

Lush lips blew him a kiss. "Actually no. One said he wanted to store his suitcase in a locker down the block, but he never came back." A shrug made a dress strap slide off a shapely shoulder and the top of his/her dress lowered to socially dangerous levels.

"Boyish nerves," joked the Herm, adjusting the strap. "Nothing unusual. Happens every day here."

I'LL BET IT DOES, scrolled Deitrich on the wrist secretaries of the news team only. HARRY, WHAT A NICE PERSON. I THINK I'LL SEND THE PALACE A BOUQUET OF ROSES IN YOUR NAME.

"Don't you dare!" bellowed Snyder at his wrist.

"What? Don't dare do what?" asked Adam, confused.

The anchor waved curtly. "Never mind!" Damn bigmouthed Brain.

In the background a platoon of Space Marines arrived and a party commenced, with immediate trampoline action.

"But he was very nice," Madam Adam went on, unperturbed. "He even paid in advance for the group discount with the rest."

Jhonny and Mike tried not to gape. A group discount? Did they also have double coupon days and rebates?

"What did he pay in?" asked Collins, leaning into the screen.

"Sanddollars." An eyebrow arched. "Okay, why are you dancing? Was that good news?"

Giddy with victory, the human reporters were arm in arm whirling about the tiny room. Whee! Found him again!

The blonde impatiently tapped a pretty foot. "Who are we talking about?" he/she demanded.

"Top secret," said Jhonny, finally joining the conversation. "Hush-hush. Burn before reading, that sort of thing."

Cavalierly Madam Adam accepted the rebuff. Keeping secrets was a major part of both their jobs.

"Thanks for the help. Call you later."

"You better," pouted the beauty. "I'll keep it warm for you." A gay laugh. "Bye all!"

The screen went dark.

Snatching the bottle of Scotch off the table, Harry up-ended the container and did something he hadn't done since his last phone call to The Pleasure Palace. Hacking and coughing, he returned the empty to the table. It would have to be the story of the millennium for him to go there in person. And an exclusive too.

HEY, MIKE, EVER THINK ABOUT VISITING THE PALACE? asked Deitrich mischievously. YOU'RE NOT A LAWYER SO IT SHOULD BE OKAY. MIGHT EVEN GET A DISCOUNT FOR BEING THEIR FIRST ALIEN.

"Oh, I couldn't do that," said Michelangelo resolutely. "And not for any religious or physiological reasons. It's just that human females are . . . I mean they're so . . ."

"Tiny," asked Rikka, hiding a smile. What a pleasant compliment.

"Ugly!" cried the leviathan alien. "Ye gods above and below! You have no hair worth mentioning! And the size difference. Human women resemble malnourished children with the mange!"

Rikka turned to stare at the alien with eyes of flame.

"But very pretty malnourished children," the tech hastily amended.

Quickly Harry spoke to save his friend. "What's in the area?" asked Snyder, scanning the map frantically. They were so close. Minutes might count. For both Yertzoff and Mike.

"Could the prince have taken a cab?" asked Mike. Then he frowned. And leave a clear trail? No. Not this human.

"Look!" shouted Jhonny, stabbing a finger onto the lunar surface. "Just down the block. There's a used space shuttle dealer!"

"Perfect!" said Mike, eager to cover his blunder with a mountain of anything else.

Flipping through the directory software, Rikka found the number of the dealer and they were connected.

"Yellow!" called a smiling plump man in a cowboy hat and Western string bow tie. "Honest Hobart's Used Shuttle Emporium. This is the 1,345th day of our going-out-of-business sale so prices have been slashed-slashed-slashed again! How can I he'p ya?"

Oh, give it a break. "Harry Snyder, QSNT," said the anchor, showing his station ID to the telephone. "There's a week's free interplanetary advertising for you if we can be assisted with a few simple answers."

Removing his ten-gallon hat, the space cowboy chewed his tongue and scratched head and belly as a vintage country aid to the thought process.

"Fair enough," the dealer decided with a grin. "Always happy to he'p the press. Ask away, pardner!"

"Did a man dressed as a technician from Koop just purchase a shuttle from you?"

"Sure did. Oldest junker I had. Been on the lot for years." Handshakes under the table. Hurrah!

"How old?" probed Harry. "Did it have a working bio-scanner?"

A head scratch. "Well, it had a bio-scanner, that's the law. But as to the working part, that's a matter of opinion."

So the prince could now pilot solo, eh? "Any chance the buyer used a name?"

"Course. Bob Smith."

Yes!

"What did the guy pay in?"

"Bucks."

The celebration stopped cold.

"Earth bucks?" asked Rikka, coming on screen.

A cheery wave. "Hey, Ms. Collins! Yeah, it was Earth money. Say, what is this about? The money wasn't counterfeit, is it?"

"Not to the best of our knowledge," said Harry, and the dealer relaxed with a sigh.

Rikka furrowed her brow. "Where could he have obtained the bucks from?"

"Bingo!" said Jhonny.

"Nyah, that takes too long."

Goodnaturedly, the android smacked the woman on the arm. "No, you goof. There's a money exchange store between The Pleasure Palace and the dealership."

Faces brightened. Ah, they were still on a roll!

"Did he register a flight plan?" asked Harry, feeling confident.

Tilting his hat, the man scoffed. "This ain't Earth, ya know, buddy, with stupid things like gun permits. People here fly wherever the hell they want."

Oh, well, it had been worth a try.

"What type of shuttle was it?" asked Mike from above.

Rikka relayed the question. Most folk didn't know that shuttles were only identical externally. The inside had a dozen configurations: cargo, passengers, mining, laboratory, military version, and so on.

"Standard passenger," replied the friendly Texan. "Used to be a school bus."

"Only driven on Sunday," added Snyder out of habit.

"Now how'd you know that?"

Mike leaned forward into the telephone. "What did he name the craft?"

Peering about in his screen for the source of the question, the dealer shook himself and lifted a slip from the mess of papers on his desk. "Umm . . . the *Sanders*."

"The what?" Ah, another clue! That odd a name surely meant something important!

Glumly Jhonny pointed at the map.

"Hobart, is there a fast-food restaurant across the road from you?" asked Snyder despondently.

"Why, sure. The Colonel's. Nice place. I eat there all the time."

The human, alien, and android exchanged sighs. So much for the name meaning anything. Yertzoff didn't miss a pracking trick.

Feeling as if she were moving in slow motion, Rikka calmly asked why the title was still on the dealer's desk?

A short laugh. "Shoot, lady, and how fast do you think I register these things?"

The words were plain and simple, but they hit the reporters like the rain of sledgehammers.

"You mean he's still there?!" they chorused.

A sudden wash of light filled the window behind the dealer and a soft rumble of thunder came over the telephone.

"Not anymore," smirked the man, fanning himself with a thick sheath of Earthly green.

CHAPTER FOURTEEN

ON EARTH, THE matter of the absconded prince was discussed in detail by the duly elected officials of the United Nations. But since the missing man was not a duly elected official, they decided to hell with him and went fishing for the afternoon.

Somewhere in deep space, unseen and undetected, the legendary military stealth vessel, The Ship, made discreet inquiries into the whereabouts of the kidnapped royalty. But the answers were as vague and unsubstantiated as the ghostly Ship itself.

Puzzling. Most puzzling.

On the moon of Jupiter officially known as Ganymede, but colloquially known to the rest of the solar system as the Boom-Moon, Administrator Charles "Crash" Conway watched yet another news report on his missing friend the prince. But the rocket scientist mentally sent his best wishes to Rikka Collins. His lady may have finally gotten herself into a situation where even her vaunted skills might not save the reporter or her crew.

Damn the woman! She was as crazy for danger as he was!

But then, that's why they were such a perfect pair.

Good luck, my love. And always remember to duck.

Three deafening reports volleyed from the MAGNUM OR BETTER stall of the underground target range, each closely followed by a violent concussion as the entire middle section of a distant sandbag wall exploded, imploded, vaporized, shattered, or dissolved.

Located in the sub-sub-basement of Not-Uncle-Bob's Castle on North Mars, the target range was available to anyone with the proper clearance, and was designed with the professional shootist in mind. The storage room, which doubled as the arsenal, possessed virtually every weapon known to modern human and Gremlin science. The firing stalls, which resembled a series of open-ended phone booths, were lined with acoustical baffles that retarded echoing. The target control room offered a wide variety of targets: from stationery paper bull's-eye at graduated distances, human silhouettes that danced laterally across your field of vision, to 3-D laser holograms that sprang at you from nowhere and realistically screamed-bled-died when hit. This was a gruesome, but necessary device used to help the Interplanetary Police harden themselves to the unpleasant sight of death, a harsh reality in their job.

Twice more the massive weapon fired, and at last there came a rewarding clang as a flange was blown off the old heat engine block downrange. With a frustrated sigh, Sgt. Brad Montgomery tore the sound suppressors off his head, laid the steaming Gibraltar Assault Pistol on an insulated shelf.

"Damn," he cursed, pushing aside the Plexiglas door to the firing stall. "This is no good, Thompson. I simply cannot control this new monster of yours."

Harried from endlessly working on the kidnapping, the Army Intelligence sergeant was unshaven but properly dressed in a dark green civilian jumpsuit with matching jacket, electric blue shirt, and a bright red bow tie. Fashion came before health in his book.

Uncrossing her arms, Special Agent Lulu Thompson stepped out of the target control booth and walked over. As always, the Imperial enforcer was dressed to kill: in matching knee-high boots, short jacket and skirt of blue suede, and a button-down white blouse with a solid front of frills that only served to accentuate her naturally im-

pressive bustline. An old boyfriend had once described her
as having an hourglass figure, with most of the sand yet to
fall. The man's speech pattern was a major factor in his
becoming an ex-boyfriend. Although, weapons do come in
many shapes. Her software also served nicely to hide her
bulletproof vest, antilaser shield generator, and a small ton
of lethal hardware.

Thompson gave the man a consoling pat on the shoulder. "Don't worry about it," she said with a smile. "If you
hit a man in the torso with your Bedlow laser he's dead
anyway."

Grudgingly Brad accepted that. "But still," he insisted.
"You could shoot a man in the knee with your Gibraltar
and make his ears fall off."

"If he had any remaining," Montgomery added thoughtfully.

"Graphic, but true," Lulu relented, putting her hand in a
pocket where it belonged. "My GAP has twenty-two times
the physical stopping power of your laser. But if you can't
hit anything, then that doesn't matter. Accuracy is always
more important than power. Why, even a PeaceMaker can
kill you if you are hit with enough shots."

The sergeant snorted. "A PeaceMaker stungun? Bah. A
toy for rent-a-cops and street muggers. Useless against the
Free Police."

"Who are neither," Thompson laughed. "Agreed."

His shoulder still warm from her touch, Montgomery
busied himself with deactivating the Gibraltar and thumb-
ing the safety on. Brad hefted the awesome weapon in his
hand before returning the pistol. "Heavy little brute, isn't
it?"

Amused, the Imperial agent arched a scarred eyebrow.
"I beg your pardon, sir, but my brand-new Mark I, deluxe
model, Gibraltar Assault Pistol is a handcrafted, precision
instrument and not a 'little brute.' "

Sgt. Montgomery chuckled. "Well, excuse me. I didn't
know you two were emotionally attached."

"Rumors only. We're just friends."

"Good," said the man.

Not quite sure how to respond to that, Thompson stepped into the deserted firing stall, closed the plexiglass door, and reloaded the GAP from a stack of ammo boxes, power clips, grenades, needles, and fuel tanks on the shelf. Then, assuming the regulation firing stance, she snapped off five thundering discharges, annihilating an obsolete tiger tank at thirty meters. With a screech of stretching metal, the armored military vehicle fell apart like an overcooked Thanksgiving turkey dissected by a trained surgeon in a bad mood.

Brad couldn't help smiling at that. Lulu was just about the best shot he had ever seen, in or out of the service, and he knew why too. Poor woman, it wasn't her fault that both of her parents had brown hair and brown eyes, and that their grandparents and great-grandparents had brown hair and eyes, and that all seven of her sisters and brothers were likewise colored. But Lulu had been born with black hair and hazel eyes . . . just like the milkman. At an early age, Louella "Lulu" Thompson had learned to shoot and shoot well.

Oddly, both of them came down here in the cool quiet of the gun range to blow up a few old frigates as an aid to thinking. And with this case, they needed all the help they could get. What had Vladamir done? Disintegrated into thin air?

"What sort of muzzle blast does that have?" he asked, watching her eject the spent shells, cartridge casings, exhausted fuel tanks, and drained batteries.

"Fifteen hundred foot pounds ps/ps."

"Bull."

"S'truth."

"Wow." No wonder he hadn't been able to hit that heat engine. Whew, 1,500fp per second/per second. Why, that was the equivalent of having a quick game of Catch the Meteor!

"Impressive," Brad remarked in professional admiration.

"Yar, she's a fragging beaut, tain't she?' replied Lulu, lapsing into asteroid slang.

"Not the gun," Montgomery corrected. "You."

"Oh."

Not knowing how to reply to that, Thompson laid her weapon on the nearby worktable and began to plunge out the gun with a stiff brass bristle brush, a preliminary to cleaning and oiling.

Slightly flustered from his forwardness, the sergeant turned and walked briskly past the target control booth to place his Bedlow laser in the robot gun cleaner, which swallowed it whole and began to make swishing sounds. The machine would disassemble the weapon totally, cleaning every millimeter and replacing any worn parts if need be, recharging and fine-tuning the focus infinitely faster than he could. Thompson used it too when she was in a hurry, but he knew that she preferred to clean her weapon by hand whenever allowed. Occasionally, Montgomery did the same himself.

Returning to the table, Brad drew a chair close to watch the woman at work. Her fingers moved with the assurance of intimate knowledge. "What do you think about Uncle Bob?" he asked, changing the subject ever so slightly.

"Expletive deleted," she replied, reaming out the main firing cylinder with slow sure strokes. The carbon deposits fell like black snow onto the white linoleum table.

He smiled. "Agreed, but no, I meant, what do you think about the possibility of him kidnapping the prince. Is he off-planet, hidden in the rings of Saturn, something like that. Or what?"

Thompson shrugged and reached for the cleaning solution. "Who knows? He could be disguised as one of us, having killed the agent who found him."

Thoughtfully, Brad handed her the container. "Doubtful."

"Thanks. Just an idea. A sex change . . ."

"A what?!"

The Imperial agent swabbed out the mini-bazooka barrel with carbon remover, being extremely careful not to get any of the caustic liquid on her hands. "A sex change," she repeated. "Inventory has shown over two hundred kilos of New Flesh missing from Medical."

"Interesting," mused the sergeant.

As an experiment, Lulu lifted the hem of her skirt to scratch at a thigh and was pleased to note that Montgomery's attention promptly returned to her. So that's his game, eh? And a mischievous gleam twinkled in her eyes.

With a supreme effort of will, the sergeant wrenched his mind back to their conversation.

"What is the opinion of Tars Gooden?" asked Brad, adjusting his tight collar. Damn civilian clothes.

"That the prince merely has cold feet and is hiding somewhere within the castle."

Sgt. Montgomery softly chuckled. Yeah, right. Vlad the coward. Ha!

Closing bottles and drying her hands, Lulu Thompson reached for the can of homogenized oil. That was not really necessary since modern day guns have nylon bushings to protect the moving parts from abrasive friction, but Thompson firmly believed in better safe than sorry. "The MIA thinks he's gone to join Uncle Bob. Nonsense!"

"This is not withstanding your opinion that the MIA couldn't scheme its way out of a revolving door."

Lulu concentrated on her lubricating. "As you say, irrelevant."

Brad rocked back in his chair. "The King and Queen have no fixed opinion. The House of Lords is too scared to think, Parliament never could . . . what about you?"

Thompson capped the oil can and started wiping the mammoth gun down with a silicon-treated cloth. "I think, therefore, I am."

"Thank you, Rene Descartes."

She smiled. Brains and beef, how nice. "No, but seriously I believe Prince Yertzoff wasn't kidnapped but departed of his own will."

With a flourish, Brad returned the chair to the floor. "Coercion? He was forced by blackmail or threats to somebody he loves?"

The woman nodded no. "His own free will. How else could he possibly evade our security? That castle was tight!"

"But why?"

Lulu shrugged and started to pack the cleaning kit.

Sgt. Montgomery leaned forward. "You know what I think?"

The Imperial agent matched his position. "What?"

After a furtive glance about the room, the man pulled her close to whisper his idea into her ear. On the table, their fingers accidentally met and became intertwined. In flushed excitement, the man and woman suddenly found their faces only inches apart.

Hours later, while Lulu tidied the storage room, Brad retrieved his Bedlow from the long-silent robot washer. Polished and oiled, the laser shone like new. He checked to make sure it was properly charged and slid the gun into the right side of his double shoulder holster, opposite the HK needler. Then the man wiped his hands clean on a towel to remove any possible traces of oil and smoothed out his rumpled jacket. Fine. Nothing showed.

Joining his lover by the door, the two agents stole a last kiss and left the gun range to find Tars Gooden. They had to tell him about Brad's exceptionally clever idea about finding Prince Yertzoff.

And not a damn thing else.

Nestled deep inside a millennium-old impact crater, at the very north pole of Phobos, was a single titanic dome emblazoned with the kilometer-high hologram letters: IN-TERPLANETARY NEWS SERVICE; and underneath in slightly less noticeable script: OUR STOOLIE LINE IS NOW OPEN, SNITCH ON A FRIEND AND EARN BIG BUCKS! DIAL: 1-800-RAT-FINK.

Inside the dome was a faceted hive of divisions and sections, endlessly complex. Deep within the bowels of the dome was the circular tower of offices for QINS executives, their staff, protégés, and toadies. At the pinnacle of the core was a spacious penthouse with deep pile rugs, extra-large real wood desks, a Jacuzzi built for twelve, and a control console designed to do anything the operator wished.

On a cluttered desk, a phone rang and was automatically answered. "Hello!" said a cheery artificial voice. "And welcome to the offices of Hardcopy and Sunshine, ace reporters for QINS."

"News, NEWS, *NEWS*!" sang a genderless choir.

A perfectly pink plump hand picked up the receiver. "Sunshine here," growled the woman, chewing on a stylus. "Yeah?. . . so what . . . who cares . . . up yours . . . lunch?. . . never." And the reporter hung up without saying good-bye.

"Well," asked Hardcopy, engrossed in his computer research into the history of the prince. In sneering contempt, Jason decided that this do-gooding sissy would never have survived a slow weekend on Venus. The wimp didn't even habitually carry a gun! What kind of a prince was that?

"It was a call from the chief of communications," said the dimpled blonde, thoughtfully scratching her hair with the stylus. "Apparently Rikka Collins called our Public Info Service pretending to be a customer and asking about explosions above Mars."

At the name, Jason stopped the scrolling of his monitor and swiveled his chair. "Was there one?"

"Yes. Right here on Phobos. Near the space port."

For a minute his brain swirled with infinite possibilities, connections, ramifications, and theories.

"Obviously a ruse," he stated curtly. "And how'd they know it was her anyway?" Suddenly his handsome face took on a terrible countenance.

"Somebody isn't watching SNT, are they?" Hardcopy roared, rising from his chair.

"Not and work here, they don't," smiled Sunshine, calmly scratching inside her shoe with the stylus. "Collins was still wearing her Wilkes Corporation earrings. Which is plainly nonsense. She'd never make a mistake that dumb. It's a flimsy ploy to make us waste time running around in our own backyard."

"The bitch," agreed their camera-op from across the

room, his nose safely ensconced behind the latest issue of *Vidiots* magazine. It was their special, once a year, all print issue. Written words, what a cute concept!

"Any results from your investigation into Prince Wholesome?" asked the blonde, toying with the computer pen. Going to have to get a new one soon. These things wore out so fast.

Hardcopy handed her a printed summary. "I say our best bet is to go visit Inga Swenson."

Chewing on the stylus, Susan read the condensed file and considered the notion. Hmm, makes sense. Yertzoff is kidnapped by unknown perpetrators and she is his only known criminal contact.

"Let's boogie!" agreed the woman, tucking the pen into a pocket, and they started for the door.

"Wait!" cried the camera-op, tossing aside his magazine. "Neptune was minus 700 degrees below zero!"

"So?" they asked impatiently, hand on latch.

Spinning about, the technician grabbed the thermos of coffee off the desk. Hey, every little bit helps.

An end to the annoying echo of his panting announced the culmination of his arduous journey, and with an explosive grunt Lord Hyde-White popped his head out of the gravity chute. Gratefully he drank in volumes of fresh air. Whew. What a crawl. Made his infamous stagger home from the Bear 'n Bull tavern in downtown London to his ancestral condo in Dublin seem but a holiday stroll in comparison.

Grabbing a hold of the top lip of the chute, the QBBS reporter levered himself up and swung his legs out. Releasing the metal tube he dropped to the floor of crushed gravel. Instantly he spied a crack in the wall and proceeded eagerly into the serpentine tunnel, uncaring of crooks, capture, or cave-ins. He was hot on the trail of an exclusive!

In a wash of warm air, the shuttle landed on the mountain ledge alongside a flat expanse of rock. At this close a distance, the sheer stone was clearly only a cleverly disguised hatchway. Ah, this looked promising!

Carefully Hanna O'Toole checked her WatchDog scanners. Yes, this was very close to the present location of Lord Hyde-White. His disappearance from the private office of the prince failed to expose any secret exits, so they must be very well hidden, indeed, but tracking the signal from his wrist secretary had been simple as interviewing an egomaniac. Getting a burglary kit from her general equipment locker, the solo reporter exited the QCNN shuttle and began working on the locking mechanism.

Inside the bare cavern, Lord Hyde-White heard someone scratching at the hatch, and with camera in hand, Alexander placed his back against the dry stone wall. Quickly he took a light reading and manually adjusted the focus on the pocket camera. There would be no mistake this time. Soon, he would have the story of the decade and the photographic evidence to prove it. Hello, Pulitzer!

With a hydraulic hiss, the hatch opened.

"Oh, there you are!" cried O'Toole, smiling.

The camera dropped. Good-bye, Pulitzer.

On Level 10 of Media, the QSNT shuttle disappeared, blasted out the hatchway and into space at four times the speed of light, breaking countless safety regulations and a couple of laws of physics. As the air suddenly realized there was nothing in that area, the atmosphere slapped together in a strident thunderclap implosion. Triplicate forms exploded off desks into a whirlwind of paper. A man's toupee and a woman's wig were violently exchanged. Coffee was sucked out of cups. A pair of dentures achieved escape velocity and flew off into the stars. The picture window of the flight control tower was sucked out of its frame and the unbreakable sheet proved its claim as it went skidding and tumbling along the dock bouncing off shuttles, stanchions, and ceilings.

Completely unperturbed, Lloyd Peterson continued to do some typing at his fantastically clear desk. Well, at least they wouldn't have to dust this week. It was funny, but the man was actually starting to get used to this sort of stuff.

Maybe it was time to retire.

"Out-out-out!" shrieked the archbishop of Rome, waving his arms.

Maneuvering frantically about the cathedral, the horde of news reporters ducked and weaved from pew to pew as a platoon of heavily armed clergy maintained constant fire toward the enemy heretics.

"But we only wanted to verify—"

Rat-atat-tat-tat-tat!

"Wasn't His Holiness in telephone communication with—"

Zzzzz! Zzzzz! Zzzzzzz!

"There was a rumor indicating that the church had prior knowledge of—"

A bazooka was unlimbered.

"Couldn't we simply see the records pertaining to the—"

Click-clack.

Uh-oh.

Whoosh . . . *KA-BOOM!*

As the smoke of the explosion cleared, the last pew had been annihilated and the bedraggled crowd of reporters were finally encircled, with only the door they came in as a means of escape. Reluctantly the newshounds admitted defeat and took off into the parking lot toward their waiting aircars sitting in the handicapped zone. Hey, weren't they handicapped by their editors? Leading the pack was a muscular technician carrying a fifty-kilo video camera and a box of chocolate-mint communion wafers.

"And don't come back!" bellowed the priest, shaking the jawbone of an ass at the vile interlopers.

Collapsing in his throne on the pulpit, the archbishop removed his crown of thorns and wiped his forehead with a gold filigree sleeve. Whew! Never in his entire life had any reporter, singularly or in a group, been so persistent in getting an interview. Walking in with fake documents, tunneling up through the floor, dropping down the fireplace chimney, scuba diving in a vat of sacramental wine! And not only that, but the infidels had rudely refused to believe that he knew nothing about the kidnapping of poor Vladamir Yertzoff and kept coming back with more questions. Constantly trying to trick him into admitting something said in the confessional, even after they had been bodily thrown out, attacked by the guard dogs, doused with boiling holy water, and finally besieged by the Sisters of No-Mercy Defense Squadron and Tactical Bingo Commandos.

Clearly, what the Vatican had here was a failure to excommunicate.

Meanwhile on the barricaded world of Mars, King Yertzoff and Queen "Boom-Boom" instituted a planetwide search for their kidnapped son; a frenzied manhunt the likes of which had not been seen since the spring of 2299 on Earth when Abduhl Benny Hassan had escaped from Sing-Sing and performed his unspeakable act upon the crack of the Liberty Bell in front of a horrified group of schoolchildren, none of whom had ever before seen a naked adult, or rubber novelty items of that caliber.

The previously ordered APB on the missing prince was canceled and changed to the much higher priority FHOE: find him or else! And the royal police—state, county, local, and lunar—scurried to the task. Across the planet pictures of Vladamir appeared in newspapers and on milk cartons boasting of incredible rewards. Advertisements were placed on cable and broadcast TV. AM and FM radio stations made it a contest, with concert tickets for life as the First Prize. There was no Second Prize. WatchDog scanners scoured the country from top to bottom. Spy satellites took some truly astonishing pictures with their tele-.photo lenses. Reward posters were placed prominently in post offices. Posses rode through the badlands of the New Old Southwest. Scuba divers plumbed the depths of dust lakes and water rivers, such as they were. Mountaineers scaled new heights. Window washers peeked in where they shouldn't have. Stool pigeons were grilled to perfection under the hot lamps of police interrogators. Royal Martian Mounted Police combed the terrain of the Arctic North, foothill by foothill. Foreign agents were hauled in from the cold and made to talk. Determined cops uniformly patrolled every big city street. Bloodhounds sniffed alleyways and forest trails. Boy Scouts scrambled for the ultimate merit badge. Mail carriers stubbornly tried to ferret out just who was "Occupant." The Imperial Revenue Service taxed its memory to the fullest. Magazine centerfolds bared their secrets. Door-to-door salesmen knocked on every door. Rabbis double-checked to see that everything was kosher. Cabdrivers demanded travel itineraries from their passengers. Prostitutes asked for two forms of ID. Scholars reread Nostradamus. The Baker Street Irregulars off-planet club, the Redheaded League, discussed the matter in detail. The computer systems of the nation were enabled and bit by bit their data banks exhausted. The full fury of the MIA was unleashed, along with that of the Imperial Marshal's office, Army Intelligence, Navy Security, InterPlanetPol, and the Royal Society for the Preservation of our Hierarchy. The Amazing Kreskin (who really was amazing considering the fact that by now he was over 540 years old) was consulted, along with every other available mentalist, spiritualist, medium, small, large, the new Dear Abbey, newspaper columnists, media reporters, TV interviewers, TV interview show guests, and even game show hosts. Everybody who was anybody was asked.

Details, facts, notes, theories, photographs, wire taps, and video recordings quickly poured into the offices of the Planetary Defense Citadel, and slowly, with infinite patience was amassed—The Vladamir File. The over 8 trillion pieces of information were enough to fill a swimming pool (where it was temporarily placed until proper storage facilities could be located), and composed the total sum result of irrefutable proof that nobody but God himself knew where the prince was.

So they prayed, but it didn't help.

However, the diligent searchers did find: all ten criminals on the Royal Police's Most Wanted List, fifty-five thousand missing people, thirty thousand stolen shuttles, twenty-four thousand missing pets, eighteen thousand runaway spouses (half of whom promptly ran away again), the lost tribe of Israel, the sunken city of Atlantis, a left-handed monkey wrench, a complete copy of Edison's *Frankenstein*, an honest cabdriver, a genuine snipe, a bucket of steam, and an autographed First Folio of Shakespeare. They found the commonplace, the bizarre, and the useless. They found the inane, the insane, and the mundane. They found items that nobody even knew were missing yet.

But they did not find the abductors of Prince Yertzoff. Or even a ransom note. And the King and Queen were starting to get real suspicious about that omission.

So, reluctantly the Imperial Council finally decided to accept Sgt. Montgomery and Special Agent Lulu Thompson's outrageous proposal on how to find the missing heir to the throne. Which would only produce a royal corpse if they were wrong.

God help the prince if they were wrong.

CHAPTER FIFTEEN

THE ENDLESS BLACK of space filled the bow windows of the QSNT shuttle as it coasted along at sublight speed, the ebony abyss sprinkled with a hundred thousand diamond-hard points of light. The stars. The unreachable stars. Humanity had Fatal engines, faster-than-light ships, but even the best engine burned out after fifty-four hours of travel, and at the greatest obtainable speed the closest star was six months away. So close and yet so far. These mixed feelings of helplessness, rage, and desire burned anew in the hearts of the reporters. And the QSNT team steadfastly came to realize they had lost the prince for good this time.

Boy, were they seriously honked off.

Using only the chemical engines, the shuttle traversed steadily along a crevasse of the asteroid belt. Staring out the windows, the reporters moved through the center of an avalanche of endlessly tumbling boulders and a trillion motionless mountains. They felt like a gnat flying through the slow-motion blast of a shotgun. Irregularly, a boulder would have a flashing warning buoy, a red glowing navigational beacon or an illuminated billboard, mostly advertising Nu-Clear window polish and Capt. Schol's spacesuit deodorizers. But the majority of specimens in the infinite collection of congealed plasma chunks were barren and still, except for the occasional stately collision that produced only a silent geyser of sparks and a spray of much smaller asteroids.

"Anything?" demanded Rikka, standing rigid at the bow window, binoculars pressed hard against the Armorlite glass. Indicators winked, lights blinked, and meters ticked on the consoles and surrounding control boards.

Impulsively Jhonny took a picture of his grumpy friend and mentally labeled it: One Hundred and One Damnations.

Tucked deep within the bowels of the newscraft, isolated in his warm jar of bubbling ambiotic fluids, the disembodied human brain ceased his use of the optical telescope mounted in the prow of the spaceship for a visual track of the stellar horizon.

"Not yet," said Deitrich over the ceiling speaker. "Hey, I'm an expert pilot. Maybe one of the best in the biz, but I don't think anybody has ever been asked to follow another shuttle traveling at Fatal Three without using the scanners! It isn't easy to track a ship that's going faster-than-light by sight!

"God, I'm good," added the four-pound pilot. "Although a bit dizzy."

Feeling the same, the news team didn't blame him. Their wild zigzag through space in hot pursuit of the runaway prince, going Fatal and stop, Fatal and stop, had been a joyride through hell worthy of a Spanish Inquisition. Half of their seat belts had snapped like string under the brutal jerks and the aft video lab resembled a garbage dump that had been bombed. The reporters now personally knew what a pinball felt like during a championship game in which the zealous players went in a full-tilt battle frenzy. They had experienced fun before and this wasn't it.

"The use of sensors would only tell him he's being followed," said Harry, both hands holding a different receiver to his ears. "We've only gotten this far by skill and luck. Can't take any chances."

Easing a slide back and forth, the man tried to listen to every alphabet radio channel at once. Come on, speak to somebody, Yertzoff. Since when was reticence an attribute of royalty? Usually the only way to make a member of the Martian aristocracy shut up was to glue their lips together, and then they'd merely blink at you in Morse code.

"Anything in the vicinity?" asked Michelangelo, nervously polishing his pince-nez glasses on a fuzzy forearm. "Space station? Mining camp? Bubble city? Sculpture school?"

Incredibly, near his boots was an untouched crate of apples. The compounded faster-than-light lurches across the center of the solar system had left his appetite, along with his stomach, somewhere near Mercury. He only hoped it was having a good time and didn't spend too much at the casinos.

"Nothing in the area that's useful," replied Collins, peering out the port window. She was happy to be doing something of value other than keeping her seat warm. "The warning buoys are to keep travelers away from a weapons test site for the USDA. This is a dead section of the belt. Most of these rocks are loaded with only gold, silver, and platinum."

"Worthless," noted the alien. With the advent of asteroid mining, the once rare metals had proven to be so commonplace that the materials were used these days only for making costume jewelry and disposable soup cans. However, tin, beautiful dull gray tin, especially in its denatured allotropic form, was what made FTL travel possible. And thus was worth its weight in the Martian Youth Drug. These days the alien carried a tiny coin of tin as an emergency source of fuel for the shuttle, but he wisely had coated it with 18-Karat gold so nobody would steal the trinket from him.

Suddenly Collins sat up straight in her chair, almost banging her head into the ceiling console. "Hey! There's a sign ahead with an arrow pointing off to starboard announcing five thousand klicks to oxygen and beer."

Killing a headset, Snyder grinned. So, Yertzoff did have a possible destination in this zone. "Are we anywhere near The Trap?" he asked suspiciously.

"I think so," answered Rikka, moving the binoculars from window to window. "Yep! There it is!"

"The what?" asked Michelangelo, pricking his ears.

Twirling dials, Jhonny answered, "The tarnished buckle of the asteroid belt."

After setting the engineering controls on automatic, Mike accessed the word in his IBM portable. Hmm, (A) *The Trap*, a play by Arthur Miller. No, that wasn't it. (B) A 2003 movie starring the computer-generated John Wayne and Bruce Lee, with Charles Bronson, Sylvester Stallone, Clint Eastwood, Steven Segal, and Herby the Love Bug. Interesting, but also no. (C). (D). (E). Ah, here we are! (F) The Trap, a group of four asteroids locked together in a natural tandem orbit in the formation of a trapezoid and jointly housing an array of speciality entertainment clubs catering to asteroid miners and other assorted criminals. Location: in Quadrant 3, Sector 9, of the main stream of the bad part of the asteroid belt. Warning: Nicknamed "The Trap" by Belt Police, the Interplanetary Tourist Bureau strongly recommends that their members avoid the place at any cost. And if you're not a member, then how the prack did you get a copy of this report?

Quickly the technician killed his borrowed duplicate of the expensive travel log. Those copyright protection laws were constantly getting really aggressive. And he was going to have a word with Jhonny about the legality of this gift.

"What are the names of the clubs?" asked Rikka, tucking the binoculars into a padded pouch on the bulkhead. "Any establishment called Thunderfish, Storm Whale, Lightning Dolphin, any kind of variation such as that?"

"Nope, sorry."

Drat!

"There's four listed in the brochure," read Jhonny, shifting slightly as the attitude jets changed the course of the shuttle. "The first is Wong & Wong's Sushi Dojo and Shiatsu Parlor. It's a private establishment almost exclusively for Orientals."

"The prince may be Oriental now," reminded Harry, still monitoring the airwaves. "After that body surgery he could be anybody."

"Even a Gremlin," added Mike absent-preoccupied as he altered the mix of the fuel.

Everybody turned to stare at him.

"Yes, he could be," said Deitrich. There could be a lot of interesting possibilities in this New Flesh.

Weighing options, Rikka decided against the Oriental club. The Two Wongs, no, somehow it just didn't sound right. "Let's save that for last. We'd be extremely notice-able there."

True enough. "The next is The Magic Club," went on the android.

"Sounds nice," smiled Harry, coiling the coaxial cable of his headphones. Maybe he could get a new spider!

"Nice? Not really," read Jhonny from the monitor. "A police report states they once sawed a woman in half."

"Old trick"—laughed the anchor—"a swing platform under the casket allows your assistant to bend her stomach and—"

"She wasn't anybody's assistant," said the android coldly. "The miner tried to rob the place, so they sawed her in half."

Oh. "Did they put her together again afterward?"

"No."

Well, that wasn't a very good trick.

Watching the steering wheel turn and angle without hu-man assistance, Rikka slumped into the copilot's seat and drummed her fingers on the armrest of her chair. "Next?" she barked irritably.

The camera-op paginated down. "The Excelsior. No fighting or rude language allowed. All pinkies must be raised while drinking tea. The use of any weapon, which includes a shrimp fork or steak bone, is cause for immedi-ate death."

"Whew," breathed Collins. Not even her mother was that strict at meals. "Why would anybody ever go there?"

"It's a challenge," said the anchor sagely. "Most of these folk are hard-boiled two-fisted hombres. To know that death awaits them if they even forget to say 'please' and 'thank you' properly is a thrill, an adventure!"

"And miners adore danger," observed Michelangelo. "So they must go. It is a challenge to their cheese!"

"Huh?" asked the ceiling, before the crew could.

The alien checked his IBM once more. "Oh, sorry. That's macho, with an M."

An asteroid the size of Cleveland passed the window, with Toledo and Akron close behind.

"What's the last?" Rikka inquired, trying not to smile.

"Mmm . . . ah! Uncle Bob's Royale. Rules are that everybody must act like a prince of the realm."

"Huzzah!" cried Harry, giving a thumbs-up. "Pay dirt for sure."

Although the reporter's instinct told her otherwise, Collins could think of no reason to dissuade the idea. "It does sound perfect. Vladamir won't have to alter his speech or habits to fit in fine!"

"Agreed," said the android. "It is the most likely of the four."

"Then let's be off," said the MainBrain. "Prepare for Fatal travel!"

There was a momentary blurring of the stars outside.

"We're here!" Deitrich announced.

"Took long enough," chided Rikka jovially.

The ceiling crackled. "Hey, I had to stop for gas."

Out the port window was a large clear area in the asteroid belt, either the careful and systematic cleansing away of debris by tractor beams and lasers, or else somebody had simply set off a really big chemical bomb, which was a much more likely event, knowing the attitudes of the folk who lived and worked around here. High explosives were just another way of saying hello, and even the town welcome wagon was armed. Just in case it wasn't welcome.

In the center of the clean patch were four huge asteroids, each topped with a single large dome of burnished steelloy. The outer natural rim of each asteroid was rough-hewn stone edged with a metallic honeycomb, each hexagon section a private landing dock for one medium-sized space shuttle. Neat and orderly, the arrangement helped reduce the daily firefights for the good parking spots near the telephone and soda machine.

In the distant past there were no fancy parking facilities; miners used to line the keels of their vessels with Velcro. It was cheap and efficient. But it sometimes took three or four miners to rip a ship off an asteroid, not to mention the fact that the secondary static-electrical charge could fry critical computer circuits and made everybody's hair stick out goofy.

The local space was chaotic with dozens of shuttles and singleships coming and going in the traffic zone about The Trap, so the news shuttle carefully maneuvered into a low-path approach to Uncle Bob's. But as they moved past Wong & Wong's, the bow monitor was filled with a direct view of the fourth asteroid club.

It was in ruins.

The dome was a jagged slagged ring, like the head of a snowman in summer. Inside lay blackened rock and congealed pools of molten metal. The honeycomb dock was dark and broken into enough pieces to qualify as a bad jigsaw puzzle, op art, or obtain a grant for urban renewal.

"Radiation is nil," announced Harry, studying his console. "This must have been done by concentrated laser beams and hydrogen lances."

Sadly viewing the wanton destruction, Mike made a face. During his mandatory study of human weapons technology he had encountered the operational specifications of the nasty things. Elemental hydrogen was excited into a state of fusion and then hurtled out a magnetic cannon, spiraling into a tight lance of atomic destruction. The quasi-solid rods of burning annihilation had an operational temperature of 5,000 absolute degrees Kelvin and no respect for personal property.

"There's a buoy in a geosynchronous orbit above Uncle Bob's Royale," said Mike, adjusting his meters.

"Where?" asked Jhonny, doing the same. "Oh, I see it. Hmm. It's a warning."

Rikka asked, "To whom?"

"Everybody! To wit: this club gave a glass of water to a member of the Free Police," recited the manchine. "They ain't going to do that anymore. Signed, the scum of the universe."

Recoiling, Mike looked over his glasses. Lawyers did this?

"Scum of the universe?" asked Rikka, pronouncing the words precisely. "Civic-minded citizen is more like it. Even criminals hate the Free Police."

Ah, miners did this. The alien relaxed. That made much more sense. A lawyer would have tried to talk the pirates to death. And probably could have succeeded.

"Well, this is where the pirates do most of their killing and plundering, so local feelings should be rather sensitive on the subject," acknowledged Harry. "Although I am surprised the attackers didn't try and kill the pirates intact to sell the bodies."

"Sell the bodies!" roared Michelangelo, clutching his head. Good gods above and below, that was the most hideous concept he had ever heard. And he had once been to Los Angeles!

"Sure," replied Rikka, acting surprised by the reaction. "It helps hold down recruits when a potential pirate knows that even chunks of them are worth hard cash. InterPlanetPol pays . . . how much, Jhonny?"

Turning from the window, the android laid aside his camcorder. "Ten thousand for a whole body, five thousand for a head, two thousand for an arm, one thousand for a leg." The android gave the standard three-second pause for the punchline. "But only a buck-an-ear!"

Expectantly, the news team waited, but the alien only nodded at the brutal wisdom of the ploy. It did make sense. Missing an arm or a leg would seriously slow down a pirate and the owner could be identified by finger or toe prints. While removing an ear would only be a minor annoyance.

With a sigh, the team turned their backs on the technician. This would be the last time they ever set him up for a gag. The big dummy.

"How old is the destruction?" asked Rikka, returning to work.

Studying his WatchDog scanners, Jhonny hurumphed.
"More than fifteen minutes," he stated. "This place is
cold."

"Okay, then the wandering prince ain't there. Is he?"
asked the anchor. This was news, albeit, Sunday supple-
ment filler.

"WatchDog scanner, radar, deep radar, EM scanner,
exothermic graphic, infrared, ultraviolet, motion, and proximity all say no," reported Jhonny, hands everywhere on
his console.

"Confirmed," said Deitrich. "I tried calling the place
and even the answering machine is toast. There's nothing
alive in there."

Suddenly Michelangelo shook as if with the ague. "A
buck an ear?" he boomed, throwing wide his chops in
laughter. "Buccaneer! *Wa-ha-ha-ha . . . !*"

As the alien began guffawing through his snout, Rikka
tugged on Harry's sleeve. "Is it too late to ask for a replacement?" she inquired, nodding at the roaring giant as
he fell out of his chair and started pounding the deck with
a fist.

"Sorry. The warranty expired. We're stuck with him."

"Oh, poop."

Regaining control of himself, the technician sat in his
chair and wiped his hairy face with a bedspread cleverly
disguised as a handkerchief.

"Good one," he acknowledged, dabbing at his eyes and
then trumpeting his nose.

Jhonny bowed to the compliment.

"Okay, which next?" prompted Deitrich, priming the
main engines. "Magic Club or the Excelsior?" A low rumble shook the shuttle.

"Magic Club," prompted Harry cordially. "Magicians
nice. Good people. No bother us. Plenty firewater. Ugh."

Accepting the decision, Collins leaned forward and then
back in her seat, putting her seat back forward. Besides,
it was nowhere near as dangerous as the Excelsior.
She didn't think they even had a copy of Ms. Manners
2300 AD onboard. Unless it was being used to level the

refrigerator. And there was no sense getting killed until after they found the prince and filed the story. The news game was purely a matter of priorities.

Swinging about, the shuttle arced away from the blackened ruin, a somber reminder that this section of the solar system was woefully lacking in patience and arms control. A most dangerous combination.

Under Deitrich's adroit control, the newscraft slid into the worn chamber of the landing honeycomb and cut the engines. A meter on the dashboard flicked in response, showing that a sonic curtain now sealed the mouth of the dock shut and the atmosphere was at Earth normal. And much cleaner.

Setting their consoles on hold, the team shuffled out of the bridge and into the mid-deck area. The place was a shambles, but the reporters still found the equipment they wanted and prepared for their covert intrusion into the deadly subworld of lawless, outer space taverns.

Sounded like fun, actually.

Eager to depart, the team crammed into the airlock and Jhonny got an exceptionally good look at the back of Harry's head. Hmm, dandruff. Should he tell the man? Nyah.

"I'll stay here and monitor the other ships," said the ceiling speaker in the airlock. "If the *Sanders* arrives or departs, I'll give you a toot on the Ameche."

"I beg your pardon," said the alien stiffly, addressing the speaker directly.

With a sigh, the airlock doors parted. "He'll call us on the phone," translated Rikka, showing everybody out.

Tramping along, the hexagon chamber led to another airlock that opened onto a catwalk, an endless array of perforated metal platforms and ladders that spanned the entire vertical band of the encircling landing dock. It resembled the inside of God's truss.

The QSNT logo long gone, Deitrich waited until they were gone before putting on the bow of the shuttle the new name of "A Sharp Whistle and a Bone." That's what he always used to summon his dog—Prince.

Clambering down the stairs, the team adjusted their disguises and proceeded along the main corridor into the asteroid proper. On route, the plastifoam walls were decorated with advertisements for Wilkes Corporation .444 Magnums "the Champagne of Guns" and "Trillo-Bites," the tasty snack that has waited 10 million years to go into your mouth. Geez, was there anything their boss wouldn't sell to make a buck? The next poster was a 3-D hologram ad for hemorrhoidal cream. Gagging, the team averted their gaze and scurried away fast. Nope, guess not.

It was twelve hours till their deadline for the story. Briefly the reporters wondered what sort of constraints the prince was under. Time? Chains? Honor? Love? Life?

Or maybe death.

CHAPTER SIXTEEN

REACHING THE END of the corridor and advertisements, Rikka and the team passed effortlessly through an ultrasonic disinfectant tube and then took a long escalator going up into the huge dome on the surface of the asteroid.

"This is one assignment we can't afford to fail," noted Harry, holding on to the handrail.

Careful of not getting his fur entangled in the serrated edges of the interlocking steps, Michelangelo asked why this one in particular?

"Because we're operating on nothing," replied the android, sliding a fresh blank disk into his camcorder. "No real proof or facts. Only a hunch and a notion."

"But hasn't the centuries of news reporters' hunches being constantly proven correct been enough to show that these crude telepathic impressions should be a matter of serious note?" asked the alien.

Rikka smiled at the huge mass of fur and brains. Lord, she wished he were in charge of Media. "It does to us, but not to Wilkes."

"And certainly not to Maria," added Snyder. "But blow this and more than losing the story, they'll never trust our hunches again."

Arching his back, Mike chewed this over. "So, we would pursue this story anywhere, under any circumstances, including without the express written consent of the owner of the station or either of our immediate superiors?"

"Damn straight," replied Harry, puffing out his chest.

"Is that immoral?" asked the technician, his stentorian voice dangerously low.

"Nyah," gestured Jhonny, bumping to a stop at the top of the mechanical stairs. "Just a direct violation of our contract."

Mike relaxed. Ah, merely illegal. No problem.

In a series of near disasters, involving one last valiant attempt of the stairs to eat pant cuffs and skirt hems, the escalator dumped the news team off at ground level of the asteroid.

To their left was the inside of the steelloy dome, its seamless surface coated with a thick cushion of purple antipuncture sealant, and regularly spaced all around the dome were boxes filled with expandable plastic fingers to plug any larger holes. It was an idea the original builders got off a Dutch submarine.

Ahead was an interior wall beautifully coated with layers of laser-cut stone decorated with bunnies holding top hats and pulling out men in tuxedos, hands fanning cards—all aces—and a smiling woman receiving a tax refund check from the Interplanetary Revenue Service. Now that was magic.

Setting their faces and demeanor into tough-guy mode, the reporters strode forward and threw open the doors to the Magic Club. Smoke and noise hit them like a sonic curtain. Pushing gamely through, the team found themselves in a carpeted hallway, both walls adorned with pictures of famous magicians, illusionists, and escape artists; most of whom were still wanted by the police, as evident by the rewards posted underneath their pictures.

A cloak room filled with spacesuits and opera capes was on the left. The hat-check girl was a grizzled slab of muscle with an eye patch and a robotic hand. A sign on the wall proclaimed that the management was not responsible. For anything. To the right was located an ammunition vending machine and a hospital's Emergency Room Closet-Doc. The implications were sobering.

An android waiter greeted the team and lifted a velvet rope to allow them entrance. In passing, Jhonny gave the brother a sign and the two artificial people held a fast, silent conversation.

Stepping down a small flight of stairs used primarily to make fleeing patrons trip and become better targets, the reporter was delighted to find the night club spacious and dimly lit, with a smoky haze of perfume and flash powder clouding the black ceiling. A mushroom forest of tables was mostly filled with people in rugged work clothes or spacesuits. Only a few were in fancy duds and the team felt immediately out of place.

Trying to dress for success, the QSNT team had copied the pattern of a famous historical crime team, The Wolf Pack, thankfully long dead. Harry was in a slick blue two-piece jumpsuit with a neck tie resembling a breathing carp. Jhonny was in the same, sans the tie, but with a clear plastic belt in which there swam a school of colorful tropical fish. His camcorder was disguised as a BoomBox, a remote control radio for setting off hidden explosions. It was the epitome of tough.

Rikka was sporting a flimsy white blouse that barely hid her body armor underneath and a blue skirt slit to her appendix scar. The shapely leg on display was clad in a white nylon stocking held in place by a living red garter snake. Michelangelo was clad entirely in a blue caftan, with sand and waving seaweed on the hem, foamy waves crashing on his sleeves, and a duplicate of Bruno on steroids endlessly circling his mighty torso.

That, they had decided, should scare the crap out of anybody.

Off to one side was the bar, its counter a perfect mirrored doughnut, yet glasses and mugs stayed rigidly wherever they were placed on the slick curved surface. The bartender was a skinny man with a full beard, pointed eyebrows, and a truly demonic smile.

Straight ahead was a huge stage with three magic acts going on at the same moment. But a hard-driven sonic curtain made the view fuzzy and kept the performance area totally silent. Patrons could see but not hear, unless they paid an extra charge and got a table on the other side of the curtain.

Harry approved. That was smart management.

As required by asteroid law, all of them carried assorted weapons in prominent display, but each privately wondered if they had remembered to load the things.

Sadly, there was no sign of the prince.

As they stepped on the carpet, the ceiling above them began to flash red and the room erupted in metallic clicks as everybody turned to point a gun at them.

The QSNT crew froze motionless, desperately trying to do the old "vanishing reporter" trick. Oops.

"Ah, newcomers," smiled a pretty dark-haired woman, stepping into view from the darkness. Although wearing a loose black jumpsuit and lumpy waitress apron, her trim figure was still quite discernible. "Hey, put away the hardware, troops," she said to her collar, the words echoing throughout the crowded establishment. "The scanners read clean, they ain't cops, pirates, or insurance salesmen."

More clicks sounded. But these had a gentler, far less dangerous noise to them and the assorted weaponry was holstered, stuffed up sleeves, down dress fronts, and back into fake meatball sandwiches.

"Welcome to the Magic Club," smiled the woman, displaying a winning battle against tobacco stain. "I'm Kit Matulich, the hostess and bouncer. Mess with me and you're dead meat." There was no direct threat in the words and the team had the impression she said them fifty times a day.

Tucking her bulletproof serving tray under an arm, Kit turned and pointed. "Over there at the bar is my hubby, Joe. He's the chief bartender and the special effects wizard. Mess with him and you'll wish you had messed with me instead."

Making change at the cash register, Joe waved hello and continued to polish a glass with his other two hands, which then snapped off his chest and ran away on tiny feet.

Just then, a baby girl in a plastic bubble floated by overhead. The infant was dressed in a fairy outfit and cooed in delight at Michelangelo.

"Teddy!" she cried and went to hug the leviathan arm.

"That's Alyssa, our baby girl," boasted Kit proudly, watching the embarrassed alien with amusement. "Go ahead and try to mess with her. Joe designed the bubble."

Behind the bar, Mr. Matulich smiled and disappeared . . . to walk out of a closet some fifty yards away. In the middle of the room he burst into flames and fell to the floor a fiery lump. Then a hatch opened in the ceiling and out dropped Joe, with an extinguisher held in four arms to douse his crackling corpse with mounds of foam. Which instantly dried up to reveal nothing underneath but a single red rose, which he then presented to the closest woman with a flourish and a bow.

The attending crowd applauded its approval.

Equipped with only a snap cane, disappearing ink, Niagara cards, a squirting carnation, and other meek tricks of that ilk, Harry felt totally out of his league. This guy was fabulous!

Hooking a thumb into her apron, Kit moved her head. "Come on, I'll find you a table without any trapdoors."

"Appreciated," said the alien, gently disengaging the aerial infant. Giggling, she wafted away in search of a more cooperative playmate.

"So, what do you folks do?" asked Kit, her swaying hips maneuvering through the maze of tables with trained rhythm. " 'Cause you sure ain't miners."

"Construction," replied Harry gruffly. That was always a favorite phony occupation of criminals. Either that or politics.

"Whole building or just the foundations?" asked Kit wryly.

"We fly the streets of big cities at night and blow potholes in the roads with miniature missiles," explained Rikka, snapping her chewing gum à la gangster moll.

The waitress stopped in her tracks. "What?" she gasped.

"Hey, potholes don't just happen naturally," stated Jhonny, trying to radiate an aura of pure evil.

"Besides," rumbled Mike. "Somebody has got to keep those union road crews working."

Listening in over the PA system, the crowd of patrons roared its approval, and then returned to their drinks and marked cards. "You folks are okay!" smiled the lady bouncer, gesturing at a safe table. "That's a load of crap, but a great bar story. What do you want?"

"Vodka martini," said Snyder, taking a seat. Oh, well, it had sounded good in the shuttle.

"Gibson sidecar," said Jhonny, reversing a chair and sitting backward. Actually, he would have preferred a Martini X, but that was a drink solely for androids and even here in the wild and wooly asteroid belt he was still illegal. Someday, his people would have to do something about that.

"White wine spritzer," said Rikka, fixing her lipstick and trying to look as brainless as possible. "With a twist, if you got."

"I'll have a double spartoon, straight, no rocks," said Michelangelo, pouring Tabasco sauce on the complimentary bowl of dill pickles.

Shifting a hip, Kit gave an approving look. "Sorry, never heard of the drink."

Which was only proper since the alien had just made up the stuff. Asking for something a well-stocked bar doesn't have made you sound important. And his stature had been severely damaged with the "teddy" incident. Internally he shivered. Did he really resemble a stuffed toy bear? Maybe he'd better order something really tough.

"Then give me a milk," he rumbled. The alien knew that in the distant past on Earth, milk was a drink for children, old people, and cowboys of questionable fighting ability. But out here in the asteroid belt, where so little usable sunlight fell, the miners needed all the vitamin D they could get to maintain healthy bones. Although they had to settle for vitamin-enriched powdered milk substitute.

"Fresh," he added. "Pasteurized. A gallon."

Impressed, the waitress scribbled on her computer pad.

Whole milk required expensive refrigeration and still went bad in only a few weeks.

"Ah . . . cow, goat, or wildebeest," asked Kit off the top of her head, struggling to recoup the dignity of her bar.

A paw was flipped. "Whatever has the highest fat content."

Whew. "Natch. I'll be back before the first show. If you have any fireworks, please explode them on your own table."

As the waitress walked away, Rikka looked at Michelangelo and tugged on an earring. Pretending to scratch under his Bruno-infested caftan, the tech did a quick scan of their table.

"We're clear of insects," he announced. "Ah, I mean bugs. And I have the hummer in operation so we cannot be overheard with a maser or directional microphone."

Harry snorted a laugh. Where was the technician when the anchor needed him during his second divorce?

"Okay, now what?" asked Jhonny, leering at a nearby woman until the female scowled back and turned away from him. Perfect. Anybody watching would be positive he was a human male. "How do we find Yertzoff, if he is in here?"

"Easy," said Collins, fluffing her hair. "The prince couldn't have had New Flesh surgery done on his feet, or else everybody would have mentioned that he was limping or walking oddly."

"Meaning?" prompted Mike, puzzled.

Feeding a cracker to her snake, Rikka grinned. Obviously, the tech had not read the medical report on the prince. A classic beginner's mistake. "Yertzoff has small feet. They run in his family."

"Most feet do," observed the alien honestly.

Snyder waved that aside. "Vladamir has really small feet. Dancer's feet. And his shoes were specially made."

Stifling a yawn, Jhonny dropped a fork on the floor and stared at it in annoyance.

"So what we have to do is get a video recording of the feet in this bar and if the smallest pair are wearing the best shoes, then we have a prince," finished Harry, giving his fish a breath of air by dunking it in a glass of water. Such wasteful things were biological ties, carp-carp-carp, that's all you did for the whole day.

Bending over, the android retrieved the fork and surreptitiously set his camcorder on the floor. Immediately the semisentient machine scuttled off on its errand.

"And now we wait," said Rikka, undoing a button on her blouse. She was sweltering under the body armor. "If he's not here, we hit the Excelsior."

"Understood."

Just then a dapper young man in natty gabardine jumpsuit approached their table, stopping a respectful meter away, and bowed toward Collins.

"Please pardon me for intruding, gentle folk," said the man politely. "But I was wondering if I may be so bold as to ask for the boon of a formal introduction to this lovely young lady, so that I may properly ask if she would deign to partake of a dance with me. At her pleasure and convenience, of course."

The disguised reporters exchanged exasperated glances. Goddamn, they had no time for midnight romance, there were important plans to be reviewed! But what could be done? Romeo here had obeyed every rule of proper conduct for polite society. There was no quick way to get rid of him.

"You wanna lick my *what*?!" shrieked Rikka at the top of her lungs.

Instantly the ceiling panel above the man exploded.

At a range of two feet, the stricken target was actually lifted into the air from the blast of the PeaceMaker. Limply he hit the floor, oily snakes of Narcolipic gases swirling about his quivering form, his chest bristly with anesthetic darts.

Instantly his pocket-doc scurried into view, hummed for a moment, and then returned to its hip holster. The man was quite undamaged. Just very seriously unconscious.

As a cushioned bulldozer hauled off the lonely inebriate, Kit arrived with the drinks. Placing tumblers and cartons on the table, she was sorting out who ordered what, when two men across the nightclub started yelling at each other and the argument quickly escalated into drawn weapons.

"Aren't you going to do anything about them?" asked Jhonny, curiously accepting his tumbler. "As the bouncer, I mean."

An empty tray tucked under her arm, Kit looked around. "Oh, those guys? Nyah. It's not a fight, that is just a gun battle."

"There's a difference?" asked Mike, sipping his milk. Horrid stuff, but it was part of the act.

Tucking the check under a clip bolted to the table, she smiled. "Sure. Watch."

Going to the aft wall, each man assumed a fighting stance before a door. An LED timer built into the wall counted down from ten to one, and at zero both doors slammed open and out lunged horrendous monsters composed of fangs, teeth, claws, stingers, talons, scales, and more fins than a Buick Continental.

Instantly the men drew and emptied their weapons into the beasts. As the riddled husks of the robots toppled to the floor, a digital meter tallied up the points.

"Ha! I win!" scoffed the older man, reloading his Wilkes .444 Magnum.

The youngster holstered his Bedlow. "Yeah, well, mine hit the ground first."

"But mine was taller. And uglier. Looked like my wife."

"Nyah, it resembled my mother."

Suddenly realizing what had just been said, each man stared hard at the other, as if seeing his enemy for the very first time.

"Dad?" ventured the smuggler.

The thief spread wide his arms. "Son!"

Standing near the QSNT reporters, Kit gave a sniff. "How sweet. Reunions always bring a tear to my eyes," she said, wiping her face with a corner of her apron. "But then, so do onions." And she sashayed away.

But the scene at the gun range went on.

"Where the prack have you been all these years?" demanded the youngster hotly, releasing his parent.

"What's it to you, ya bastard," snarled Pop.

Without warning, the kid drew his Bedlow and fired. He missed his estranged father, but winged a woman on the other side of the bar, making her drop her drink.

Yowling in pain, the victim fired back with an HK needler, the stream of lmm flechettes missing the bastard, but blowing the top hat off a beer drinker. Madder than ale, he fired an MPB Neutrino pistol from the hip. She ducked and the invisible beam of supercharged ions vaporized a bowl of popcorn on another table spraying a dozen people with hot buttered shrapnel.

After that, the exact details of the exchange became difficult to track but soon the nightclub was crisscrossed with brilliant beams of annihilation and the thundering flash of projectile weapons booming their hot lead responses.

That was when a blinding white light filled the club and everybody dropped their scalding weapons to the floor.

Behind the door, Joe rang an ancient brass pugilism bell to get their attention. "Okay, okay, it's been long enough, and we needed to redecorate anyway," he announced grudgingly. "No more guns, but the Ms. Manners security system will be turned off for the next half hour. Have fun."

In horror, the reporters could only stare at the grinning crowd of miners, criminals, and psychopaths smacking fists into palms. Above them, baby Alyssa was hauled into the back room by Mom.

"Yes, of course you can watch," said Kit with maternal pride to the bubble. "But from behind the Armorlite barrier, just like before."

"Whee!" cried the infant, clapping pudgy hands.

"Trouble, we are in trouble," said Jhonny, nervously glancing about at the impending riot. "My camera will depart the moment I do and I'm not staying without you guys for protection."

"To hell with this," said Harry, standing. "Let's go."

But leaving their table, the team saw the front door was

blocked solid with people at the cloak room checking breakables and reclaiming boxing gloves and baseball bats.

"Fire exit," said Rikka, glancing everywhere.

"None," answered Michelangelo, towering above the crowd doing calisthenics and stretching exercises. "And the stage door has been closed with a steel grill."

"Service entrance," snapped Snyder, feeling the tension in the atmosphere build around him like a brisket in the pressure cooker. "We'll leave by the pantry or garbage chute."

Collins located the goal in question. "Over there!"

But approaching the area, they saw a sheet of Armorlite glass slide from the jamb to seal off that doorway. Obviously, the kitchen crockery had often been involved in the donnybrooks and the Matulichs wanted to minimize the damage.

"Shit!" cursed Rikka, stomping a foot.

"I'm thinking about it," replied Harry, chewing a cigar not in his mouth.

Cuffs rolled to the elbows of their muscular hairy arms, a pair of stevedores from an ore freighter waddled forward.

"I want a piece of the big guy," declared one, indicating Mike.

"Yeah, me too!" echoed his second, cracking his knuckles with relish. "He don't look so mean."

Michelangelo was terrified. Oh, dear, physical violence. Only one thing to do. Baring his long canine fangs, the alien spread his powerful arms wide, allowing his talons to extend to their fullest length.

"Come to me, tasty humans!" he bellowed in bestial fury. "Yes! Attack! Now!"

The toughs paused in concern.

Mike frowned angrily. "Don't make me order out for lunch!"

"The fop in the belt?" asked one.

A nod. "Fop."

And they charged Jhonny.

Sidestepping a rush from one, a flying bottle caught the

camera-op in the chest. The container shattered with a crash and down he went. Sprawled on the floor, the android rolled under a table. Then grunting with the exertion, he grabbed the stem of the table and hoisted it in the manner of an umbrella shield. He took that from no *man!* Besides, they were trapped.

"Silicon can!" the android bellowed as a war cry and charged straight for the drunkards.

Retreating to a corner of the room where their backs would be protected, Rikka turned on her pocket camera, while Harry moved a chair in front of them for protection. Then erecting menus, the reporters tried to crouch as low as possible. A bar fight. They were about to become embroiled in a real old-fashioned bar fight!

Where was QINS when you needed them? For cannon fodder, that is.

"Hey, ain't you with the fop in the fish belt?" asked a gnarly specimen of humanity.

With a sigh, Harry used a shoe to shove the chair forward and it slid directly into the man exactly where a gentleman doesn't hit another with a chair, except for the best of reasons. The hulk went down and Rikka smashed a bottle over his head for good measure.

Then a wave of patrons engulfed the reporters and gone was any semblance of such polite tactics. Fighting and fuming, screaming and cursing, ranting and raving, the night club exploded into a bare-knuckle brawl of deadly serious, but nonlethal proportions.

His table shield broken, Jhonny started to use his pocket camera flash to blind the oncoming horde. But that was kicked out of his hands by somebody swinging from the rafters. From his burglary kit, he next tried squirting oil on the floor, but the slippery lubricant seemed to have no effect. Jumping over a table, Jhonny scrambled for the safety of the Closet-Doc, but the android was directly confronted by a snarling specimen of spacemanhood and was soon duking it out with the milkman. While the artificial male lacked the awesome strength of humans, under the plastic skin of his hands were bones of titanium steelloy, and each punch was greeted with grunts of surprise. In short order, the dairy driver went down for the count, and his final coherent thought was how could this little guy hit that hard without brass knuckles?

Then a dozen men and women swarmed over Jhonny and he disappeared in a tangle of arms and legs. Magic coins, cards, cups, and guppies went flying from the wrestling group.

Braver, or dumber than the rest of her brethren, a navigation officer from a tramp liner relentlessly advanced upon the giant Michelangelo with a broken bottle in one hand; the jagged glass gleamed evilly under the smoky lights.

Although his PeaceMaker stun pistol was still in his hip holster, it was only there for show and the devoted alien pacifist tried not to show his fear. Uh-oh. Think fast, *aaraa-ting!*

"Excuse me, but do you believe in God?" asked Michelangelo, smiling.

Temporarily, the burly woman was confused. Was this some sort of a weird plea for religious clemency?

Roaring like thunder, the alien hauled the navigation officer bodily into the air with a single paw, holding her high above his snarling head.

"Ya wanna meet him in person?" he breathed hot and wet into the human's exposed belly.

The spacer promptly fainted.

Gently, placing the limp form into a whole chair, Michelangelo beat his chest with both fists as he had seen in the old Earth jungle movies. A critic of his singing voice came in the manner of a thrown vending machine, so the alien made a catch and dramatically tore the mechanical device apart. Then, stalking about the drunken battle, he offered the parts to others as ready-made weapons as an incentive to fight him.

Politely the kind offer was endlessly refused.

In a martial arts crouch, a very drunk asteroid miner used a karate chop to splinter a table and then leaped at Rikka. Spinning about, Collins grabbed a chair and busted it over the fool's head. With a sigh, the ninja slumped to the debris-littered floor.

The investigative reporter tossed aside the bit of wood still in her grip and dusted off her hands. Damn fool. This fracas was a tea party compared to a budget meeting.

Igniting a cigar, Harry puffed the tip to a cherry-red and extinguished the tobacco onto a man's exposed neck. Screaming from the stinging pain, the surly steward pivoted and got a face full of disappearing ink and then a snap cane shoved into his mouth. As the fellow tried to spit out the prop, Harry slapped him in the face and suddenly his cheeks gave a valiant effort to become three feet wide. Staggering off, the gagging man went in search of a mirror.

"Thanks," panted the android, struggling to his feet.

Harry gave his friend a hand. "No problem."

"Duck," said the camera-op.

The anchor did and an occupied spacesuit went sailing through the spot his head had just occupied.

HEY, scrolled Deitrich. WHAT THE HECK IS GOING ON IN THERE? WORLDS WAR II?

For the moment his request for information went unanswered.

On the stage, a man and a woman were engaged in a furious fight with quarterstaffs cobbled from wooden dowels stolen from the cloak room. Holding the makeshift staffs in the middle, the two combatants slammed the dowels together in a flurry of overhead smashes, sweeps, parries, and jabs. The wood shafts became only blurs of motion as the trained opponents attacked and countered in a series of clacks too fast to even describe.

Clackclackclack. "I got what it takes." Clack.

"I can take what you got." Clackclackclack.

"What you got ain't so hot." Clackclack.

"I'm so hot," Clack! "What you got." Clack! "Don't mean zot!" Clackclackclackclackclackaclackclackclackclackclackthud.

And the two mighty warriors broke apart gasping for breath.

In the orchestra pit, a drummer asked, "This looks serious. Should we give them a hand?"

"Certainly," replied a pianist and the musicians started applauding.

Out of bottles and chairs, Rikka kneed an incoming monster directly where Harry had hit the other. Only this titan merely grunted at the impact.

"Body armor," he growled, grabbing her by the throat with one huge hand. The other cocked back a fist roughly the size and general shape of Montana.

"I've been in bar fights before," he chuckled insanely.

Facing an obvious pro, Collins played her last card.

"Yeah?" she squeaked through her crushing larynx. "Well look at this!" And grabbing the lapels of her blouse she yanked the shirt wide apart, buttons flying.

Contemptuous at first, the goliath blinked twice in amazement and could only stare agog at what was underneath.

Respectfully, he released Collins, stood ramrod straight and saluted. The reporter accepted the token of respect as her due.

"Hey, guys!" he thundered, leveling a sausage-thick finger. "Look!"

A few turned at the summons, but then word quickly spread and soon the whole bar stood gaping at the display. Dutifully, Rikka pulled her blouse farther apart so that her Media-issued, USDA-approved, Emergency Identification T-shirt underneath was totally visible.

"QSNT!" gasped a burly fellow with another patron clenched in a fist like a club. "These folk are the Satellite News Team!"

A bloody lump broke in half with a grin. "Gosh, I watch you guys every day!"

"These are the folks who orchestrated the destruction of the Free Police base on Io moon!" added another. "Now that took guts!"

"Collins!" cried another. "She's Rikka Collins!"

A pile of sweaty freighter captains parted and a bedraggled Harry was hauled to his feet. "And this is Mr. Snyder!"

"Wow!"

"This was Mr. Snyder," mumbled Harry, having trouble standing by himself. "I think I'm dead." Thank goodness he had written himself an obituary years ago.

Somebody shook Rikka's hand. "Ma'am, you put my brother in jail for fifty years," rumbled the jackdaffer, identifiable by his robotic elbows and knees. "Can't say how pleased I am that you did. Keep up the good work."

"Thanks," said Collins, removing her blouse entirely. This was the first time taking her clothes off in a bar had ever gotten the reporter out of trouble! On the back was a hologram of her and the team before the reception desk at Media. An electronic wafer sign at the base of her spine scrolled, "All News All the Time!" Wisely, she had disconnected the audio long ago.

Bruised but smiling, the young lady Jhonny had been leering at earlier now handed the android his camcorder. "Sorry about trying to set you on fire, Mr. Smith, sir."

"Hey, it happens," he managed to say while attempting to focus his eyes. "Now please tell me what planet this is again?"

"Construction, ha!" chuckled Kit, moving among the battered throng, dispensing bandages, Bactine, and beer from her tray.

"Teddy okay?" squealed Alyssa in delight from above. Closing his pupilless eyes, Michelangelo assured the bubbly infant that he was perfectly intact. Maybe he should dye his fur blue, or get a mohawk.

Suddenly everybody was smoothing hair and straightening clothes. Seltzer was used as a crude shower and pocket combs were broken in half to be shared by bitter enemies.

"Are you filming yet?"

"Where's the camera?"

"Want me to throw Fred out the window again?"

"Mention the name of the club!" shouted Joe from three different places at the same time.

"Here's ya BoomBox," offered a clean vacuum salesman, handing Jhonny his camcorder. "Better get it tuned, mister. Damn thing almost walked out the front door following that miner over there."

The team swiveled so fast, it took their clothes almost a full second to catch up. Limping past the broken vending machine in the foyer was a small female Gremlin. Standing barely two meters tall, alongside Michelangelo she was almost a dwarf.

Especially considering those tiny feet.

"Get her!" cried the reporters and they plowed through the crowd, bowling over their astonished admirers, to tackle the alien just as she was reclaiming a spacesuit.

"Awright!" grinned a gap-toothed stevedore, popping his knuckles with relish. "Is da fights back on?"

"*No!*" chorused the whole bruised room in unison.

Wrestling the petite titan to the floor, Harry and Jhonny each grabbed an arm, Mike lay flat across the legs, and Rikka climbed on top of the fuzzy chest.

"What? Who are you? Help!" squealed the Gremlin.

"Hi, Your Majesty," whispered Collins, straddling the hairy torso to hold a microphone right in the astonished face.

There was a pause. Then with a heartfelt sigh, the trapped alien went limp under the combined bodies of the news reporters. Yet another helpless victim to the power of the press.

"Oh, hell," she said in an amazingly masculine voice.

CHAPTER SEVENTEEN

ESCORTING THEIR PRIZE back to the QSNT shuttle, the reporters gave the impotentate a few moments of privacy in their Closet-Doc to remove his New Flesh disguise.

Stepping from the door of the robotic physician, obscured by clouds of minty steam, Prince Vladamir Yertzoff strode on the middeck. His clothes were the vented green jumpsuit of a common medical tech, but the face bore a striking resemblance to a former president of the United States of North America who was not a crook. Hooking a thumb under his chin, the runaway royalty pried loose a flap of skin and peeled off the mask with the most nauseating sucking sounds imaginable. Underneath was a younger, friendler set of features; blond hair, blue eyes, and dazzling smile. Only a small patch of discoloration marred his right cheek where a Neutrino blaster had nearly crisped his head in the famous battle with the Free Police at the children's hospital. Obviously, the Royal Martian Youth Drug had some limitations on its healing powers.

"Ah," Vladamir sighed in relief and he tossed the New Flesh mask into a corner. It lay there staring at them with hollow eyes, just like the original man had in real life.

Mike had arranged a semicircle of chairs on the middeck and the prince took the largest. The team was amused watching the man move about their ship as if he owned it. Probably just habit from living most of your life on a planet where you did own everything.

"If you don't mind," said Prince Yertzoff, shielding his face with a hand. "The T-shirt, please, miss?"

Eh? Oh. Fondling a cuff, Rikka cut the hologram off and the shirt dimmed to white cloth mottled with wafer electronics and microcircuitry.

He bowed. "Thank you."

"No problem," she curtsied.

"First off, how did you know it was me?" he asked bluntly.

"With those feet?" chided Snyder, pointing.

Going motionless for a second, the man then bent double and stared down as if seeing the extremities for the first time.

"Why, is there something unusual about them?" he asked, astonished.

Rikka waved that aside. "Why did you run?" she demanded, going for the jugular. "Had a fight with your fiancée? Tired of being the prince? Sided with Uncle Bob for a takeover of your own homeworld?"

On cue, Jhonny activated his camcorder.

Placing ankle atop knee, Yertzoff gave a half smile. "What incredibly unique ideas," he acknowledged. "They're totally wrong, but fascinating. How much of your news is usually this accurate and how much fiction?"

The reporters went livid from the accusation. Even Mike, who first had to access the word on his IBM portable before becoming a) adj., deathly pale induced by anger; see blanched.

"Actually, I had a fight with my . . . fiancee and came here to hire some of the locals and arrange for transport to . . . Titan. The new government there is in shambles and a fine place for me to disappear. Start a new life."

Every member of the news team heard the microscopic pauses. Ah, the prince might be a wonderful liar at a podium before large crowds, telling them how low taxes will be soon and other such prack, but he was absolutely untrained to dodge answers while under pressure.

"So you came to The Trap, the very place where your troubles in life started, to merely pass on through," detailed Collins, her very being denying the statements.

"Yes, exactly," answered the man, crossing his arms and legs in the classic denial position of body language.

Resting an elbow in a palm, Snyder let his arm arc over his lap and hit a thigh. The rest of the team heartily agreed. A great try, but it got a solid one hundred on the baloney meter.

"Royal bull," said Rikka, estimating it was time to crack this haughty composure. She decided to go back to the basics and try a sniper tactic on their first avenue of thought. Inga Swenson.

"When is the prison break scheduled?" demanded Collins loudly.

"Prison?" squeaked Yertzoff, eyes going round.

Smiles abounded. Ah, how satisfying. It had been a shot in the dark and those didn't always draw blood. But when one did, it was a geyser!

"So the coded signal you received on the private Z-band watch was the notification that Inga's escape was imminent," composed Rikka off the top of her head. "You immediately departed the party, where you would not be missed for several minutes, by using your carefully planned route, to rendezvous here with Inga Swenson before hiding permanently."

"What? Nonsense!" denied the sweaty man. "You're mad! I'm merely here to make her jealous by having a last bachelor fling with the local ladies."

"Make who jealous?" asked Jhonny softly, zooming in for a close-up.

"Inga. No! I mean, ah . . . Eta. Henretta!"

Fascinated, Michelangelo watched the verbal sparring. This was his favorite part of blowing the lid off a conspiracy. It was a lot like having sex; the harder the other person wiggled, the better it felt when you finished.

Starting to use his broadcast voice, Snyder angled himself toward the camcorder and took a dramatic stance. "Your Highness, we have tracked you from the secret exit in your office activated by the box of war medals, through Koop Memorial, to the used shuttle dealer, and to this very asteroid. We know about the explosion on Phobos, the thirty men who went to the moon, and why the shuttle was named *Sanders*!"

The jaw of the prince threatened to hit the deck.

"No," he gasped in disbelief. "Nobody is that good."

"Why here?" demanded Snyder hotly, driving his wedge home. "The old Purloined Letter trick? The most obvious place is the last they'll look?"

Eyes full of fear, Vladamir Yertzoff looked around at the reporters. Breathing hard for several minutes, his face became grim as the man finally came to a decision.

"Occam's Razor," relented the heir, sagging. "I own The Trap."

"Eh?"

"What?"

"Huh?"

A regal nod. "After so many years of digging for information here, I found it was easier to solicit local cooperation if I was their boss."

Four bobbing heads. When in doubt, become the king. Made sense.

"And we weren't going anywhere else. Inga and I planned to live here in our retirement. You would be surprised at what royalty owns these days," he added for edification. "Especially on Earth."

So there was an escape planned. Fabulous! Rikka crossed her legs, nearly crushing her snake. "Yes, we wondered why you didn't go there. Billions of people on one planet. It's the perfect place to disappear."

"We thought of living there, but simply can't stand the awful air," the prince said, crinkling his nose. "Too damn much ozone!"

Everybody chuckled. True enough.

Way back in the pre-space era, Earth had been facing a major problem. The use of fluorocarbon gases in aerial spray cans had seriously depleted the protective ozone layer of the homeworld allowing harmful UV rays to penetrate freely. The ecosystem was thrown off balance from the rising heat and mutations became as commonplace as

TV evangelists. Some believed it was a combination of the two that spawned the birth of the Free Police.

Fortunately, there was a solution. Whenever lightning struck the ground, a natural, if somewhat smelly, by-product of the violent action was ozone. But humanity needed lots of ozone and fast.

So, with the advent of tokamacs, clean operating nuclear fission power plants, every nation on the world altered thousands of power relay stations. Their only task was to function as poorly as possible and in their crackling, smelly, dangerous innards, the miniature lightning bolts playing among the busbars steadily recombined loose oxygen to produce ozone. And ruined television reception for kilometers, but that was a problem for another government group to solve.

Within a few decades, the protective layer about the Earth was replenished, the global warming ceased, and the mutations slowed to only those that naturally followed any major nuclear war.

But as always, humanity took a good thing too far, still producing stinky ozone in an insane fear of ancient ills long cured. So now the planet smelled horribly bitter to off-worlders and few, if any, could stand wearing the exceptionally unattractive breathing apparatus needed to filter out the stench of healing technology.

Secretly, Rikka had heard rumors of a growing cult of hair-spray worshippers who were using fluorocarbon gases again in a crazed effort to rebalance the ecosystem. Earth, sheesh! Dirt was the name and general level of intelligence for the indigenous population. Anybody with brains went into space.

The prince cleared his throat to speak further.

WE HAVE COMPANY, scrolled Deitrich on the team's wrist secretaries.

A blank section of the hull parted to reveal a sizable monitor; it flickered into life showing a clear view of the dock outside. A platoon of Marines in full battle armor was marching along inspecting everything. The room was swept by a sudden chill that had nothing to do with the life support system.

"Martian Security," identified Yertzoff. "Damn! They mustn't find me!"

"Silence," ordered Collins. "Deitrich, do a dead man."

"Roger," the MainBrain acknowledged and the lights cut off. Then the Sterling generators went still, the operating meters of the Closet-Doc darkened and the gentle hum of life support disappeared.

Sitting motionless in the dead pitch-darkness, the team heard nothing until a dull pounding sounded on their hull at the door. A scratching, clicking noise came as somebody tried to key open the airlock and failed. Time passed. The lights came back on.

"Whew, close one," said the ceiling.

Harry thumped the floor furiously, with a fist. Followed by the cops like cub reporters on their first assignment! They had been concentrating on the prince so hard, it had never occurred that somebody might be following them!

"They tried for a scan, so I gave them the impression the hull was full of birds," said Deitrich.

Curiously, the prince glanced about to see who was talking.

"Birds?" asked Jhonny, amused and relieved.

The pilot chuckled. "First thing I thought of. They almost caught on when I changed the name on the hull from QSNT to 'Yellow Journalism, the magazine about canaries.'"

"You're a sick man."

"Thank you!"

"Outside view, please," asked Rikka, worrying her hands.

Deitrich complied and the bow monitor darkened into a panoramic view of nearby space. An armada of Martian warships had The Trap completely surrounded. The asteroid cluster had finally become its namesake.

"Sensors indicate that the warcraft are fully armed and totally pissed off," noted the speaker.

"What an amazing computer," acknowledged the prince,

in spite of the dire situation. "Is it an IBM 37? Omega 99?"

"A Donovan Four, sir," replied the sixty-four-ounce Brain in a fake mechanical monotone.

Chewing on a fresh cigar, Harry kicked over his chair and started to pace. "But now we're totally trapped," he growled in annoyance. "If we run, the military will track us to the ends of the solar system in hot pursuit. Enabling us to do nothing. But if we stay, then Inga will break out of jail and come running straight here into them."

Frowning, Rikka agreed. Either way, Swenson would be executed as an escaped criminal and their story of the year becomes the tragedy of a lifetime. This was a classic no-win scenario! In their efforts to uncover a mystery, the news team had inadvertently ruined the lives of two desperate lovers. And that was unacceptable. Damn what the other networks did. QSNT was dedicated to helping people! Well, the innocent ones, anyway.

"Okay, when is the jail break?" barked Collins.

The prince glanced at his pinkie nail watch. "In four hours."

Prack! "More than enough time," she said aloud.

"Enough for what?" asked Michelangelo.

"To prove that Inga was framed," replied Harry, smiling, a rush of adrenaline flooding his body. "If we can show her innocence and get the proof to an IP magistrate before she escapes, everything will be fine!"

"No offense, gentle folk," said the prince, choosing his words carefully. "But I have had the best minds in the system working on this for ten years. What makes you think this group can do, or find, something they missed?"

Rikka tilted her head. "And how long did you work on the perfect escape?"

A moment passed.

"How can I help?" asked Yertzoff, the rising excitement adding a touch of color to his cheeks.

CHAPTER EIGHTEEN

"HERE IT COMES again!" cried the Media janitor over the chattering roar of the electric feather duster in her hands. "Retreat!"

Steadily beating their mops and brooms, the makeshift commandos pulled back and the door to the QSNT office was slammed shut.

"Geez, that's one tough Danish," sighed a security guard, wiping his sweaty brow with a sleeve. To hell with calories, he was sticking to doughnuts from now on.

"Okay, that didn't work," growled a plumber, slamming a fresh battery into his Weedwacker. "So, what are we going to do next?"

"I'm working on it," replied the chief janitor hostilely.

Slumped against the wall catching his breath, a life support technician perked up. "Hey, chief! Remember how we took care of that infestation of bad pizza rolls last year on Level 6?"

"Brilliant!" cried the woman, adjusting the blades of her faithful gardening tool. "Hannigan, contact MacKenzie in The Horny Toad."

"Yes, sir!"

A wailing roar came from the decimated office and a horde of wiggling tentacles lashed out from underneath the closed doorway. The maintenance troops and security guards battled the monster with their assorted weaponry, but it only served to temporarily repel the advance of the hideous desert mutation.

Oh, lord, she sure hoped Bruno was hungry!

* * *

"Nothing, nothing, nothing!" cried Rikka, throwing the pile of printouts and photographs across the workroom of the shuttle. The fluttering storm settled to the deck back in their original disorganized mess.

"I truly appreciate your help," said Prince Yertzoff, daintily removing a manila folder of unsolved murders from his face. "But it is plain that—"

"Aw shaddup!" barked Collins, nostrils flaring.

Retreating a step, the ruler of Mars wisely took a position behind Michelangelo. Too busy to notice the minor altercation, the alien sat at a computer console paginating through his hundredth computer file on the laws, regulations, ordinances, bylaws, common laws, unwritten laws, obsolete rulings, precedence, procedures, taboos, and etiquette on gunfighting in space. So far, his only hard conclusion was that this definitely was the place to shoot another sentient. Who designed these social regulations, a cadre of morticians?

Staring at her clean workbench, Rikka grabbed the hair at her temples and tried to think even harder. The reporter knew she was missing something. An important piece of the puzzle lay in her grasp and she was constantly overlooking it. Why? Something too small to notice? Or too commonplace?

"Well, I found a magistrate in the Black Pages of the com-link directory," called Jhonny, down the hallway from the bridge. "Judge Richard Tucholka over at the bubble city, Iron Nose. The asteroid is only about fifteen minutes away at Fatal Two."

"Geez, is that all?" puffed Harry, a pile of dead cigar butts sprinkled around the hooded monitor he had his head stuck in. Blindly, the anchor was touch-typing on two different keyboards.

But at those words, Rikka jerked alert. All. That was it. She didn't have every one of the files! Most, but not all!

* * *

Boldly, Hardcopy and Sunshine knocked on the door to the warden's office and entered before any response was possible.

"Warden Thorson? Hello," said Jason gruffly, petulantly slamming the door behind him. "Apparently your idiot guards foolishly believe that *we* need your permission to hold an interview with Inga Swenson!"

"Correct," chewed the warden around a mouthful of toasted sandwich. His desktop was bare except for the hovertray loaded with assorted foodstuffs and its own independent Mr. Beer automatic brewery. With optional pretzel maker. "So suppose you two tell me why I should interrupt my lunch, and do the same to a prisoner, merely to accommodate a couple of snooping bozos?"

The news duo was rendered speechless. Almost.

"Why?" throated Susie in outrage. "Because we're Hardcopy and Sunshine, ace reporters from QINS!"

"News, NEWS, *NEWS*!" obediently echoed their robotic belt buckles.

With a grunt, the man returned to his lunch. "So pracking what? I hate the news."

Furious by this cavalier ignorance of their vaunted status, Hardcopy and Sunshine immediately launched into their standard number two spiel on their incredible accomplishments, accompanied by slides, a musical soundtrack, and a hefty bribe. Suddenly the warden was paying close attention.

And smiling.

"What do you mean they haven't posted any reports?" shouted a hologram of Maria Valdez in the middle of Box's office.

"Hey, they're only two hours over their one-hour schedule," answered Ambocksky, shuffling papers on his desk as a prelude to shuffling even more papers in time for the midnight summary of the news of the day. Only what day was this? And when had he last had some sleep? And who was he talking to like this?

"This is justifiable cause," stated the translucent Valdez,

slim hands akimbo on belled hips. "Fire them!" And with a flounce, the beastly beauty faded out.

Using the intercom, Box asked the yawning Mrs. Seigling for doughnuts and triple black coffee to fortify him for the night. Then munching on an entire pack of antacids, Paul decided that, no, he wouldn't fire them. Not for something this minor. But when the SNT did phone in a report, the team had better be on top of a hot story. And he meant hot! With proof this time!

Or else.

Retro-rockets gently flaring on the prow of an unmarked space shuttle, the sleek craft eased to a halt among the tumbling boulders just outside the perimeter of The Trap. In the cockpit of the bridge, Hanna O'Toole of QCNN and Lord Alexander Hyde-White of the QBBC stared in delight at the massive armada of Martian warships filling the rift in the asteroid belt.

"He's here," breathed Hyde-White, releasing the steering wheel. "I can smell the prince."

Holding a sensor clip to her ear, O'Toole nodded agreement. "But sneaking in there past the troops is going to be most difficult."

"Sneak?" repeated the British lord. "Nonsense! I'll simply place a call to the commanding officer of that flotilla and ask to be admitted."

A rough and ready street reporter, Hanna was flabbergasted at the bizarre tactic. Ask? What a wild idea! "Think it'll work?"

"Always has before," replied Lord Hyde-White as he started to punch numbers into the console telephone.

"Hello . . . Mars?"

Orbiting among the thousand ships about The Trap was the Martian dreadnought *Indestructible II*. The first *Indestructible* had accidentally blown up in dry dock as it was being built. Sporting an arsenal of spacial weapons, the ship wasn't classified as a super dreadnought, although its crew did personally think very highly of the craft.

On the crowded bridge, a Space Marine marched out of a turbo-lift and stamped his boots in the regulation one-two before smartly saluting a scowling lieutenant.

"Sir! No sign of His Highness, sir," reported the trooper, Gibraltar Assault Rifle neatly clipped to the metal shoulder of his spacesuit. The first thing he had learned in boot camp, right after how to tear out an enemy's gizzard and where it was located, was the indisputable fact that in the Marines, neatness counted.

"Then search everywhere again!" stormed the uniformed officer, hands locked behind his back. "Rip the clubs apart, offer a reward, and bore holes in the asteroids themselves, but find Prince Vladamir Yertzoff!"

"Sir, wouldn't it be simpler to just get another heir?" asked the weary Marine.

"Out!" ordered the lieutenant, and the soldier scurried away.

Geez, he was only asking.

"Got it!" cried Rikka, holding aloft a piece of paper triumphantly.

Lurching from their workbenches across the shuttle, everybody came charging in to see what the woman had unearthed.

"The photo of Inga shooting Schwartz was faked!" offered Jhonny. That was his pet theory.

"Nope!"

"It wasn't really Inga but an impersonator," delivered Harry dramatically. That had to be the answer.

"Wrong!" sang the happy woman.

"It was a justifiable shoot?" the prince hopefully asked. That would make everything fine in one fell swoop.

What was a fell swoop anyway?

Rikka faced the prince. "Sorry, sire. While Inga and Schwartz were both drunk, somebody started making jokes about the nutty aristocracy of Mars. They got into a cursing match and reached for their guns. Inga drew first." She laid a hand on his shoulder. "In the asteroid belt, this type

of gun battle is commonplace. But since she was the un-
wanted fiancée of a prince . . ."

Vladamir nodded solemnly in understanding. Such treatment was the curse of royalty everywhere. Alongside pre-
mature baldness and paternity suits. Endless paternity
suits.

"So what did you find?" demanded Snyder, chewing a
cigar butt to bits and then swallowing in his excitement.

Sliding a sheet into a slot on her lab bench, Rikka typed
a recessed set of controls. Instantly on the wall was displayed the picture taken from the files on the Club Royale,
showing Inga with a smoking gun and Schwartz getting
his brains blown out.

With a flair, the woman added a second sheet to the slot,
and alongside the first was projected the classic picture of
the young prince fighting off the hordes of Free Police at
the hospital.

Everybody craned their necks trying to look at the two
pictures at the same moment. Although there were some
differences, the resemblance between a pirate cadet and
the miner in the space bar were too overwhelming to ignore.

"Steven Schwartz was a space pirate?" cried the prince.
"Wah-hoo!" And he began to dance about the shuttle in a
jig.

"How did you do this?" breathed Harry in admiration.

The woman smirked. "I did what nobody else thought
of doing. I accessed all of the files. Not just the pertinent
ones. But everybody's files: Inga, Schwartz, the prince, his
parents, the man who installed the security camera, Uncle
Bob, the arresting officer, the judge, everybody!"

"Kid, my congratulations," he said, and standing
straight, he gave her a military salute. Jhonny did the same
and Mike put a clenched fist to his chest.

Urp. Heartburn again.

"We've got to locate a magistrate and have her verdict
changed from Murder One to a Murder Won!"

"A what?"

"The public slaying of a space pirate." Not only would

Swenson get of jail, but she'd receive a reward! Gosh, was this becoming a banner story.

"Madam, I owe you my life for this," said Prince Yertzoff, tears of joy upon his cheeks. "Ask and it's yours. Anything within my power to give! Ask!"

Wow. A carte blanche. She hadn't expected this level of gratitude. Hmm, cancel the contract for QINS? Nyah, too childish. Ask for a million sanddollars? A pound of the Youth Drug? Her own town?

"Do you still do beheadings on Mars?" asked the divorcee, thinking about her ex-husband.

"Oh, dear," said the big alien, touching the com-link in his ear. "QSNT has just replayed an exclusive from QINS. Hardcopy and Sunshine are at SnowBall Hell and a jailbreak is in progress."

The good mood in the shuttle shattered like a glass goblet at an opera singers convention.

"No," gasped the prince, staggering backward. "It's early! Too soon!" Yertzoff stared at his pinkie as if to defy the timepiece, then in consternation he remembered that he had never reset the watch to the time difference between this section of the asteroid belt and Neptune!

He'd been too busy avoiding the SNT.

"We've got to stop her!" cried Rikka, pushing her chair away from the workbench. All of their hard work was not going to go up in flames down on the ice world.

"Let's go," said Jhonny and he started for the bridge.

Turning off his monitor, Harry matched the android's stride. "We'll find a way past the blockade, sire!"

At first, Mike didn't understand the concern, but then he recalled one of his early classes in human law, which was a very convoluted thing indeed. If proof of Inga's innocence surfaced, then the woman would be set free. Unless, of course, while incarcerated she performed any illegal activities, and then she would have to serve the time for those crimes before getting released! Obviously justice and the law were two very different things to humans. Same as sex and love. Or tomatoes and tomotoes. Potatoes and pototoes.

"Let's call the whole thing off," suggested the alien hesitantly.

"Maybe that's best," lamented the woebegone prince.

Ignoring the rhetoric, Rikka turned on the aristocrat. "Your Highness, how is Inga getting out of SnowBall Hell prison?"

"I arranged for a thermal mole to burrow an escape tunnel from the outside in."

"And how does she get off planet?"

"Singleship at the end of the tunnel."

"Who made the delivery?" asked Harry, getting a bad feeling that the prince was hiding something again.

A cough. Another. "The . . . ah, Free Police."

Gagging noises were the only sounds the team was capable of making.

"Who else would even try such a task?" explained Yertzoff, spreading his hands.

"And how did you contact the Free Police?" asked Collins, her lips white.

Coughing a few more times, the prince informed his hosts that this was a potentially embarrassing situation.

"There's . . . a person the royalty of Mars can call," he offered hesitantly, "when we need circumspect information, or to arrange . . . illicit events."

"The MIA?" asked Harry. They were supposed to be the master of dirty tricks on Mars. Their infamous motto was "Ha! You got any proof we did it?" Real nice folks.

At the suggestion, Prince Yertzoff barked a laugh. "Good God, no! The MIA is nothing more than a group of mad dog assassins with a good dental plan."

Unfolding her telephone, Rikka punched in numbers. "This the number?" she asked coldly, showing only Yertzoff the integers on display.

Stepping close, Vladamir hid the phone from the others with his body. "Why, yes! But how did you get it?"

"Son of a bitch!" she cried, making a fist and deleting the sequence.

Trained professionals, the team recognized that special tone in her voice.

"Your ex?" asked Deitrich from above.

"He stole my contact numbers and has been passing them around to his royal pals!" Steam threatened to shoot out of her ears. Beheading wasn't good enough! Hanging wasn't good enough! She should remarry the slug and give him a real taste of misery!

Sensing that his friend was temporarily out of service, Harry took control. "Deitrich, you'll have to take the prince to Neptune to stop the escape, his old clunker has nowhere near the speed of you."

"Naturally," replied the ceiling proudly.

"And can you do it?" asked Snyder honestly. "Can you move too fast for the military to track you? What's your top speed? Absolute maximum, full out, stops pulled, damn the safeties, balls to the wind, kill the engines maximum?"

"Mike?" asked the speaker.

"Fatal Five point one," stated Michelangelo, joining the conversation.

"Beg pardon?" asked Jhonny, cupping an ear. Even his camcorder wasn't sure it had gotten that correctly. Four was their max.

"Five point one," repeated the technician. "I will have to baby the engines for the whole trip, and there's a percentile chance of an explosion. But for this short a journey, I think we can do it." And if not, then they could shave his butt bare in heaven. Or roast it in hell.

"Great," smirked Harry confidently. "We can do Fatal Five. Vlad, can those big warships out there do the same?"

A fleeting smile passed across the face of the heir. "No, they can't! The inverse power spread ratio of their mass—"

"Interceptors?" interrupted Snyder.

"Fatal Four point two is their top speed!"

Grabbing the prince by an arm, the anchor shoved the heir toward the bridge. "Then let's get the hell out of here and stop Swenson!"

"I'll find Judge Tucholka and fax him the photos. You just get Inga back into the hellhole jail where she's safe!"

added Collins, moving to the hologram booth and shoving in some quarters. Damn cheap Wilkes. Her plans for revenge on her ex-husband would have to be placed on hold. Besides, revenge was like ice cream, a dish best served cold. And eaten slowly. Yeah.

"Remember this is the asteroid belt!" warned Jhonny.

Organizing the papers in her lap, the investigative reporter frowned. That was a good point. Not every judge or cop out here was going to be totally honest. Prack! Getting this story was like disassembling a live nuclear bomb, the closer they got to the core the more trouble they were in.

Facing his friends, Michelangelo touched his temples and outstretched both palms. "Luck, wisdom, and speed, my friends."

Harry just gave a game thumbs-up. "Piece a cake, big guy."

"And remember to duck," quoted Collins, already punching numbers into the telephone. "Hello . . . Judge?"

With tools in paw, the alien dashed down the service corridor that led to the engine room. Below the deck they felt the main engines come on and begin to throttle to full power. The whine of the Sterling generators steadily increased and the shuttle started to softly vibrate.

"Showtime!" cried Deitrich from the cockpit.

Harry, Jhonny, and Yertzoff hurried to the bridge.

"We'll waste valuable time pulling out to turn around," said the prince, assuming the engineering console. "My Navy may be able to stop us if we depart too slowly." He resembled a child on his parents' couch and none of the controls moved without extreme effort on his part.

"Are you kidding?" scoffed the android, taking his usual spot at Navigation. "Flying backward at light speed is our specialty!"

"I thought it was a cheese lasagna in pepperoni sauce," said Snyder.

"Lying to the boss," corrected Michelangelo's voice.

"All of the above," amended Deitrich sagely, removing their name from the hull.

As the engine lights flashed ready, Jhonny punched the

button and backward the QSNT shuttle blasted out of the honeycomb dock faster than its own reflection could follow. In gradual stages, the afterimage of the asteroid slowly faded away to be replaced by the red and blue stars of space. On the bow monitor, the reporters watched as The Trap shrank into view and then dwindled out of sight.

"Ohmigod!" Harry smiled, adjusting the controls on his communications console. "This is a first for me!"

"Racing in a flying bomb?" asked Jhonny, checking the supply of disks for his camcorder.

"No. We're off to save a princess!"

"Alas," sighed Vladamir Yertzoff, buckling his safety harness. "If she really were a princess, then none of this would have been necessary."

Hmm, true enough. Oh, well, still sounded good, though.

Amid the humming machines and vibrating FTL motors down in the engine room, Mike finished ripping out the safety seal on a surge protector circuit and reached for the strategically placed drum of heavy-duty aspirin. Whatever happened, this was going to be a memorable trip. He only hoped they survived.

And how do you duck in a spaceship?

CHAPTER NINETEEN

BLINDING CRACKLING LIGHTS filled the small underground tunnel, and the shivering prisoner walked steadily along behind the lumbering mechanical mole. Fueled with hydrogen, the mole generated a soft atomic lance that boiled away the rock before it, the condensed material lining the tunnel like a supporting sleeve.

Normally, the mole required massive amounts of water to cool the wall, and the operators wore modified Samson armor to protect them from the awful heat. But here on Neptune, the lance perfectly formed a livable zone of warmth behind it as the escapee trundled along chattering and shivering. Ten feet behind was icy death, two feet ahead was burning lava, but exactly here, it was a balmy 10 degrees Fahrenheit. At the extreme end of the tunnel was a gaping hole in a fifty-meter-thick wall of dura-steel and a small jail cell, its armored door now locked from the inside by a million-sanddollar web of Florentine Plastic.

The guards had been most annoyed.

Originally, Vlad was going to have a singleship waiting in the ravine for Swenson, but a message smuggled in from a new convict said that the prince had changed his mind and would have a fully armed ship of the line waiting for his sweetheart.

Into the blistering, freezing darkness the mole advanced. Freedom was only a thousand kilometers away and nothing this side of SnowBall Hell, or the original, could stop the escape now!

* * *

On through the starry black of space streaked the QSNT shuttle at slightly over Fatal Five. The meters on the dashboard had neatly wrapped their indicators around the pegs past the red danger line, and unbeknownst to the news team, a secretly installed monitor by Wilkes Corporation had recorded the destruction of the safety circuits and already canceled their insurance.

"We lost 'em," announced Jhonny in victory at the sensors console. "No pursuit from The Trap."

"Great!" gulped Michelangelo at the wall speaker, running a diagnostic program on the FTL motors and himself. Both were operating a bit hot and shaky.

"Whee! Watch us fly!" said the ceiling. "Now we're cooking with microwaves!"

As a bachelor, that statement puzzled Jhonny. Was there any other way to prepare a meal?

On the middeck, Rikka savagely slapped the off button on the hologram phone. Damnation! She had already called five judges and not one of them was sober enough or willing to listen to her tale. Plus, she was running out of quarters!

What a way to get a story!

Brrring! "Hello, Judge Notlessube? Rikka Collins here, QSNT."

Click!

As the streak of white erupted from the asteroid and disappeared into the star, the blockade of Martian warships stayed intact for a heartbeat. Then the military formation shattered into a thousand separate ships, each turning and racing at top velocities. A thousand ships erected a tighter blockade about The Trap and four went off in hot pursuit.

"Hot rockets, skipper, they're gone, sir!" cried an ensign at the sensor console.

Swiveling her command chair about, Captain Kiya Murphy faced the bridge station and arched an eyebrow. "Incredible. They're actually trying to escape? Helmsman, full speed. Fatal Four point two. We'll overtake them soon enough."

"Ah, sir," started the helmsman hesitantly. "Sensors show the shuttle traveling at Fatal Five."

There was a pause.

"Nonsense," said the woman gruffly. "Double-check those readings."

"Aye, sir. Did, sir. Still correct, Captain."

"Then prepare all weapons," said the woman coldly. "We may have to use Option 9."

Silence filled the bridge, broken only by the tiny machine noises of the consoles, controls, and a distant video game from some uncaring soul on a break.

"No," breathed an ensign at the communications console. "Sir, not that!"

The dreaded Option 9 was a possibility the crew had been briefly briefed upon before leaving Mars. In the event that royal forces cannot stop the prince from being kidnapped, they had explicit orders from the King himself to terminate the man, so his vast knowledge of the Imperial defense could not be used against the homeworld.

Ashamed, the captain hung her head. Shooting at her own sovereign ruler. God, sometimes this was a real pracking job. Why didn't she go into something nice and cushy, like the news biz?

"Weapons status!" Murphy barked.

"Missiles one through forty-five ready!"

"Forward, port, and starboard hydrogen lances ready!"

"Main disruptors ready!"

"Bedlows fully charged!"

"How soon till they're out of sensor range?" asked the captain, buttoning her shirt to the collar.

"Fifteen minutes," replied the ensign.

"Give me a thirty-second countdown at fourteen," said Captain Murphy, raking fingernails along the thigh of her uniform. "And God help us, that's all we can give him."

In the cockpit of the shuttle, Prince Yertzoff was busy accessing a coded file on a computer cube while the reporters ran a last-minute diagnostic on the craft. If they maintained this velocity, they'd be out of scanner range of any possible pursuit in less than ten minutes. Great!

By coincidence, the QSNT newscraft rocketed by a corsair owned by The Wolf Pack chasing after an Earth luxury liner full of tourists. Since that event was flatly impossible, the puzzled mercenaries stepped outside the warship to see why they weren't moving and promptly tumbled off into limitless space.

"Hey," asked Jhonny, jerking up his head. "What was that we passed?"

"Didn't see it," said Harry, busily operating controls on every side. "ETA to Neptune?"

"Five minutes," replied Deitrich. "Prince Yertzoff, are you ready to feed me the defensive stats on the prison?"

A royal hand wave. "They're in the computer."

It only took a moment for the Brain to pass the numerous security seals, code phrases, and counter-phrases and access the information requested. And fourteen military manuals poured into his secondary computer. It came in a whirl of words and a stream of figures; graphs and three-dimensional charts flowed through his brain. The pilot reeled with the info dump. Deitrich knew he could assimilate data pretty fast, but nobody can keep pace with this! Geez, he was only a cyborg.

When the download was finished, Deitrich culled through the material. Did the prince really think they could pull this off? He had a lot of answers to defeating the Neptune security systems, but the main stumbling block was a battery of Bedlow gigawatt lasers capable of zapping a fifty-ton space shuttle into vapor faster than playing touch tag with the sun.

But maybe Deitrich himself was an answer to those.

"Actually, not too bad," he reported aloud to the prince. "We have an estimated success rate of seventy-three percent."

"Excellent!"

"Ah, against, sire."

A frown. "Oh."

"Alert!" cried the ceiling. "Incoming!"

On the bridge, the crew jerked back to reality. Nothing was visible through the windows. WatchDog and radar showed clear.

Cautiously, the MainBrain did a passive EM bounce scan. Ah, somebody was trying to get a computer-guided weapons lock on the shuttle. Smugly, the pilot allowed them to have the target acquisition, but a good hundred meters away. Seconds later the fiery darts of ultra-fast interceptor missiles lanced harmlessly past the newscraft on either side.

"Hey, those weren't attack missiles," stated Jhonny, checking his scrolling monitors. "There was no warhead. They were drones!"

"I do not understand," said the prince. "Is my Navy trying to kill us, or not?" Oh, dear, perhaps the dreaded Option 9 was in play here?

"Kill us? No way," Harry explained. "We're flying faster than them, but they have missiles which fly faster than us!"

"So they're launching reconnaissance missiles to track us?"

"Yep."

Pretty darn clever actually.

"But that means we're taking them straight to Hell!"

An apt observation.

"What do you mean he's dead?" barked Rikka on the telephone. "This is no time to be dead!" Slamming the off button, she frantically dialed the next person on her list. "Hello . . . Judge Reinhold?"

Orbiting peacefully above Neptune were sixteen ships painted dead black with a glossy white skull 'n' crossbones on their forward prow. The bones were made of flame, the skull was laughing and sported a policeman's riot helmet. The hulls of the vessels were pitted with repaired wounds, and bristly with gun ports of every size and caliber.

On the bridge a young admiral threw a fold of his scarlet cape over a shoulder and assumed a dramatic stance in the bare middle of the combat bridge. There was no chair for the dapper commander; he preferred to be an example to the crew and used a gravity net in the floor to keep him standing motionless during the most fierce confrontations. Impressed the troops no end, and helped to maintain that oh-so-important crease in his trousers.

On every side of him, officers and technicians worked frantically at their consoles, watching for trouble and monitoring the progress of the escapee from the prison below. The con man Stitt had already passed the bogus message on, and when Swenson came out of the tunnel, she would blithely climb directly onboard one of their frigates. Soon afterward, they'd force the prince to come to them, and afterward Mars itself!

Then the worlds!

"Hey, Killer," whispered a gunnery officer. "Know why the boss always wears that cape?"

Curiously, the other weapons operator shook his head no.

"Because the Earth Defense Force shot his arse off."

The second man started to snicker, then the first joined him. But their merriment was cut short as the floor under their chairs dilated and they dropped screaming from sight. Seconds later two frozen corpses tumbled past the portside windows.

The standing admiral touched his throat mike. "Personnel? Admiral Brainbasher here. I need two replacement gunners for the bridge. And try and make sure these have a better sense of humor?"

"Aye, sir!" Somebody must have told the old "why does he wear that cape" joke. A pirate's life was a dangerous lot.

Good dental plan, though.

"Neptune is on the screen," announced Jhonny, setting the onboard cameras to full automatic.

"So what's the plan?" asked Prince Yertzoff, holding on to the armrest of Mike's huge chair.

"We'll dive straight toward the prison until we're inside its defensive shield," responded Harry, preparing a recorded message for continuous broadcast. "Then we can holo the warden proof that Inga is innocent and land." A smile. "After that, it's all a matter of sorting out who gets blamed for what."

"Harry, can't we somehow force a message through the shield around the prison?" asked Deitrich.

The anchor shook his head. "Forget it. That place is immune to any form of EM communication short of an A-bomb."

Damn! And they didn't have a bomb.

"Fair enough."

"Holy prack on whistling toast!" cried the android, staring agog at the console monitor. "There's six, no, seven, ten . . . a lot, there's a lot of Free Police warships in orbit above Neptune!"

"What?!"

And to Prince Yertzoff the rationale was suddenly clear. They had been instrumental in assisting Inga's escape. But now the pirates wanted to capture her as a lure for him! A bit of royal torture to obtain security codes and soon they would have Mars to plunder at will!

Snyder followed the same line of reasoning and didn't like the conclusion any more than the prince. It was a great story, but a horrible idea. Yet what could they do? There was a war fleet breathing down their neck and an ambush of pirates dead ahead. Stop and Inga died. Keep moving and they died. Damned if they do, damned if they don't, and damned if he knew what to do!

"Black," said the prince in a voice of command.

His camcorder humming as it took endless pictures of everything, Jhonny tried for a soothing tone of voice to calm the hysterical aristocrat down. "Now, I understand the pressure you're under, sire, but giving up—"

"I am not giving up!" shouted the man, standing in the cockpit. "Neither did I say go back. But get black!"

"Gotcha," cried Deitrich in comprehension, and the entire outer hull of the shuttle went pitch-black.

Shutting down all unnecessary systems, the newscraft got as close to a dead man as it could and still fly. Rikka put the judge on hold and Jhonny turned off his legs. Swift and silent, the near-invisible vessel streaked directly toward the orbiting warships of the space pirates. The crimson vessels loomed larger and larger, until the tiny ebony blob passed directly under a huge red cruiser and between a brace of bloody destroyers, close enough to one to see the line of gas station silhouettes painted under the main airlock tallying their total kills.

Wow. These guys had been busy. Must work the weekends.

Holding their breaths, the crew finally sighed in relief as the shuttle exited out the other side of the pirate fleet. That had almost brought a whole new meaning to the term Fatal speeds!

However, when the fleeing ship went off the scanners of the Martians, the rescue fleet stayed on the original course searching for debris. And suddenly the Martian war fleet noticed the Free Police at the exact same moment the pirates did them.

The irresistible force met the immovable object with the expected results: total chaos. Scintillating beams of ravaging destruction lanced out to impact on shields in blazing pyrotechnica. Salvos of missiles were launched, and countered by antimissiles. Rockets battled torpedoes for the right to explode anywhere. Limpet mines were dumped in swarms. Red laser beams and green disruptor rays added a festive holiday feeling to the wholesale destruction. Magnetic cannons volleyed kilotons of high-explosive shells. Coronas of energy lashed from shield to enemy shield as the titanic outpourings of military violence reached staggering proportions!

The odds were sixteen to four, but the Martians didn't care.

They liked a fair fight.

CHAPTER TWENTY

WITH A LURCH, the QSNT shuttle slowed to sublight and the planetary refrigerator called Neptune lay before them.

"Mains are gone," announced Michelangelo's voice over the intercom. "Permanently. You could fry an egg on the engine housings and the FTL elements are toast."

"Lunch later, I promise!" yelled Jhonny, erecting their own meager shields. "Just get us out of here before we get shot!"

With a kick, the chemical engines burst into flame and the vessel angled downward into the bitter atmosphere of raw methane, elemental hydrogen, primordial ammonia, and stinky ozone.

Taking a moment in reflection, Prince Yertzoff noted that there was a certain poetic justice in using the very troops searching for him to battle the criminals he hired to save his love.

Sometimes it felt good to be the center of the universe.

"A prison buoy has just warned us to go away or die," reported Harry, hand to his ear.

"Roger," acknowledged the MainBrain.

Preparing for evasive maneuvers, Deitrich did a visual scan of the planet, but nothing was in sight. He switched to infrared. Nothing. The prison must be heat-shielded. Running the menu, he tried ultraviolet, alpha radiation, mass proximity, mailing address. Blank, blank, blank, a post office box? Bah, useless.

The whole damn complex must be underground and/or painted white! A stealth prison? Thoughtfully, the cyborg increased visual magnification, punched for maximum computer augmentation, and tied in a geographical map of the glacier continent. Bingo! There was a mountainous outcropping of ice where none was supposed to be located in sector four.

"Incoming, sector four," announced the prince, hands everywhere on the console, as the shuttle registered weapon acquisition from below.

Frantically Harry started to broadcast their Media Station ID on every channel of the alphabet even though he knew it wouldn't work. All the prison could see was a black shuttle rocketing out from the middle of a bunch of Free Police. They thought the reporters were the enemy! Well, generally they were, but not at this particular time.

"We're white again and say HI, I'M PRINCE YERTZOFF on the hull," said Jhonny. "Don't know if it'll help, but it can't hurt."

Scrambling signals and erecting shields, the MainBrain tried for a disengage, and failed. Neither could he jam the lock, nor reallocate the weapon off target.

Igniting the belly jets, Deitrich violently jerked the shuttle to starboard and aft of them somebody exploded from the hit. The deadly dance had begun. But it was a contest he had fought and won many times before in video game simulations. Living human mind pitted against simple mechanical computer. No problem.

Unless the computers of SnowBall were also MainBrains themselves! Could the plucky pilot have finally met his match in skill, hardware, and raw ruthless skulduggery?

Nyah.

Fuel level dropping with alarming speed, Deitrich kept up the wild gyrations, knowing that success meant never doing the same thing twice. Judging the time ripe, he did the same thing twice, which only seemed to drive the enemy computer into a bestial frenzy.

Which was exactly what the crafty Brain wanted.

Suddenly the Bedlows stopped, as if trying to draw them into a lethal straight line approach. But Deitrich had calculated that the accumulators were momentarily drained and this was their one chance.

Demanding maximum thrust, the solid-fuel emergency chemical boosters rumbled into action, kicking the shuttle forward in a burst of speed. For one full second the vessel traversed a true course. Vulnerable. Helpless. Easy prey. Then the spaceship rocketed below the attack horizon of the Bedlows. Blocked by the prison itself, the mighty lasers could no longer focus on them.

They skim the surface of the frozen world, clipping in half countless icicles and snowmen wearing guard uniforms in passing, and a tremendous slab of blue-white ice completely filled the forward monitor.

"Damn it," cried Harry, beating on his console. "The prison shield isn't a generated forcefield but propagated through the metal walls of the pracking place!"

"Then we have to go inside to tell the warden?" asked Jhonny, a camera in each hand clicking away.

"Yes! Damn it, yes!"

"Window or door?" asked Deitrich calmly as the glacier zoomed toward them at frightening speed.

"Observation room second floor, on the main map," snapped the prince. "Visual shows nobody there!"

"Got it!" cried Rikka, waving a fax as she stepped onto the bridge. "Swenson has been cleared on all charges!"

"Not yet," exclaimed Harry, grabbing his friend around the waist and pulling her into his lap.

Cutting the engines, Deitrich applied full retros and the shuttle savagely turned to brake. The hull of the craft groaned from the forces unleashed, control panels erupted in sparks, but the craft did slow. At subsonic speed, they only got a fleeting glimpse in the Plexiglas observation dome—empty chairs and tables clearly visible for a split second—before the scene shattered in a million pieces.

The deafening crash-crash-crash filled the world as the shuttle plowed through the triple sheet of Armorlite; shards twinkling in the cold sunlight. Hull scraping against the walls, thousands of white tiles were ripped from the shuttle in a spray of shredded lithium. The QSNT shuttle twisted from the impact, sparks flying from the bare metal to metal contact. Violently the battered craft jerked to a halt as its nose brutally slammed against the inner wall, the thick dura-steel bending dangerously inward.

Already in their spacesuits, the team untangled themselves from each other and scrambled for the airlock.

"Gee, are we back on Media?" asked Michelangelo, holding the hatch open for them.

With a hydraulic hiss, Rikka sealed on her helmet. "Sure sounds like it."

"No, the tone of the crash was different," stated Jhonny over his suit radio.

Harry only grunted agreement as he hawked and spat the remains of the cigar out of his throat and into the waste spittoon in his helmet. Flash!

As the inner hatch of the airlock closed, the reporters wasted no time in cycling through, but simply detonated the explosive bolts on the outer door, blasting it free from the twisted craft.

THANKS, I NEEDED THAT, scrolled Deitrich on the spacesuit cuffs.

Jumping from the ship, the team and prince raced across the decimated room, the killing wind from outside stopping abruptly as a sonic curtain sealed the wound in the prison. Throwing aside the double doors, the team turned to the left and sprinted for the warden's office at their top speed. But just then, an armed guard holding a Peace-Maker stun pistol stepped in front of them from around a corner.

Actually, this did remind them of an average day on Media.

"Halt!" cried the guard as he fired the PeaceMaker.

Moving fast, Michelangelo stepped in front of the team and took the full barrage of Narcolipic gases and darts in his chest. But did not fall.

"These chemicals have no effect on my species," he said, yanking the gun out of the trembling hands of the guard. Who promptly fainted. "And the sonics are too weak."

Another hurdle vanquished, the team raced on.

"Hey, Gremlin!" cried a second guard, bigger than the first, and with a PeaceMaker Mark G.

Closing his eyes, Snyder jumped in front of the alien and got feathered with darts and splashed with an oily fluid that tasted like coconut and shoe polish. Bleh, what a combination! Definitely needed Scotch.

With a curse the guard holstered that gun and drew another.

Jhonny dove forward and got that charge. Designed for humans, the stun charges were futile against the disguised android.

"Will you guys please stop doing that!" admonished a guard furiously as the reporters ran away.

Then he paused. Hey, that last guy had been human and hit with the correct PeaceMaker! Experimentally, the guard triggered a charge into his palm and limply hit the floor. Nope, worked fine . . . ow . . .

Uncaring, the group charged down the main corridor of the chilly prison, made a right, and barged straight into the office of the warden. As the door slammed open, a sheet of Armorlite glass descended from the ceiling dividing the room in half. Safe behind the meter-thick barrier was Warden Thorson and his desk; on the other was the news team and the prince.

The prickly Mike and Harry took a position blocking the door and Jhonny stepped aside filming everything. Throwing herself forward, Rikka hit the barrier hard and pressed the writ of habeas corpus and a stamped IP release form against the cold glass. Prince Vladamir Yertzoff was one second behind her.

Drawing a Bedlow laser from a belt holster, Thorson glared suspiciously at the unannounced intruders. What was this, an invasion of human porcupines?

"Warden Thorson, please pay close attention, we're trying to save an innocent life!" cried the reporter, her words forming clouds in the air. "Please look at these! Please! Your escaping prisoner has been declared innocent! Totally innocent of all charges!"

The barrel of the laser never wavered, but the man's eyes squinted as he read, then went wide in surprise and his mouth silently formed the words "holy prack." Hitting a switch, the Armorlite slab ascended into the ceiling as the warden holstered the Bedlow and grabbed for the command microphone on his desk.

In the background, the sky was filled with crisscrossing energy beams and the pyrotechnic explosions of missiles, bombs, and other deadly military stuff. A gentle rain of black ship parts began to meteor into the frigid atmosphere of Neptune, long tails of flame dangling behind the melting chunks of pirate hull.

"Alert all prison officials!" bellowed the warden, his words echoing a thousand times through the under-ice complex. "We have a Code 9-99. Repeat a Code 9-99. Prisoner 40586 has been cleared of all charges. Do not harm the escapee! Repeat do not harm . . ." He touched a com-link receiver clipped to his earlobe. "Eh? Repeat, please, guard forty-seven! Oh, no.

"I am afraid you were a minute too late," Thorson softly apologized, placing the microphone on his desk.

Fear distorting his features, the prince rushed over and grabbed the man by the collar. "What has happened to my love?"

"Dead," said the warden in a wooden tone. "Shot in the tunnel while trying to escape."

Bursting into tears, Yertzoff slumped to the floor, his entire body wracked with heaving sobs.

Thick silence filled the room and Jhonny respectfully turned off his camcorder. Some things were simply not meant for public consumption.

"But what I can't understand," continued the puzzled prison official, "is why such a fine man as the prince here would care about a crawling hunk of slimy filth like Stitt."

Yertzoff stopped his tears. "What?"

"Who?" whispered the news team in unison.

"Well, that's who was in the tunnel," explained the warden, surprised at their growing smiles. "Prisoner 40856. Stitt. Zultar Dameon Stitt. Our new arrival from Luna."

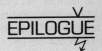

ON MEDIA STATION , down on Level 2 in The Horny Toad, an anxious crowd of extremely well-dressed people strained their ears to hear the fateful words.

"And so, by the power invested in me, as the sovereign political entity of Luna," said the Justice of the Peace from amid the flower-draped trestle on the altar, "I do hereby pronounce Vladamir Yertzoff, Inga Swenson, and Henretta Caramico husband and wives."

The crowd erupted in cheers as the three happy newly-weds embraced and then promptly left for the privacy of Table Zero to consummate the vows before anybody got sober, dethroned, or assassinated.

Behind the counter, Alonzo MacKenzie was in full highlander regalia and serving drinks with his usual aplomb. Floating listlessly in the aquarium in the wall, a very plump Bruno was barely ambulatory and had a toothpick sticking out of his choppers. Occasionally a bubble rose to the surface as he burped again from his homeric meal of Danish.

Over in the corner, the CD player generated a hologram of a happy fat man in rough work clothes, his belt dripping string. The fellow shook his fist at the heavens and his belly at the world as he started singing about the values of tradition. Perched precariously atop his head was a tiny fiddler who played and danced with amazing agility.

"I love happy endings," Harry sighed, watching the tiny TV monitor in his lap that showed the team breaking into the warden's office on Neptune, the prince collapsing, and with the flaming wreckage of the Free Police dropping in the background, in walks Inga for the joyous resolution. Ah, now that was good news!

"Define happy," slurred Jhonny, a wall of empty martini glasses protecting him from the encroachment of sobriety. Hic!

"The lovers are reunited," said Collins, counting off on her fingers. "And the prince gets the political marriage Parliament wanted that forges Mars into a single unity."

"Good thing polygamy is okay on Mars and that Lady Caramico is a good sport about sharing," mouthed Snyder, slopping a bit of his drink off an already stained sleeve. Damn, no cigars tonight, or he would personally be providing the fireworks. The firewaterworks! Hic.

Collins agreed. "We got an exclusive story that is still playing across the solar system. We scooped QINS."

"Hurrah!" chorused the team, lifting their glasses high and fast, the contents continuing on to splash the ceiling.

"Plus, the Free Police have probably been destroyed as a viable military entity, forever!"

"Zoltar Stitt isn't happy," noted the android, giving a pout. "Poor bastard."

Watching the dancing parents go by in a conga line, Harry smiled and shrugged. "Prack him. Don't do the crime if you can't do the time. He knew the punishment for attempting an escape from SnowBall Hell, and if he hadn't lied to Inga about the prince targeting the wrong cell for the mole to break in, she most likely would have been killed by the guards."

"So, don't lie, kiddies," scolded Collins, waggling a stern finger. Then she glanced upward as a drop of moisture impacted on the tip of her nose. What, was it raining in here?

At the front doors to the bar, a very angry Maria Valdez was trying yet again to gain entrance to the royal party. But her charms and bribes had no effect on the stern barrier of the agents of the Martian Secret Service. In a huff, she stomped off to find Danny J and have another relaxing massage. Or two, or three.

"By the way, where is your ex?" asked Snyder, refilling his tumbler from the champagne bottle in the silver ice bucket on their table. Chateau la Yoo-Hoo, 2235. A classic vintage.

Grinning evilly, Collins did the same to her crystal Dixie cup. "In the bathroom, polishing the moose."

"And he'll be there for the whole party?" asked Jhonny slyly, crouching low behind his shaky wall of perfectly balanced empties. The crystal segmented his view into a thousand different colors and directions, which rather clarified things nicely.

A devious wink. "For the next two weeks!" corrected Rikka.

He offered a glass. "You are a bastard, madam."

"Thank you!" And they clinked.

HEY, GUYS! scrolled Deitrich. YOU SHOULD SEE OUR NEW SHUTTLE. SHE'S A BEAUTY! A SLEEK, SILVER, SUPERCHARGED BMW DELUXE.

"Well, beamer me up, Scotty," laughed Harry, raising his glass in a toast.

I NOW HAVE A FLORENTINE PLASTIC SUPERSTRUCTURE. IF NEED BE I COULD PROBABLY FLY STRAIGHT *THROUGH* MEDIA.

"Perhaps tomorrow," advised Collins.

STILL NO NAME, THOUGH.

"How about the 'Tropical Crush,' " offered Jhonny, addressing the table instead of his wrist. "In honor of your most memorable crash landing!"

In his bubbling tank onboard the new shuttle, the disembodied Brain imagined walking up behind the android, grabbing his pants, and giving the manchine a severe wedgie. Geez, sink one small Pacific Ocean island and you never hear the end of it!

Suddenly appearing at the door was Gardner Wilkes. The Martian Secret Service agents dutifully parted and a hush came over the crowd as he stepped right to the very jamb of the doorway and stopped.

"May I enter this establishment?" he asked cordially toward the distant bar.

Poised behind the counter, MacKenzie chewed a lip

thoughtfully and then checked his watch, looked at the wall calendar, made some quick calculations on his wrist secretary.

"Sure," he waved grandly. "Come on in!"

The crowd released a collective sigh and Wilkes joined the boisterous aristocrats, trying his best not to stomp on any feet.

"Lord, would I ever love to know what Mac had on the boss which allowed him to have The Horny Toad on this station and Wilkes had to ask his permission just to enter!" rambled Michelangelo, toying with the gallon mug in his paws. A specially blended caffeine champagne had been brewed for the alien, since alcohol had no inebriating effect on his species. But caffeine got them "tight." Already his fur was sticking straight out from his hide and the alien was moving slower with every drink.

"Maybe it's best we don't know what the secret is," admonished Harry, turning off the TV. " 'Cause then we might get barred from the only place on the station not under the direct control of Wilkes Corporation."

"And the only source of booze," added Jhonny, giving a sip of yet another Martini X to his camcorder. Twirling its lens madly, the semisentient device shuddered and toppled over into the bowl of caviar and Cheez Whiz.

"Amen!" toasted Rikka, having trouble staying in her chair herself.

"Knowledge is power," quoted Michelangelo stiffly. "But then so is magnetically induced 440 cycle direct current!"

The anchor chuckled. "Ah, Mike, you're incorrigible!"

Confused, the alien blinked and checked his IBM portable. "I won't rust?"

"Ah, no," corrected Snyder. "That's uncorrodable."

"I don't matter?"

"That's inconsequential."

"I'm not endorsed by the government?"

"That's unconstitutional!"

"I can't be bribed?"

"That's incorruptible!"

"I can't be reformed?"

"*That's* incorrigible!"

"Ah!" sighed the alien contentedly. "I won't rust."

Moaning softly to himself, Harry acknowledged that, yes, the alien technician could not rust.

"Didn't think I could," mumbled the hairy leviathan around his gallon pitcher of aged ice tea.

"But *I* can!" sang out Jhonny.

The rest of the team ignored the drunken interruption, content in the knowledge that they had pulled another one out of the fire, saved the good guys, helped beat the bad guys, and assured their jobs . . . for at least another week.

Hic.